The Duke's Guide To Winning a Lady

The Strongs of Shadowcrest
Book Seven

Alexa Aston

Malcolm Ware
Euphemia Strong

© Copyright 2024 by Alexa Aston
Text by Alexa Aston
Cover by Dar Albert

Dragonblade Publishing, Inc. is an imprint of Kathryn Le Veque Novels, Inc.
P.O. Box 23
Moreno Valley, CA 92556
ceo@dragonbladepublishing.com

Produced in the United States of America

First Edition October 2024
Print Edition

Reproduction of any kind except where it pertains to short quotes in relation to advertising or promotion is strictly prohibited.

All Rights Reserved.

The characters and events portrayed in this book are fictitious. Any similarity to real persons, living or dead, is purely coincidental and not intended by the author.

ARE YOU SIGNED UP FOR DRAGONBLADE'S BLOG?

You'll get the latest news and information on exclusive giveaways, exclusive excerpts, coming releases, sales, free books, cover reveals and more.

Check out our complete list of authors, too!

No spam, no junk. That's a promise!

Sign Up Here

www.dragonbladepublishing.com

Dearest Reader;

Thank you for your support of a small press. At Dragonblade Publishing, we strive to bring you the highest quality Historical Romance from some of the best authors in the business. Without your support, there is no 'us', so we sincerely hope you adore these stories and find some new favorite authors along the way.

Happy Reading!

CEO, Dragonblade Publishing

Additional Dragonblade books by Author Alexa Aston

The Strongs of Shadowcrest Series
The Duke's Unexpected Love (Book 1)
The Perks of Loving a Viscount (Book 2)
Falling for the Marquess (Book 3)
The Captain and the Duchess (Book 4)
Courtship at Shadowcrest (Book 5)
The Marquess' Quest for Love (Book 6)
The Duke's Guide to Winning a Lady (Book 7)

Suddenly a Duke Series
Portrait of the Duke (Book 1)
Music for the Duke (Book 2)
Polishing the Duke (Book 3)
Designs on the Duke (Book 4)
Fashioning the Duke (Book 5)
Love Blooms with the Duke (Book 6)
Training the Duke (Book 7)
Investigating the Duke (Book 8)

Second Sons of London Series
Educated By The Earl (Book 1)
Debating With The Duke (Book 2)
Empowered By The Earl (Book 3)
Made for the Marquess (Book 4)
Dubious about the Duke (Book 5)
Valued by the Viscount (Book 6)
Meant for the Marquess (Book 7)

Dukes Done Wrong Series

Discouraging the Duke (Book 1)
Deflecting the Duke (Book 2)
Disrupting the Duke (Book 3)
Delighting the Duke (Book 4)
Destiny with a Duke (Book 5)

Dukes of Distinction Series
Duke of Renown (Book 1)
Duke of Charm (Book 2)
Duke of Disrepute (Book 3)
Duke of Arrogance (Book 4)
Duke of Honor (Book 5)
The Duke That I Want (Book 6)

The St. Clairs Series
Devoted to the Duke (Book 1)
Midnight with the Marquess (Book 2)
Embracing the Earl (Book 3)
Defending the Duke (Book 4)
Suddenly a St. Clair (Book 5)
Starlight Night (Novella)
The Twelve Days of Love (Novella)

Soldiers & Soulmates Series
To Heal an Earl (Book 1)
To Tame a Rogue (Book 2)
To Trust a Duke (Book 3)
To Save a Love (Book 4)
To Win a Widow (Book 5)
Yuletide at Gillingham (Novella)

King's Cousins Series
The Pawn (Book 1)
The Heir (Book 2)
The Bastard (Book 3)

Medieval Runaway Wives
Song of the Heart (Book 1)
A Promise of Tomorrow (Book 2)
Destined for Love (Book 3)

Knights of Honor Series
Word of Honor (Book 1)
Marked by Honor (Book 2)
Code of Honor (Book 3)
Journey to Honor (Book 4)
Heart of Honor (Book 5)
Bold in Honor (Book 6)
Love and Honor (Book 7)
Gift of Honor (Book 8)
Path to Honor (Book 9)
Return to Honor (Book 10)

The Lyon's Den Series
The Lyon's Lady Love

Pirates of Britannia Series
God of the Seas

De Wolfe Pack: The Series
Rise of de Wolfe

The de Wolfes of Esterley Castle
Diana
Derek
Thea

Also from Alexa Aston
The Bridge to Love (Novella)
One Magic Night

PROLOGUE

Waterside, Kent—June 1810

MALCOLM WARE, DUKE of Waterbury, rose, not having gotten much sleep, thanks to his wife's caterwauling while having her babe. He hadn't realized it took so long to produce a child. Mama had Ada while he was away at school, or else he might have had an idea about the length of the birth process.

He rang for his valet, and Barker appeared with hot water, shaving Malcolm and helping him to dress. As he opened his door to go down to breakfast, he paused in the corridor and listened a moment.

Silence.

Perhaps Imogen had finally had the babe. Malcolm hoped it was a boy because he wanted to get his heir and spare off his wife as quickly as possible. His father had not even wed until his mid-thirties, and Malcolm had wondered if his father's advanced age had anything to do with the trouble Mama had birthing children. He had come along quickly enough after their marriage, but a decade stood between him and Ada, his younger sister. That was why he had wed Imogen as early as he had. The sooner he could get sons from her, the better.

The door opened to the duchess' rooms, and a woman stepped out. For a moment, before she closed the door, he caught sight of Imogen in her bed, the sheets tangled and bloody. Malcolm recoiled seeing the glimpse of his exhausted wife.

"Ah, Your Grace," said the woman, stepping toward him, tears swimming in her eyes. "I am Her Grace's midwife."

"How is her labor progressing?" he asked, frightened to hear the answer.

Wearily, the woman shook her head. "Not well, I am afraid. The poor thing has screamed and cried herself hoarse—and still the babe has not come." The midwife paused. "It is because it is a breech birth, Your Grace."

She looked at him as if he was supposed to know what she meant. "Does that make it . . . difficult?"

"Almost impossible," the midwife admitted. "You see, a babe is meant to come out head-first. Most all of them turn in the womb when it is time, and that is how they exit the birth canal. Your child . . . well, its feet are now first."

Tears began to flow down her cheeks. "One foot has appeared. The babe is stuck. I did my best to turn it before that happened. That is why Her Grace was in so much pain."

"What are you saying?" Malcolm asked, cold fear pooling in his belly.

"I cannot push the babe back, Your Grace," the woman explained wearily. "Most likely, the babe has already suffocated." She shook her head sadly. "And Her Grace will soon be gone. I came to look for you. So that you might tell her goodbye."

He heard the words and yet could make no sense of them.

"She is only turned nine and ten," he said, as if her youth protected her from such things.

"I am sorry, Your Grace. Please. Go to her. Offer what comfort you can," begged the woman.

Though it was the last thing Malcolm wanted to do, he nodded in agreement, following the midwife as she returned to the door and opened it.

Malcolm eased inside, treading lightly as he moved toward the bed. Imogen looked completely worn out, so small and frail. Her hair was damp with sweat and matted terribly. A sour smell lingered in the air. For the moment, her eyes were closed, and he looked at her as if looking at a stranger. That's how he truly saw her.

Imogen had made her come-out last Season, when he had decided it was time to take a bride. She was quiet, elegant, and incredibly boring. His duchess was also thick as two short planks, having no conversation. She was like a pretty flower, opening to her peak at the Season, and then withering and dying once they had wed. Malcolm had avoided her as much as possible after the first month of marriage because he had gotten her with child. Imogen had been sick the entire time, vomiting with great regularity, keeping mostly to her rooms.

He had spoken to the village doctor about it, learning that while most women experienced some degree of nausea, it usually subsided after a few months. In rare cases, a woman might be ill throughout the time of her increasing.

That had been Imogen.

Looking at her, so tiny and exhausted, he could not recall the last time they had even spoken. And now, they never would after the conversation they would now hold.

She must have sensed his presence because she opened her eyes. Pity moved him, and Malcolm removed his handkerchief, dabbing the tears from her pale cheeks.

"How are you?" he asked, immediately wishing he could withdraw the question.

"Not well, Your Grace," she responded, pain in her eyes. "I am sorry."

"You have nothing to be sorry for, Imogen," he said softly, taking her hand for the first time in months. Had he even held it any time after their marriage ceremony?

He couldn't recall doing so—and guilt filled him.

Brushing her hair from her brow, he forced a smile. "Trust in your midwife. You will be fine."

"You think so?" she asked hopefully.

Malcolm hadn't the heart to tell her the truth. "Of course, my lady. Close your eyes now and get some rest. Your babe will be here soon enough."

His duchess did as directed, having faith in him.

Turning to the midwife, he asked her a silent question, wanting to know how much longer his young wife had. No words passed between them as she shrugged.

He could do nothing further and decided to leave the room. As he did, he glanced over his shoulder, seeing the midwife had raised the sheet covering Imogen's body. A tiny foot protruded from her body.

His child's foot...

Yet Malcolm felt no connection to it or the mother. He blamed his father for that. The previous duke had been cold and distant, rarely engaging with his family. Once, when Malcolm had been feeling especially brave, he asked his father why the duke never bothered talking to him. His father had seemed stumped by the question and had impatiently flicked his wrist, indicating for his son to leave with receiving an answer.

He went downstairs, forcing one foot in front of the other, knowing he had no appetite. It would be important to prepare his family for the events which would soon come.

Mama and Ada were already at breakfast. Both looked up expectantly. Seeing his face, his mother's mouth tightened. His sister bit her lip, looking distressed.

Looking to Calley, Malcolm said, "Clear the room."

The butler did not have to utter a word as the footmen on duty quickly exited. Calley followed them out, shooting a sympathetic look at Malcolm before closing the door.

Taking a seat, he said, "Imogen and the babe will not make it. The midwife said the babe is breech."

Mama sucked in a quick breath. "Oh, no!"

"That is bad?" his sister asked. "They will die?"

"Yes."

"But surely she can—"

"No," he replied, cutting Ada off. "There is nothing to be done. Most likely, the babe has already died. That is what Imogen is doing now."

Ada began weeping softly. She pulled her napkin from her lap and buried her face in it.

Mama's gaze met his. "This is my fault."

He frowned. "How so?"

"She was too small for birthing babes," Mama said dismissively. "I let my head be turned by her beauty and family's name. The next time we will—"

"The next time?" he asked, his tone low and deadly. "My first wife has yet to expire, and you are already planning for a new one to take her place?"

Mama glared daggers at him. "It is not as if you are attached to the girl, Waterbury. I cannot recall the last time I have even seen the two of you together. Yes, she was beautiful but lacked for conversation. You need someone more lively. I will find you a better bride next Season."

Malcolm couldn't begin to think of attending the whirl of social events. He had been grateful of his babe's upcoming birth conflicting with the Season, giving him an excuse to remain in the country.

"I will find my own bride, Mama. In my own time," he said, his tone brokering no questions. "Make yourself useful and plan Imogen's funeral."

Ada burst into tears. "I never thought you cruel, Waterbury, but that is a horrible thing to say."

"Life is not always easy," he told his sister. "Death is a part of it."

He pushed to his feet and exited the breakfast room, finding the footmen waiting outside. He gestured for them to return to their posts, as Calley approached him.

"Your Grace, I just received word that Her Grace passed while delivering her child," the butler said solemnly. "The babe is also gone."

"Thank you," he said brusquely. "Send for the clergyman. He can meet with the dowager duchess and discuss the service to be held."

"I shall have the staff wear mourning bands," Calley said.

Malcolm recalled the black bands worn about the servants' upper arms after the death of his father.

"Yes, see to it. Inform Cook that mourners will be returning to Waterside after the burial. She will know what to do."

"Yes, Your Grace."

He walked woodenly to his study, locking himself in. Seating himself behind the desk, he wondered what was wrong with him. Surely, this feeling of detachment was wrong. He had just lost his wife and child.

And felt nothing.

He cursed softly. His father had been an unfeeling man, remote, withdrawn from his family, even aloof with his friends. Malcolm was repeating those same mistakes. He had wed Imogen because his mother had told him she would make for an excellent duchess with her looks and breeding. Instead, he had gotten her with child and Imogen had retreated even further within herself as she spent the majority of her time in the duchess' rooms. Malcolm had gone days—even weeks—without thinking of her or remembering that he was married.

Now, he was a widower at six and twenty.

He knew he would shed no tears for his wife and child. It struck him he did not know what gender the babe had been. He sat for hours, his thoughts drifting, knowing he was unhappy and yet not having a clue what might make him so.

When he finally emerged, Calley informed him that his mother had asked to see him. He found Mama in her sitting room, as dry-eyed as he was.

"Sit, Waterbury," she said, so he did so.

"I have met with the clergyman and Cook. The service for Her Grace will be held tomorrow afternoon, with mourners being allowed to call upon us after the burial."

"Thank you for handling the matter," he told her.

She sniffed. "It was the least I could do. I know her death has not truly affected you, but it has your sister. She spent hours each day with Her Grace. Reading to her. Talking. Doing her hair."

"I was not aware of that," he admitted.

She studied him a moment. Malcolm refused to flinch under her scrutiny.

"You were not aware of a great many things regarding your wife," Mama said bluntly. "Not that it would have prevented her tragic death and that of her child. In that regard, you remind me of your father."

"I am not Father," he quickly protested, ignoring the truth.

"Not yet. But you are growing wintry and distant as he was. Oh, I am not saying you must make a love match the next time around, but it would not hurt to take *some* interest in your next wife, Waterbury."

"That will be a while," he told her. "But I am *not* like him."

Yet Malcolm knew his denial rang hollow, like the Apostle Peter denying the Christ three times before the cock crowed.

Her mouth trembled. "I hope that is not the case. While I always knew a typical *ton* marriage meant a couple usually going their own ways, your father took it to the extreme. Each time I lost a child, I thought perhaps *this* would be the time he offered comfort to me." She paused. "He never did."

"Each time?" Malcolm asked. "What do you mean?"

She shook her head, impatience in her tone as she said, "You are oblivious to anything that does not revolve around you, Waterbury. In that respect, you are exactly like him. Surely, you do not believe that when Ada arrived, it was the first time I had been with child since you?"

"Actually, I did," he said. "How would I know differently?"

Her mouth thinned. "I suppose you are right. Suffice it to say there were several babes. None of them survived. Some, I lost after only a few months. Twice, I gave birth to stillborn ones."

"I . . . never knew," he said, feeling terrible.

"I tried my bloody best to give that man another son," Mama said bitterly. "Over and over, I allowed him to come to my bed. To touch me. To give me hope when he planted his seed. And time and again, I was sorely disappointed." She swallowed. "After Ada came, the doctor said there could be no more attempts."

Malcolm took her hand. "I wish I had known, Mama. That must have been lonely for you."

"As lonely as it was for that poor girl you wed," she snapped, yanking her hand from his. "She was as abandoned as I was. I am sorry she did not challenge you enough, Waterbury. Try harder with the next one. At least share tea with her. Or dinner. Attempt to see her some each day. It is not much to ask."

Guilt weighed heavily in him now. He had spent far too little time with Imogen. No wonder he felt so disconnected to her death and that of their child's. *Their* child. A babe which the two of them had created. He had forgotten about both mother and child for most of the time Imogen had lived at Waterside.

He could not do the same the next time around.

Malcolm vowed to be a better man—a better husband—when he finally did decide to take another wife.

"Excuse me," he said, leaving his mother and heading to the duchess' rooms.

The midwife was long gone. The bloody sheets, as well. The bed had been made up with fresh linens. A lone maid was tidying the place.

"Where is Her Grace and the babe?" he asked.

The maid looked at him nervously. "We washed them and dressed them, Your Grace. They are in the library now. Mr. Calley had them taken there."

"Thank you."

He passed through the hallways, heading straight for the library before he lost the courage to do so. Opening the door, he saw a footman standing nearby, while his sister sat next to a long table in the center of the room. Imogen was laid out on the table.

"Wait outside," he ordered the footman, who exited, closing the door behind him.

Crossing the room, he placed a hand on Ada's shoulder. "You are sitting vigil?"

She nodded. "I was too young to do so when Papa passed. It is the least I can do for Imogen."

"Mama tells me you spent quite a bit of time with the duchess."

"I did. She was not very bright, Waterbury, but she was sweet." Ada's lips trembled. "She was also frightened about giving birth. Since her mother died when Imogen was twelve, she had known nothing about her wedding night or how a babe was made or born."

Ada brushed tears from her cheeks with her fingers. "She was afraid of you. She said you hurt her that first time you came to her."

Regret filled him. "I did not know she had no knowledge, Ada. Yes, the first time a man and woman come together, it does hurt the woman. Not for long and only the one time, but I wish I had known. I tried to be as gentle as possible with her."

His sister nodded. "She said you did. That you talked to her and tried to help her relax. But she did not like what you did to her, Waterbury. It makes me afraid of what is to come when I wed."

He pulled her to her feet and wrapped his arms about her. "You are but ten and six, Ada. You have a couple of more years before you make your come-out. Everything will be fine. I promise."

Gently, he stroked her hair as she wept.

"Will Mama tell me more about what happens?" she asked.

"If she does not, then I shall tell you what you need to know myself."

"Thank you," she said meekly.

Malcolm released her, retrieving another chair and placing it beside Ada's.

"We will sit vigil together," he told her.

"All night?" she asked.

"If that is what you wish."

Ada took her seat again, while Malcolm went to view his wife and child. Imogen looked as if she slept. The babe was nestled against her, Imogen's arm about it.

"Do you know if it was a boy or girl?" he asked.

"A girl," she replied. "She does not have a name, though, Waterbury. And she should have one."

"I agree."

Malcolm leaned down and kissed the babe's brow. He placed his hand on her head.

"You are Eunice," he said. "That was your grandmother's name. Your mother missed her own mother a great deal. I think calling you Eunice would have pleased her very much."

He went to the chair and sat, taking Ada's hand in his.

His heart might be one of stone, but he did care for his sister's feelings. She had lost a sister-in-law and friend, and he wanted to bring comfort to her.

"Thank you, Malcolm," she said, calling him by his given name for the first time since he had taken the title five years ago.

"You are welcome."

The next day, he watched as the coffin was sealed and taken to the

Ware crypt. He would not come and visit this wife and child of his. They were his past.

Instead, Malcolm would look to his future—and hope he could become a better duke and better man than his father.

CHAPTER ONE

Shadowcrest, Kent—March 1812

LADY EUPHEMIA STRONG awoke, a sense of dread filling her.
Today would be her last day at Shadowcrest.

In the morning, Effie would leave Kent for town—and her come-out. She was the last of the six Strong girls to make her debut into Polite Society, and she was only doing so to please her mother. Effie had never really considered marriage. She enjoyed life in the country, wearing her breeches, and taking care of her many animals. Her cousin Caleb, who was the steward at Shadowcrest, had also taught Effie quite a bit about estate management, and she would be content remaining here forever, assisting him in the running of the estate.

She was making her come-out this spring because it was important to Mama that she do so. Her mother had given everything to her four daughters and two nieces, whom she had raised, living for them and not herself. Thank goodness, after her mother was widowed, Captain Andrews came into her life. The former sea captain—and best friend of Effie's brother James—had swept Mama off her feet. It had been good to see her mother giddy with happiness, especially now that she had a new babe. James—or Jamie, as the family called him—had been born last September and would be the only child Mama and the captain had, thanks to her age. They lived in town for the most part because the captain helped run Neptune Shipping Lines, the business owned by Effie's sister-in-law Sophie.

Daffodil, her cat, nudged Effie, wanting attention, and she stroked her, scratching Daffy between her ears and watching bliss fill the animal's face. Her cat would be the only one of her pets which would accompany her to town. Daffy was her constant companion, and it would break the cat's heart—and Effie's—if she were left behind at Shadowcrest.

Rising, she rang for a maid, washing and dressing for the day before heading to the breakfast room. She entered, seeing James, Sophie, and Caleb. The only one missing was Aunt Matty. Her aunt had been away from Shadowcrest for a month, helping to care for Mirella and her newborn, Daniel. Aunt Matty was like a second mother to all the Strong girls, having never wed. Instead, she had remained at Shadowcrest and helped Mama in raising them.

"Good morning," Effie greeted, being seated by a footman, who then poured her a cup of tea.

Caleb dabbed his lips with a napkin. "I must be off. Will I see you later today, Effie?"

"Of course," she promised her cousin.

She tucked into the eggs and rasher of ham brought to her by a footman as Sophie said, "I hope you do not mind that we will not be leaving with you tomorrow. The captain is coming to talk over business with me today, however, and so he will be the one to escort you back to town."

"It will be good to see him," she said, happy she would spend the carriage ride to town with her stepfather. He had taken all Mama's ducklings under his own wing and was very protective of them.

"I am certain your mother has already scheduled appointments with Madame Dumas," Sophie continued. "She is the modiste we have all used for the Season."

"Yes, I am familiar with her work. She has made up gowns for me the last several years when I have come to town for visits."

"This will be different, Effie," her sister-in-law said. "You will wear more gowns and change outfits more time in a single day than you ever have."

She tried to hide her displeasure, but James caught her eye and started laughing.

"I know you are not happy about making this come-out, Effie. I am glad you agreed to it, though, because it will make Dinah happy. I will repeat what I have told those before you, though. If you do not fall head over heels in love with a gentleman this Season and wish to wed him, you are welcome back at Shadowcrest for as long as you like. No more Seasons required of you."

"Thank you, James," she replied, knowing he truly meant it.

All five of Effie's sisters and cousins had wed in the last couple of years, with all now having children. Some of them had missed the Season because they were increasing or had just had a child. This spring would mark the first time the six of them would be in town at the same time. She felt immense pressure, knowing they would be there, cheering her on as she made her debut. Effie also knew her entire family hoped she would make the love match they all had.

Strongs were known for their love matches, something almost unheard of in Polite Society. Most marriages were strictly business arrangements between a couple, with dowries being handed over and families using marriage as an opportunity to join together for prestige.

Effie liked her life the way it was, helping Caleb on the estate and caring for the strays she brought home, as well as the injured animals she nursed back to health. Daffy had been one of those strays, severely underweight and her fur matted, but Effie had taken time and patience to bring the kitten back to good health. Now Daffy was sleek and loving. Truly, Effie did not wish for any man to be her husband, someone who would tell her what to do.

Then again, Strong women *were* strong—and she did not see any of her sisters or cousins being ordered about by their spouses. Instead, they were partners to these unique men.

James was the best example. As the Duke of Seaton, he had inherited Strong Shipping, the family business and rival to Neptune Shipping, which had been owned by Sophie. Not only had her sister-in-law owned the shipping empire, Sophie had also run it on her own.

When James and Sophie wed, her brother made certain in the marriage contracts to allow Sophie to maintain sole ownership of the company, something unheard of, which had shocked the *ton*. Their son George, who was the heir apparent to the dukedom, would not only inherit his father's title but also Strong Shipping, while their other children—male and female—would have ownership in Neptune Shipping and run it.

"I thought you were always eager to return to town, James," she commented, slathering blackberry jam on another toast point.

"I am fond of town simply because it is where Strong Shipping is located. When I am there, I am able to go into the office daily."

He reached for his wife's hand, lacing their fingers together. "But I have come to enjoy the country immensely and want George and Ida to spend as much time at Shadowcrest as possible."

"Do you ever miss being at sea?" she asked.

Her brother grew thoughtful. "Yes and no," he finally said. "Having spent my life at sea, working my way up from cabin boy to the captain of a ship, it was the only life I ever knew. Yes, I miss leading a crew of men and the camaraderie I experienced being on a vessel for long stretches. At the same time, I exercise my leadership in Polite Society as the Duke of Seaton and am head of the Strong family. The new friendships which I have formed with Caleb and all my brothers-in-law more than suffice. Why, I see Seth almost daily, since he is our neighbor, and you know that we visit with August, Sterling, and Silas as often as possible. Drake is still my closest friend of all, and seeing him wed to your mother warms my heart."

James got a faraway look in his eyes. "While I enjoyed going up on deck at night and staring out into the vastness of both sea and sky, I can do the same thing here when I ride out at Shadowcrest and view all my land."

She grinned. "I told you those riding lessons I gave you would come in handy."

He chuckled. "You are an excellent riding instructor, Effie. Yes, it is far easier getting about the estate having become comfortable on the back of a horse. For those lessons and the patience you showed while teaching me to ride, I am grateful."

"What do you have planned today?" Sophie asked her.

"I will be checking on all my animals a final time. One of our grooms has promised to take over for me in their care, especially that goat whose leg is broken. He is on the mend, however. The next time I see him, I hope he will be running freely about."

"I assume Daffy will travel to town with you," her brother said.

"I never leave Daffy," Effie declared. "Why, not only does she accompany me anytime I journey to town, but remember that I took her to our tour of the Lake District."

She had accompanied Aunt Matty, along with Mirella and Miss Feathers, her governess, to the Lake District a year and a half ago while Mama hosted a house party for Allegra and Lyric at Shadowcrest. Not only had her cousins found their husbands at this house party, Mirella had met Byron, the man destined to be her husband.

A moment of sadness filled her. Miss Feathers had searched for new employment with Effie ready to make her come-out. The governess had departed from Shadowcrest a week ago, headed for York and a new position with two young boys, aged five and six. It had been hard seeing Miss Feathers go since she had been such a part of Effie's life for so many years.

"I thought I would ride over to see Pippa today," she said, sharing what she planned to do first on this cold March day.

Of all the Strong women, Effie was closest to Pippa. They were both tomboys, and Pippa had taught Effie how to ride, hunt, shoot, swim, and fish. It had been hard to picture Pippa wed and as a mother. But now that she was, Effie could see how easily her sister had made the transition, and how comfortable she was in her role as Viscountess Hopewell and mother to Adam and Louise.

"I am glad you will go and see her and the children," Sophie said. "And one last ride through the countryside will do you a world of good."

"I also want to go to the nursery and play with George and hold Ida sometime today," she said.

Sophie's face softened at the mention of her two children. "They will be coming with us when we go to town."

Effie knew that a majority of married couples in the *ton* left their children at their country estates, not seeing them for months while the Season went on. Mama had never done that, insisting all her girls come to town so she could spend time with them. Effie believed she would see just how different her family was when she made her come-out, but she was grateful the Strongs were a close, loving group. She looked upon their spouses as her own brothers and sister, as well.

She only hoped those who had wed would not urge her to do the same, because although Effie had stated she was going into this Season with an open mind, she could not see herself falling in love, much less marrying. It would be too hard to leave Shadowcrest. The odds against her finding a love match after all her siblings and cousins had were too great. She saw herself returning to the country and devoting her time to Shadowcrest and its people.

Finishing her meal, she left breakfast and headed straight for the stables. Most women would have needed to go and change into their riding habit, but Effie's daily attire in the country consisted of a coat, shirt, and breeches. It was more comfortable dressing in such a manner with the work that she did on the estate and with her animals.

She rode to the lake which separated Shadowcrest land from that of Hopewood. The two estates had shared the lake as long as anyone could recall, and she had spent many happy hours picnicking by it, swimming in it, and rowing about in a boat, fishing. She supposed she might attend a picnic in town but knew the other activities would not be ones available for her to partake in. She laughed just thinking of asking a suitor to take her fishing in the Serpentine.

More than anything, though, was something she had not confided in anyone about. Effie worried about fitting in with the other girls who would be making their come-outs. The fact that she would have to wear gowns for several months during the Season already bothered her enough as it was. She had no idea how to behave around other young ladies.

At least she would have her sisters and cousins with her, along with Mama. With all of them being wed now and living away from Shadowcrest, she would cherish the time she had together with them this spring and summer.

She reached the Hopewood stables and handed her reins to a groom, cutting through the kitchens, as usual. She was a regular visitor to the viscount's estate, and no one seemed to blink an eye when she did so. Cook even greeted her, calling out to her by name.

"Lady Effie, it is good to see you. When do you leave for London?"

"Tomorrow, Cook. That is why I have come to say my goodbyes to you and the others at Hopewood."

Hearing that tickled Cook, and she laughed heartily.

Effie left the kitchens and found Mrs. Robb, the housekeeper, who told her that Lady Hopewell was in her sitting room. She went straight to it, finding her sister at her writing desk. She slipped her arms about Pippa's neck and kissed her cheek.

"Oh, it is so good to see you, Effie," Pippa declared, setting aside the letter she worked on. "I am glad you came for a last visit."

She chuckled as they took a seat on the settee. "It is not as if I will not see you for months. You are coming to town for the Season."

"You are right. We will arrive in a couple of weeks. I have already written to Madame Dumas so that she will reserve time for me to see her. I will not have nearly the number of gowns made up as you, however. Why, a girl making her come-out has the largest wardrobe of anyone at the Season."

"You act as if you know all about the Season when you yourself did not make your come-out, Pippa. Why, this will be the first time you have attended a Season, now that I think about it."

A dreamy expression crossed her sister's face. "No, I did not. And I am very glad I met Seth here at Hopewood and did not have to go about all that nonsense. Oh, I know I should not voice such opinions to you since you are on the cusp of your own debut into Polite Society, but I find the idea full of nonsense. I only wish that Seth had a brother whom I could introduce you to so the two of you might fall madly in love. Then you wouldn't have to bother with all this fuss."

"I am counting on you to help temper the others," Effie said. "It will be the first time all the Strong women will be together for a Season. I am most worried about Georgie and Mirella. They are the ones who have always enjoyed the company of others and talked about the many social affairs held during the Season. You know me, Pippa. I would rather be around animals than people."

Pippa reached up and stroked Effie's hair. "I know that, little sister. I do think, though, that both Georgie and Mirella have changed since they have become mothers and the Season is not as important to them as it once was." She laughed. "That is because they got out of their Season what they went into it for—a husband!"

They both laughed. Effie only hoped she would not feel bored or stifled by the events she would need to attend.

"Let me go to the nursery and see Adam and Louise now. From what I gather, I will not have much time to play with children because of the large number of scheduled events."

"You will be busy," her sister said. "Only as busy as you wish to be, however. I suggest that you only go to the social affairs you are interested in, Effie. It is important to stay true to yourself throughout this entire process. I am certain James has already spoken to you about not worrying whether you find a love match or not."

"He reminded me of that very thing this morning at breakfast," she confirmed. "I know they all wish for me to find my soulmate—even you—but I just do not see that happening, Pippa."

"My advice to you? Do not look for him. if you seek out love, you will be trying to force something to happen. If fate wishes you to find a husband this Season, it will intervene and guide you. If you finish the Season and have found no one to your taste, you have a home to return to and a loving, supportive family."

Her sister studied her a moment. "I know you, Effie. All too well. I sense that you will merely go through the motions, and you have no intention of finding a husband."

She flushed guilty. "Perhaps I am not quite as . . . open-minded about it as I should be. I will do my best to try and enjoy things. Hopefully, I might even like some of the activities. Thank goodness, I do enjoy dancing. Not as much as Mirella, of course, but I will not embarrass myself on the ballroom floor."

"Go into this Season with the idea that you are going to enjoy new experiences and make new friends. Remember how Georgie and Miss Bancroft became friendly during Georgie's come-out Season?"

"Yes, I do recall. My family has been my only friends up until this point." She grinned. "Well, besides my animals." Sighing, she added, "I will do my best, Pippa, to be open to whatever comes my way. The events. The people."

"Even love."

Her sister smiled warmly. "That is all any of us will ask from you, Effie. Now, let us go up to the nursery and see Adam and Louise."

Soon, she was playing with her niece and nephew, feeling the same pull she did when she spent time with George and Ida at Shadowcrest. Perhaps she wouldn't make a love match as her family members had. It was possible she might find a gentleman who would be a good friend to her and still allow her to be independent, while giving her children. The more Effie was around her various nieces and nephews, the more she realized she would like children of her own.

She took her leave and rode home to Shadowcrest, ready to ride about the estate a final time with Caleb and tell her sweet animals goodbye.

That night at dinner, James and the captain kept them laughing, telling stories of their time at sea. Effie couldn't recall the last time she had laughed so much.

The next morning, she awoke with trepidation, knowing even though she had been to town many times over the years, she would be going into the unknown, as far as the Season was concerned. She kissed the children and Sophie goodbye, and James enveloped her in a bear hug.

"We will see you in about ten days," he told her, kissing the top of her head. "And we will stay in town the entire Season with you and escort you to all the events."

Her eyes misted with tears. "I appreciate that, James. More than you know."

The captain handed her into the carriage, then gave her the basket which contained Daffy and climbed in himself. They waved goodbye. George kept waving and calling out her name, which tugged at her heart.

The coach drove down the long lane and turned on to the road which would take them to town.

"Are you ready for all this bloody nonsense?" the captain asked.

Effie burst out laughing. "No. Not really. I am already uncomfortable wearing a gown and wishing I were on a horse, going with Caleb to fix a fence or talk to a tenant."

"No matter how many times Dinah tries to explain it to me, I simply don't understand this Season. I watched Mirella go through it last year, though, and she was happy enough, especially when it led to Byron offering for her."

He slipped his arm around her shoulders, pulling her to him. Effie leaned her head on his shoulder, feeling safe with him beside her.

"I will not let anything happen to you, sweetheart," he told her. "You will only go to something if you really want to. Just because an invitation comes doesn't mean you have to attend every affair. While Mirella was a butterfly, flitting from one event to the next, I think you will be more judicious. Don't tire yourself out by trying to do too much."

"I appreciate hearing that, Captain. I suppose I will have to see what invitations come in and discuss them with Mama."

"These gentlemen will pester you. They'll come sniffing around every afternoon. Send you flowers. Smile at you and give you pretty compliments. Ignore all that, Effie. Go with your gut. You're a smart woman with a good head on your shoulders. You have a full life. Only say yes to a proposal if you truly love the man offering for you."

He kissed the top of her head. "And tell me which ones you wish for me to chase off."

Effie covered his hand with hers. "Thank you for looking out for me. For taking care of Mama and all of us."

"I may not have been there when you born or for most of your growing up, but you are my family. My daughter. I would bleed for you. Die for you," he proclaimed gruffly.

"Well, let us hope it does not come to that, Captain," she teased.

They changed horses at one point, and finally the great city of London came into view. Effie swallowed, calming herself. She would either find a husband she was mad enough for to wed—or she would return to Shadowcrest. This Season was as if she stood to where a road divided.

It would be up to her to make the choice of which path to follow.

Chapter Two

"I AM SO excited that Madame Dumas will be making up my entire Season's wardrobe," Ada gushed at the breakfast table. "Mama says she is the most exclusive modiste in town and rarely takes on a new client."

Malcolm only listened to his sister with half an ear. They had arrived in town yesterday, coming over a month before the actual Season began because of the extensive wardrobe his sister would require for making her come-out. He had the necessary funds and did not mind spending them on Ada. She was very dear to him. He simply did not like being in town so early. At Waterside, he always seemed to have things to accomplish. London was another kettle of fish.

His father had passed away a few weeks before Malcolm had finished at Oxford. The dons had all agreed that since he was such an excellent student, they would award him his degree. It had allowed him to go straight to Waterside and take up his new duties as the Duke of Waterbury.

He had not known how frail his father was until he returned home from his studies at Oxford, with only a final year left in his studies. It seemed as if overnight the duke had aged and grown shaky, constantly out of breath, his balance fragile. Returning to university a last time, he had awakened every morning, hoping this would not be the day he received news that his father was gone.

It did surprise him that Waterbury had passed away at Waterside instead of in town. His parents had always gone to the Season for as long as he could remember. Mama had gone without her husband that particular year, though, and so word had also been sent to her to return to Kent for the funeral. It appalled Malcolm how put out she had been, vocalizing how she would have to go into mourning and miss the rest of that Season.

Since he became the duke at so young an age, Malcolm had never spent several years in town as many young men did, carousing and sowing his wild oats. He thought of London beyond the events of the Season as being nothing more than a playground for young bachelors to gamble, drink, and wench. When he attended the Season with Mama a few years ago, wishing to find a bride, he had dutifully attended the events in search of his duchess, skipping out on how other bachelors spent their time.

"Did you hear me, Malcolm?" Ada demanded.

He turned to his sister. "I was woolgathering. I must admit talk of gowns and how many buttons a spencer should have, and the number of hats required of a lady had me turning to other things."

Ada smiled indulgently at him. "I was asking about the first ball. I will need you to introduce me to all your friends so that they might dance with me."

Malcolm had no friends.

Outsiders would never have guessed that. Oh, he knew a great many people from his schooldays and had an abundance of acquaintances. Everyone his entire life remarked upon what a true leader he was. Decisive. Responsible. Confident. A man who always was aware of his destiny and followed through with his promises. Malcolm simply was the best at everything he did, from academics to sports to riding and dancing. Everything came effortlessly to him and always had.

And yet because of that, the majority of his classmates had been envious of him. Yes, everyone wanted him on their team, to earn the necessary points—but when all was said and done, they paired off in twos and threes, going their own way with their friends.

Leaving him alone.

His tutors praised him at every turn, which only increased his alienation from his other schoolmates, and their jealousy grew. It was as if all wanted to be his friend—but none were. It had caused him to grow to be very detached around others. He put a smile on his face and was friendly to everyone who crossed his path. He cheered on others and rewarded them with slaps on the back and a shake of the hand.

But in reality, he kept to himself. He thought it prepared him for the future, when he would be the Duke of Waterbury. His father was cold and distant from all others, including his own family, and Malcolm grew up believing that was the way things should be. He merely had been set upon that path at an early age. Yet he grimaced inwardly, thinking of how disastrous that line of thinking had been and what a terrible husband he had made.

"Of course, Waterbury will introduce you around, Ada," Mama said.

He almost snorted, knowing she had no idea about anything of his growing up or private life.

Then again, as obsequious as his classmates had been when they wanted to gain his favor, Malcolm could only imagine how magnified their behavior would be since he was now a duke. Three Seasons ago, when he had found his wife in Imogen, he had only attended a handful of social events and had never gone to White's or any gaming hells with anyone he knew. Even then, making only rare appearances, others had practically groveled at his feet.

This time, he would be attending a majority of the hosted events because of Ada. He also wanted more time to peruse the Marriage Mart. Mama had made the choice of his bride the previous time. Despite what she thought, Malcolm intended to take matters into his own hands and make that decision himself this time around. He would need to get to know some of these eligible young ladies before he committed to one of them. She would need to take the title of being his duchess seriously. He realized how Imogen had been too immature to do so. While he did not expect a worldly bride, this second marriage would require a woman who could at least hold a decent conversation, both with him and others in Polite Society.

Trying to relax, he told Ada, "I am acquainted with a good number of gentlemen. It has been a few years since I have been around Polite Society, though. I will introduce you to as many appropriate gentlemen as I can, but I will also be asking questions behind the scenes to ascertain if they are good enough for you or not."

The same would be true of his bride. Malcolm would not be rushed this time. He would find a suitable duchess by the end of the Season and wed her. He hoped the same would be true of Ada and that she might possibly wed by Season's end. He wanted his sister's husband to be a man of good character, have no debt, and be respectful to Ada. If it took hiring a Bow Street runner to investigate the backgrounds of Ada's more serious prospects, then he was not above doing so.

His answer seemed to please his sister.

"Thank you, Waterbury," she said, her smile wide. "I worry that there will be so many pretty girls making their come-outs. That no one will wish to dance with me, and I will be relegated to sit with the wallflowers, tapping my toes to the music instead of actually dancing."

He shook his head. "First, you *are* one of those pretty girls, Ada. Second, Mama will tell you that you are the sister to a duke. You will have absolutely no problem attracting gentlemen. It will be up to me to weed out those who are paying attention to you for your dowry, and I will send those men packing."

Ada frowned, her worry obvious. "Oh, I had not thought about someone only wanting me for my fortune, Malcolm. That is most troublesome."

"As I said, let me handle your suitors. All are free to call—but they will always have to speak with me before they do you. I will purge your group of suitors, eliminating those whom I believe to be avaricious or untrustworthy. Only the best will do for my sister."

She leaped to her feet and flung her arms about his neck. "Thank you, Malcolm. I am grateful to have you looking after me." She gazed at him. "I will also help you to find a bride."

"That is not necessary, Ada," he said crisply.

"Oh, but it is," she declared. "I am certain to get to know the girls in my come-out class, and I will be able to let you know if they are shallow gossips or if they have some substance to them." Grinning, she added, "I will be your spy, rooting out those who would merely wish to wed you so that they might become a duchess, and informing you which ladies you might find to be strong candidates."

He couldn't help but laugh. "Ah, poppet, you do my heart good. We shall help one another, then. Hopefully by the end of this Season, two betrothals will be announced, with two weddings taking place."

Mama snorted. "And what of my role in these important matters? Am I a cipher in all this? I would expect that you would clamor for my opinion. After all, I am your mother. I will be full of good advice and direct you to whom I deem acceptable spouses."

Quickly, so as to appease Mama and her quick temper, Malcolm said, "Ah, Mama will be ever so helpful to you, Ada. She will be able to tell you which color of gown looks best on you and what hat and reticule you should make part of your ensemble. She will know which hairstyle is most becoming, and she will chaperone you every afternoon as your many suitors come to call. Mama is quite discerning. She will be of great help in finding you a husband."

He made certain to leave out that she would not be helping him to choose his new wife.

His words seem to soothe her, and talk turned again to gowns and things Malcolm had no interest in.

Rising, he said, "If you will excuse me. I have things to do."

"You will not escort us to the modiste?" Mama said, clearly put out with him.

Irritated, he tried not to show it. "Would you like me to do so, Mama? I merely thought you would be at the dressmaker's shop for several hours, looking at materials and making your selections. I would not be helpful in the slightest."

His mother considered that. "Then take us to Madame Dumas' shop and see us inside. Go and do as you wish after that, but return for us in three hours' time. That should be long enough to see things are started in the proper fashion."

"Very well. When is your appointment?" he asked.

"We are to be there at ten o'clock."

Mama told him where the shop was located, and Malcolm said they could leave at half-past nine.

He went to his study and first made a list of things he wished to discuss with Mr. Pace, his solicitor. After doing so, he composed a note to Pace, asking for an appointment tomorrow morning in order to discuss these items with him. Malcolm made a copy and thoughtfully included the list in his note, ringing for Williams and asking the butler to have a footman deliver the note to Pace's office.

"Shall he wait for a reply, Your Grace?" Williams asked.

"Yes, see that he does. I am requesting to see Mr. Pace tomorrow morning. If that is not convenient, I want to know when I can visit with him."

That accomplished, Malcolm flipped through the first of the invitations which had already arrived for the first week of the Season. As usual, there would be an opening ball as the inaugural event of the festivities. This year, it would be hosted by Lord and Lady Simmons. He combed through his memory, thinking Lord Simmons was two or three years older than he was. If it was the same man, he had gone to

Eton with Malcolm but then chosen to further his studies at Cambridge. Lord Simmons had also become betrothed the same year Malcolm had. He recalled the future Lady Simmons being friendly and polite. That was more the type of woman he hoped to wed by Season's end.

He combed through the rest of the invitations, seeing the usual events occurring that first week. Obviously, more would be received as the Season drew near. He set aside the stack, thinking he would give these to Mama after they came home from their errands today and let her respond to them. It would give her something to do and less time to dwell on the wife she thought she would be choosing for him.

What he would do while his mother and sister discussed gowns still puzzled him. He supposed he should go to White's. It was the place to see and be seen by gentlemen of the *ton*. Malcolm had only visited it a handful of times the year he had come to town. It was a place he could peruse the morning newspapers and gossip with others or, in his case, be left alone. He would do his best to appear the very essence of a duke and hope others might leave him in peace.

Then again, this might be the very place he would need to seek out others because of Ada making her come-out. If he could get to know a few of the bachelors before the Season began, he might steer her toward the ones he approved of. Yes, he would definitely go to White's. He assumed his membership had continued during his absence from town, his club fees paid by Mr. Pace. If that were not the case, surely White's would not turn down a duke wishing to spend a bit of leisurely time within its walls. He could then see that Pace paid any outstanding fees if they were due.

Hearing the clock chime, he knew it was time to meet Mama and Ada in the foyer and went there. Though he had not informed Barker he was going out, the well-informed valet held out Malcolm's hat and walking cane to him.

Ada floated down the stairs, but they waited a good ten more minutes for his mother. He had yet to see her ever be on time, and that stuck in his craw. Once the Season began, he would make certain that he was quite clear on the time to leave. It would be leave when he wished—or be left behind.

Chuckling to himself at what her reaction to that statement might be, he saw her coming down the stairs. Still attractive for her age—and still highly opinionated about every topic introduced. Malcolm decided a private chat with Mama would be in order soon, not only to discuss leaving for engagements at the appropriate time but informing her of his decision to select a bride of his own choosing.

Without her interference.

As they got into his carriage, he decided he knew why Mama had wanted his escort. She wanted to be seen pulling up in the ducal carriage. He knew it had put her nose out of joint when he wed and she had become known as the Dowager Duchess of Waterbury. If anything, Mama thrived on the prestige that came from being a duchess. If this modiste was as exclusive as Mama claimed, she would want to be seen arriving in style.

They reached the modiste's shop, which was located in a fashionable part of town. Malcolm handed down Mama first and then Ada. He offered an arm to each and took them inside the dress shop. There, Madame Dumas fussed over the pair, in effect, dismissing him. He wanted to remind the dressmaker that he would be the one paying the bills she submitted, but would not be so petty.

He left without a goodbye, seeing another carriage had pulled up to the same destination. As he moved to his own vehicle and ordered his driver to head to White's, he saw a tall, handsome man of about forty years of age step from the carriage, handing down a handsome woman with hair the color of honey. She was quite petite when compared to him and while close to the man in age, still a beauty.

Just as Malcolm's footman opened the door to his carriage, another passenger descended. She was tall for a woman, thin, with a small waist and small, high breasts. He thought her quite pretty and assumed she was the daughter of the pair.

As he settled against the cushions and the carriage began to roll, Malcolm wondered if the girl might be making her come-out this Season.

And if she were still at the modiste's shop when he returned for his mother and sister, so much the better.

Chapter Three

Effie looked out the window as they traveled through the busy streets of London to the dressmaker who would make up Effie's entire wardrobe this Season. She longed to be back in the country, tending to her animals and breathing in the fresh air, but she would keep a positive attitude. She owed Mama that much because of the sacrifices she had made for her girls. Though she doubted she would come out of it with a husband, she did hope she would make some friends beyond her sisters.

"I have used Madame Dumas for years," Mama remarked. "You will remember her, I am certain, for she has made a few gowns for you in recent years."

She did. "I like her because she is no-nonsense. She is a woman who is talented at what she does."

"Madame rarely takes on new clients, especially for the Season," Mama told her. "She has always been good to me and all you girls, especially as you have turned older and your needs for gowns have increased." She paused, hope in her eyes. "I want you to enjoy today, Effie. Oh, I know you are not one to relish talking about and wearing gowns, especially fancy ones, but you are striking with your height. I believe that Madame will enjoy dressing you for this Season."

Placing her hand over her mother's, Effie said, "I promise I will not be difficult, Mama. I actually am looking forward to this Season because I will get to see all my sisters and cousins. It seems as if it has been a long time since were together, thanks to marriages and babes appearing."

Her mother smiled gently. "Yes, it will be good for all of us to be together again, even if we are not under the same roof. That is what makes the Season so special. You get to be with your loved ones, as well as see your friends. Old ones—and even new ones you make each year."

"I am looking forward to making friends with others," she declared, determined to do that very thing.

They sat in contented silence until they reached the dressmaker's shop. A footman handed them down, and they entered.

Immediately, Effie sensed something was wrong. She spied Madame Dumas with another, older woman and a younger one who looked painfully embarrassed. The older woman looked none too pleased and spoke sharply with the modiste.

Mama turned to Effie. "That is the Duchess of Waterbury. Actually, the dowager duchess. I recall reading in the newspapers of her son's marriage. Shall we try and rescue Madame?"

They moved through the shop toward the three women. Effie noticed the younger girl's beautiful dark hair and luminous green eyes, which reminded her of Daffy's. She looked as if she wished for the floor to swallow her up.

"I insist this is the date which you provided to me, Madame Dumas," the dowager duchess said emphatically. "No, I am *not* confused, and we will *not* return tomorrow. You will see to things now, or I shall ruin you."

Effie winced at such a threat, but she trusted her mother to handle the situation with aplomb.

Mama smiled brightly and said, "Good morning, Your Grace. How lovely to see you. And you, as well, Madame Dumas. My daughter and I are so looking forward to our appointment with you today."

"It is good to see you, Your Grace," snapped the dowager duchess, a strained smile on her face. "Madame has obviously confused our appointments, however."

Effie looked at the modiste and knew no confusion had taken place. That it was this dowager duchess who had mistakenly come to the dressmaker's shop and now refused to admit her error. She did wonder, however, if Mama would correct the two women, both whom had addressed her as the duchess she once had been.

Mama said, "May I present my daughter, Your Grace? This is Lady Euphemia, the youngest of my six girls. And this is Her Grace, the Dowager Duchess of Waterbury."

The dowager duchess smiled grimly. "It is nice to meet you, Lady Euphemia. Might I present my own daughter, Lady Ada. She is to make her come-out this Season, and that is why it is imperative we begin on her wardrobe immediately."

"Ah, my daughter is also making her come-out," Mama said calmly. "What a wonderful opportunity for our girls to meet prior to the beginning of the Season. It is such an overwhelming task, trying to choose all the fabrics for a come-out wardrobe. Why, I would feel privileged if we accomplished this difficult task together. I would appreciate your input, along with Madame's, of course. Might we share this appointment with you and allow our girls to get to know one another better?"

Effie could see the dowager duchess thinking over the request. She decided to help sweeten the pot.

"Oh, Mama, what a wonderful idea. You know I have been looking forward to making friends with the other girls in my come-out group, and I think Lady Ada and I will become good ones." She looked to the girl and said, "Would you like to share this time together, Lady Ada.? I would enjoy being able to visit with you while we are looking at sketches and materials for our gowns. I am certain your mother has excellent taste, as does my own. Together, we will be the best-dressed girls making our come-outs this Season."

Lady Ada smiled shyly and looked to her mother. "It would be rather fun, Mama. Would you please consider doing so?"

They all waited with bated breath until the dowager duchess gave a quick nod. "It will take longer, but this will be good for Ada to make her first friend, especially the daughter of a duke and duchess."

She thought her mother would now remind this woman that she was no longer a duchess or at least inform her of her marriage to Captain Andrews. Mama kept silent, however. Effie realized her mother did so because she was using her former status in Polite Society to convince this disagreeable woman to stay and keep the peace. Effie glanced at Madame Dumas, seeing that she looked hopeful.

Smoothly, Madame said, "I have enough assistants. We will be able to accomplish quite a bit over the next several hours, Your Graces."

Effie noted even the modiste, who was certainly aware of Mama's second marriage, was using Mama's former title in order to keep the peace.

"And your girls are quite different, so it is not as if they will be competing for the various styles of gowns I design for them. I am known for dressing women of all ages and flattering their figures."

Mama beamed. "Then it is settled. We will share this appointment, and if for some reason we do not finish our work today, we can come back tomorrow and extend our time together."

"Let me take the young ladies to the dressing rooms to be measured," the modiste said, "while Your Graces enjoy a bit of conversation."

Effie followed Madame Dumas to the dressing room, slipping her arm through Lady Ada's and guiding her along.

When they were out of sight, Lady Ada said in wonder, "Your mother managed Mama so easily, Lady Euphemia. She can be . . .

difficult. I am so glad we get to stay. I have longed to make friends. We live in Kent, and I have never been to town before."

"Never?" she asked, remembering that it was the habit of most couples to leave their children in the country during the Season. "I, too, live in Kent. My brother is the Duke of Seaton, and I grew up at Shadowcrest. It is about thirty-five miles southwest of Maidstone."

"My brother is the Duke of Waterbury," Lady Ada said. "I, too, grew up in Kent. Waterside is close to Canterbury, on the coast."

"We are practically neighbors," Effie declared. "And you must call me Lady Effie. Euphemia is a mouthful, and I never go by it. My entire family calls me Effie."

"Is your family small or large?" Lady Ada asked as Madame had Effie stand on a raised platform and her assistants removed Effie's gown so that she might be measured properly.

"Oh, we are quite large," she said. "There are six girls in all, and my brother, along with my cousin Caleb. He is the Shadowcrest steward. I am thrilled that all my sisters and cousins will be in town for the Season, minus Caleb. He never attends."

While she was measured and then Lady Ada was, Effie ran through the roster of her family, explaining how Lyric and Allegra had been raised alongside the four daughters of the household and how she considered her two cousins to be more like sisters. She named each of their husbands and children, as well.

"All these marriages have taken place within the last couple of years," she explained. "I am the last of the girls, but Mama also has a baby boy. Little James, whom we all call Jamie, so as not to confuse him with my brother James."

Lady Ada's eyes grew round. "Your mother has a *babe?*" she squeaked.

"Yes. She was a widow and married Captain Andrews. The captain now helps to run Neptune Shipping, which my sister-in-law Sophie owns."

The other girl looked flabbergasted. "A duchess... *owns*... a business?"

She laughed as the assistants redressed Lady Ada. "She most certainly does. James was most insistent that his bride keep her company. My brother is an unusual man. You will meet him when the Season begins, if not before. Why, you and your mother must come to tea soon so that we might become better acquainted."

"You keep calling him James, but you said he is a duke," Lady Ada said. "Why do you not refer to him as Seaton?"

"He is my brother. James is his name. What else would I call him?"

"But dukes go by their titles, Lady Effie. Never their names. Even Mama and I call my brother Waterbury at all times."

Effie was beginning to see her family was quite different from others.

"James prefers us to refer to him in that manner, just as he wanted Sophie to keep her business. Their son George will become the Duke of Seaton one day and inherit Strong Shipping, our family's shipping line, while their other children will own and operate Neptune Shipping."

"You mean the sons will inherit," Lady Ada corrected her.

"No," she said. "The company will go equally to their other sons *and* daughters. James and Sophie are quite insistent about that. They both believe that girls can do anything boys can. My sisters believe the same."

Confusion filled Lady Ada's face. "But their husbands cannot believe that. Or... do they?" she questioned, clearly rattled by what Effie was sharing with her.

Madame said, "We may return to your mothers now and talk about styles and fabrics, my ladies."

Once more, Effie slipped her hand through Lady Ada's arm. "I think my family is most unusual. I hope you will become friends not only with me but also my sisters, cousins, and sister-in-law, Lady Ada.

If you would like, I can show you a bit about town. We came every year during the Season, and Mama always took us about to different places. Museums. Hyde Park. Bookshops."

Perplexed, Lady Ada asked, "You did not remain in the country?"

She felt almost guilty, saying, "No. Mama would have been beside herself having to leave all her girls for several months. Papa rarely saw us, so it did not matter to him where we were."

Lady Ada viewed her with new eyes. "You—and your family—are quite different, Lady Effie. I find it . . . refreshing." She smiled widely. "I am eager to get to know all of you."

They joined Mama and the dowager duchess, who were seated at a large table. Effie took the seat next to her mother, while Lady Ada sat beside her mother.

Madame Dumas sat at the head of the table. "All the measurements have been recorded, Your Graces. I have several ideas already how to dress each of your daughters."

"I look forward to hearing them," Mama said before the other woman could respond. "I have always trusted your judgment these many years we have worked together, Madame Dumas."

Mama turned to the dowager duchess and said, "Madame has dressed me, as well as my six girls. I trust her advice immensely. I am certain you will do the same. No one has quite the command of fashion as our modiste."

"This is the first time I have tried Madame Dumas," the dowager duchess replied. "She came highly recommended."

"I would not have anyone but Madame Dumas dress my family," Mama said firmly. "Not only will she create my wardrobe again for this Season, but she will make up the Duchess of Seaton's and the other women's in my family. Though my other daughters and nieces have all wed now, they know a gown designed and sewn by Madame Dumas is the only gown worth wearing during the Season."

The dowager duchess smiled, and Effie felt the entire table let out a sigh of relief seeing it.

"Shall we view some sketches, Your Graces?" the modiste asked.

They did so, while Madame sketched gowns as they spoke and came up with new ideas. Effie learned more about the types of events which she would be attending and the gowns expected to be worn to each. When Mama mentioned there would be over fifty balls to attend, Effie bit back a curse. Not that she was one to do so, but Caleb released one every now and then when he was frustrated, and she had picked up the habit.

She would have to watch herself around Polite Society's members and make certain she did not slip up.

The more the three older women talked, the more Effie realized just what a large investment James was making in her. It became apparent that she was expected *not* to repeat wearing a gown the entire Season. The thought of having over fifty ball gowns alone appalled her. That did not even include the many day gowns she would be required to wear, especially when suitors came calling.

Then there were other events held, both day and night. Venetian breakfasts. Garden parties. Card parties. Routs. Musicales. Trips to the theatre and opera. The number of gowns that must be made up astounded her. Effie promised herself she would wear these gowns for the next decade and never ask her brother for anything again. The fact that James had provided entire wardrobes for other women in their family did not surprise her, but she began to have a greater understanding of the Season. How important it was to be seen wearing the right gowns, created by a few, select modistes.

Once they had decided upon a large number of designs, Effie thought they would leave the shop, but they were only getting started. Assistants began bringing out bolts of material, and Mama and the dowager duchess had to examine each, fingering the fabrics and matching them to various sketches. That process took another two hours.

By the time it concluded, Effie was exhausted—and she had done nothing but sit there and agree every now and then. She had told Mama to make these kinds of choices for her, and she was glad to have done so because her mother had exquisite taste in matching a design to the right color and fabric.

Even Madame Dumas acknowledged Mama's skill, saying, "You have quite the eye for fashion, Your Grace."

"Yes," the dowager duchess agreed. "My Ada will stand out in every ballroom she enters, thanks to your advice in selecting designs and fabrics. I am grateful we decided to share this appointment, Your Grace. Thank you for all your help today regarding Ada's wardrobe. Because of it, she—and Lady Euphemia—will be the most elegantly-clad girls of their come-out group."

Sensing things were coming to an end and wanting to see Lady Ada again, Effie spoke up. "It would be nice if we could continue this friendship, Mama. Might we ask Her Grace and Lady Add to tea tomorrow afternoon?"

"What a delightful idea, Effie," Mama praised. "We would be happy to host you. My husband and I live in a wing of my stepson's townhouse."

Mama gave the dowager duchess directions to the Seaton townhouse. Effie saw the other woman was a bit perplexed.

"So, you and your husband live with your stepson, who now is the Duke of Seaton."

Her mother smiled warmly. "I was widowed several years ago. I have since remarried. You might not have been aware of that, Your Grace. Actually, I am plain Mrs. Andrews now. I should have reminded Madame Dumas of that. One just becomes used to being called Your Grace. It quite slipped my mind."

"So, you are Mrs. Andrews," the dowager duchess mused.

"Yes, I am. His Grace and my husband are the closest of friends. More like brothers, in fact. Their Graces would be delighted if you and your daughter came to tea. Unfortunately, they are in the country now and will not return to town for another week or so. Until then, I am charged to act as hostess in Her Grace's absence. I would very much like for you to meet my husband, Your Grace. Would you mind if I asked Mr. Andrews to join us at tea?"

Before the older woman could reply, Lady Ada said, "That would be wonderful, Mrs. Andrews. Might we also bring my brother with us? Waterbury would be happy to escort us to tea."

The girl's mother frowned at her a moment, and Lady Ada's gaze dropped to her lap. It was apparent the dowager duchess was always the one to speak up and make decisions. Effie felt sorry for Lady Ada. She had always been both outspoken and opinionated, and her family had taken that in stride because it was simply the way she was. Once again, she gave thanks for growing up in the family she had.

She watched as the dowager duchess mulled over things a moment and then said, "We would be happy to come to tea tomorrow afternoon, *Mrs. Andrews.*"

Effie heard the emphasis on the Mrs. part and suppressed a chuckle. Apparently, this woman thought she had been duped by both Mama and Madame Dumas, as they both had pretended Mama was still a duchess. Still, the Dowager Duchess of Waterbury hadn't been able to pass up an invitation from a former duchess and most likely only accepted it because Effie was the daughter of one duke and the sister of another, and would make a suitable friend for Lady Ada.

"Then we will see you at four o'clock tomorrow afternoon," Mama said cheerfully.

The outside door opening caught Effie's attention. They had been in the shop the entire time without a single customer entering. She believed because it was still early March that browsers were not in town, and the only clients Madame was seeing were those wishing to discuss their wardrobes for the Season.

A tall, lean man with a serious countenance moved across the shop toward them. It was obvious that this was Lady Ada's brother because they resembled one another so closely. Both had hair as dark as midnight and those incredibly green eyes. The duke was about six feet in height and possessed an athletic frame. He moved with catlike grace.

All the women stood as he approached, and the dowager duchess said, pride evident in her voice, "This is my son, the Duke of Waterbury. Your Grace, this is Mrs. Andrews and her daughter, Lady Euphemia."

The duke took Mama's hand. "Enchanted to meet you, Mrs. Andrews." He kissed her fingers before releasing Mama's hand and turning to Effie. "Equally charmed, my lady," he said, his voice low.

He claimed her hand and brought it to his lips, his gaze fastened upon her. The duke kissed her fingers and lowered her hand, not releasing it. Thinking he must have forgotten to do so, Effie tugged gently and then pulled harder to reclaim her hand again.

"Mrs. Andrews has just invited us to tea tomorrow, Waterbury," Lady Ada said, her happiness plainly written across her face. "Lady Effie is also to make her come-out this Season. We are going to be the best of friends."

"It is good you have made a friend, Ada," Waterbury said.

"Mrs. Andrews was formerly the Dowager Duchess of Seaton, but she has remarried," Lady Ada continued, earning a disapproving look from her mother.

"Is that so?" His Grace said. "Regardless of your title, Mrs. Andrews, I would be happy to escort Mama and Ada to your house for tea."

"You are invited as well, Your Grace," Mama told the duke. "In fact, my husband will be joining us. I am certain you will find plenty of topics to discuss with him."

Waterbury nodded. "Then I accept your kind invitation, Mrs. Andrews." He looked to his mother. "I came inside to find out what was taking so long."

"We are done for the day, Waterbury," the dowager duchess replied.

"Since you have agreed to accompany your mother and sister to tea, Your Grace, why don't you bring Her Grace, as well?" Mama asked.

A pained expression crossed his face, quickly passing. Effie wondered why.

"I am a widower, Mrs. Andrews."

Mama smiled sympathetically. "I am sorry to hear that, Your Grace."

"These things happen," he said vaguely, not offering any details of his wife's passing.

"We should be going, Effie," Mama said. She turned to the modiste. "Thank you again, Madame Dumas, for taking on so many Strongs this Season." She smiled graciously at the pair of women. "We look forward to continuing our conversation with you tomorrow, Your Grace."

They left the dress shop and climbed into the waiting carriage.

Mama sighed as the carriage took off. "My, that was certainly challenging. Her Grace is a bit snooty."

"But you handled her beautify, Mama. I feel sorry for Lady Ada, though. She seems quite cowed by her mother."

Mama patted Effie's hand. "I believe you will be a good influence on her."

She thought the same but had not voiced it, deciding she would need to practice curbing her tongue a bit while in town.

"I do think Lady Ada and I are going to be friends."

"I think so, as well," Mama agreed. "I wonder when His Grace lost his wife—and if he is looking for a new one yet."

"No matchmaking, Mama," Effie warned.

Mama laughed. "I was not thinking about that."

"You were. You simply are not admitting it," she said, teasing her mother.

"Well, perhaps the thought did cross my mind, but I know you have a very strong will, Effie. You will need to be the one who decides which gentlemen you are interested in and which ones you will allow to call."

"I am glad you will have the captain present tomorrow. He can keep His Grace occupied, while you can sacrifice yourself and do the same with Her Grace. That will give me time to visit with Lady Ada. In fact, I may even suggest a tour of James' townhouse so we can spend some time alone. And she has never been to town before, Mama. Ever! We must take her on a few outings with us before the Season begins."

Mama laughed. "I am pleased you are so enthusiastic about making a new friend, Effie. We will most certainly ask Lady Ada to go with us to a few places. Preferably, *alone*."

They both began laughing, and Effie was glad she was having this special time with Mama. Ever since her marriage to the captain, the couple spent a great deal of time in town, while Effie preferred staying at Shadowcrest with all her animals. She had missed being around Mama, who always approached life with such joy.

"I know where we take Lady Ada first," Effie decided. "A trip to Gunter's!"

CHAPTER FOUR

MALCOLM ESCORTED MAMA and Ada to the carriage, intrigued by Lady Euphemia. Effie, as her mother had referred to her.

She was even prettier than he had thought when he had seen her from a distance. Ada was obviously taken by her, as well. The only thing that worried him was that Lady Euphemia had been so quiet. He'd already had one wife who had barely spoken before they wed and rarely spoke after they did. This time, he was looking for someone he could carry on a decent conversation with. To be fair, he *was* a duke. That might have inhibited conversation. Most likely, she had been in awe of him.

Ada was extremely chatty on the way home, which was most unlike her. Usually, his sister was very reserved, and he wondered if Ada's loquaciousness was due to having made a new friend today. If the two were truly to become friends, then it might be possible for Malcolm to know more about Lady Euphemia before the Season even began. If fortune were with him, he might have already found his new bride, which would make the Season more tolerable.

Then again, he knew not to rush into anything, with Lady Euphemia or any other woman. Malcolm hoped his second marriage would be one which would last—and bring him some peace of mind.

"While it is good you have met someone your own age," Mama cautioned Ada, "you do not have to be overfriendly with Lady

Euphemia and her family."

Ada frowned. "You sound as though you disapprove of her and Mrs. Andrews, Mama. I do not see why you would. After all, Lady Euphemia is the daughter of a duke and duchess."

"And that duchess was unwise enough to wed again and forgo her title," Mama said accusingly. "Who would do such a thing? Give up the highest rank in Polite Society to wed a man of absolutely no social standing? If the mother has such little common sense, I fear the daughter might also lack it."

Wanting to smooth things over, Malcolm said, "Mama, let Ada make her friend. It is good that she is not worried about where Lady Euphemia ranks in Polite Society." Smiling at his sister, he added, "You are correct. Her bloodlines are good since she is the daughter of a duke and duchess. That alone makes her appropriate company for you."

"She just is so . . . kind and refreshing," Ada declared. "Why, we took to each other from the start as Madame Dumas and her assistants measured us. I like her quite a bit, Waterbury. I could not be more pleased when she suggested that we come for tea tomorrow." She smiled sweetly at him. "Thank you for agreeing to escort us."

Then his sister said something which Malcolm wished she would have kept to herself.

"Who knows? You and Lady Effie might also enjoy one another's company. Why, she might not only become my friend—she could become as a sister to me if the two of you wed!"

Seeing the sour look appear on his mother's face, Malcolm quickly said, "You are putting the cart before the horse, Ada. It is simply tea between new acquaintances. Whether I decide to wed again this Season is not what you should be thinking about. We must focus on you and the match you will make."

"Waterbury is right," Mama said. "I need to find out more about Mrs. Andrews and her situation. Something about Seaton is nagging at me. I will recall it sooner or later."

Pouting, Ada said, "Or you could find out at tea tomorrow, Mama. Just come out and ask what you wish to know."

His sister's outburst earned a sharp rebuke from their mother. "I simply do not know what has come over you, Ada. You are never this outspoken. If this is the poor influence Lady Euphemia and Mrs. Andrews have had upon you, perhaps I should beg off from tea tomorrow."

Immediately, tears filled his sister's eyes, and she pleaded, "No, Mama. Please do not do that. You know how much I have wished to make friends my own age. I have truly had no one before now. It is something I have longed for as this Season has drawn near."

"You should be focused upon finding a husband, Ada. Not friends. And especially not unsuitable friends." Mama paused. "Still, Mrs. Andrews was once a duchess, and she continues to live in the Duke of Seaton's household. I suppose since we are already committed to going to tea, we should keep our appointment for it."

"Oh, thank you, Mama," gushed Ada. "You will see. Lady Effie is wonderful. She will make a good friend for me. Mrs. Andrews is quite respectable. After all, Madame Dumas has kept her as a client, even after she remarried, and Madame still dresses all of Mrs. Andrews' daughters."

They rode home from the modiste the rest of the way in silence. Malcolm could still feel the waves of disapproval coming off his mother. She had always been conscious of rank and social standing within the *ton*, and it had been her—even more than his father—who had drilled into him what his duty would be when he became the Duke of Waterbury.

He knew that his mother had been the daughter of a viscount, so it had been quite a leap up the social ladder for her to have wed a duke. He realized now how much his mother clung to her title and position and all they afforded. Since he had been born into it and destined to become a duke, Malcolm had never really given the matter any thought. Even when he had wed Imogen, he had not thought of her being the daughter of an earl, but he was certain Mama had been aware of that, which would have made Imogen more suitable in Mama's eyes. Perhaps he should be more aware as he selected his new wife from the eligible ladies in Polite Society, keeping in mind the family she came from and their connections within Polite Society. After all, certain expectations fell upon a duchess. She was to be a leader within the *ton*, as Mama had proven to be all these years.

All Malcolm knew was that he had to be the one responsible for choosing the right woman to be his duchess. He had left the task to his mother the first time around, and those results proved disastrous. Yes, Imogen had been gently bred, was an earl's daughter, and quite pretty. Part of him thought Mama had gravitated toward Imogen as the perfect choice *because* of her youth and inexperience. Instinct told him his mother had wanted to mold Imogen into what she considered the ideal duchess. His bride had proven to be too timid and unassertive. Frankly, she had bored Malcolm.

This time, he would be much more involved in the hunt for a bride. Perhaps instead of one of the girls making her come-out, he might look for someone slightly older, a woman with a bit more maturity about her than Imogen had possessed.

Not every girl wed after her come-out Season, so he might look to those who already had a bit of polish on them. He might even consider a young widow, preferably one without children. While he knew he must provide an heir and hopefully a spare, he was not fond of children and did not see himself spending a great deal of time with any of his own offspring. He would leave the raising of them to his duchess and the servants designated to aid in that.

They arrived home, and Malcolm retreated to his study. He wanted time to himself.

Time to consider his future.

They rode in the carriage to the Duke of Seaton's townhouse, which was located less than half a mile from Malcolm's own townhouse. As they pulled into the square, he saw it was even grander than the residence he owned. He would need to learn all he could today about this duke and his sister. Not only would Lady Euphemia be under consideration to become his duchess, but he wanted to make certain she was the type of woman his sister should be friendly with.

"Calm yourself, Ada," Mama cautioned. "You appear too eager."

"Well, I *am* eager, Mama," Ada said defiantly, shocking him.

Where was his docile sister?

If this was the result of being around Lady Euphemia for a few hours, Malcolm had to agree with his mother in questioning the budding friendship between the two girls.

"You never want to appear the way you are now," Mama warned. "What I tell you goes for Lady Euphemia, as well as any gentleman you meet during the Season. If you appear too eager, the other party will realize they have the upper hand."

"Pish-posh," Ada said breezily. "I do not believe you have to hide your feelings in such a manner."

Mama glared at her daughter. "You will do as I say," her sharp tone even giving Malcolm a chill. "You are to be polite to all and remain distant. Even unapproachable. You are the daughter of a *duke*, Ada. Others are to come to you, not the other way around. Never display your true feelings to anyone. Appear aloof at all times. Even uninterested. That is what will attract others to you."

"But Mama, I think—"

"That is where you are wrong," Mama snapped. "You are not to think. You are merely to do as I tell you. *I* will be the one making the decision for you, Ada, in regard to your husband. Along with Waterbury's input, of course. Your brother knew enough to allow me to select his wife. I will do the same again. For him—and now you."

Tears misted Ada's eyes. "What if I do not like the gentleman you choose for me, Mama? I thought the Season was for me to get to know all the eligible bachelors and then choose the one I would be happiest with."

Mama snorted. "You have stars in your eyes, girl. Liking has little to do with choosing a husband. We are looking for a match that is suitable for our family, not simply for you. Marriage is a business arrangement, Ada. You are a duke's daughter. I wish for you to wed a duke. A marquess, at the very least."

"But... what if there are very few of these titled men available?" Ada asked, a stubborn set to her mouth.

"You leave that to me," Mama said briskly. "The same is to be true for the girls you befriend. You want to keep to those near your station, and I can help you do so. Oh, be polite to all as I have taught you, but you will wed a gentleman with a lofty title, and you will only make friends with the wives who hold a similar position to yourself. Be glad that Lady Euphemia is the daughter of a duke. For the present, that is the only thing in her favor. If you continue these outbursts and remain pouting, as you have, I will forbid you to even speak to her, much less see her."

Ada dabbed her eyes with the handkerchief which Malcolm offered her. "Yes, Mama," she said, and even he heard the resignation in her voice.

Wanting to stand up for her, he said, "There is no need to dash Ada's hopes, Mama, much less break her spirit even before the Season begins. Let us go to tea now and see if Lady Euphemia is a suitable companion to our Ada."

His sister flashed him a grateful look.

"Very well, Waterbury," Mama said. "I will try not to judge anyone before we become familiar with the Duke of Seaton and his family."

The carriage had come to a halt several minutes ago, but no footman had opened the vehicle's door. Malcolm tapped on the ceiling with his cane, indicating they were ready to exit. Immediately, the door opened. He handed down Mama and then Ada, and they approached the front door. They were greeted by a butler who showed them to the drawing room, announcing their arrival.

His eyes immediately went to Lady Euphemia, who smiled brightly at Ada.

As they crossed the drawing room, Malcolm took in the space, seeing it tastefully furnished, with a bit of homeyness about it. His own townhouse looked as if it were a museum, the lavish decor not welcoming in the least.

"How good of you to come today, Your Graces," Mrs. Andrews said graciously.

"Thank you for your kind invitation," he replied, greeting her, then looking to the man standing next to her, recalling him as being the one who had exited the carriage yesterday.

"Your Grace, may I present to you my husband, Mr. Andrews."

He shook Andrews' hand, the man's grip firm, his gaze assessing Mr. Andrews' dress and demeanor.

"Thank you for having us, Mr. Andrews."

He then introduced his mother and Ada to the man before turning his attention to Lady Euphemia.

"It is good to see you again, my lady."

"Likewise, Your Grace," she said pertly, immediately turning her attention away from him and back to Ada.

Mrs. Andrews asked them to take a seat as the teacart was rolled in. Their hostess poured out for the group, her manner elegant and graceful.

"How did you and Mrs. Andrews meet?" Malcolm asked Mr. Andrews, knowing it was something his mother was curious about.

"My best friend is the Duke of Seaton," Mr. Andrews replied. "My wife was his very young stepmother."

"I was Seaton's second wife," Mrs. Andrews explained. "His first had passed away, and His Grace was looking for someone who might give him sons." She smiled. "I happened to present him with four wonderful daughters instead."

"And do not forget Allegra and Lyric," Lady Euphemia prompted.

"Yes, I also raised my two nieces. My sister-in-law passed away after giving birth to the twins, and her husband was not quite certain how to raise girls. It was left to me to bring them up alongside my own. Five of the girls are now wed. Effie is my youngest, and I have high hopes she will find her husband this Season."

Mrs. Andrews took a sip of her tea and added, "Mr. Andrews and I are also parents to a son. Jamie. He is named after my stepson."

"We call him Jamie so as not to confuse him with my brother James," Lady Euphemia offered. "It would be difficult calling them both James and having them respond each time someone did so."

"His Grace is gracious enough to allow us to live here while we are in town," Mrs. Andrews said. "It is convenient since my husband helps run Her Grace's business, Neptune shipping."

Malcolm saw his mother's reaction to this statement and from her eyes, he could tell she had recalled what she wished to remember about this family.

"Oh, I do recall hearing about this," Mama began. "His Grace's family owns Strong Shipping, and he wed the widow of the man who owned Neptune Shipping."

He had heard of both shipping empires since they were the two largest in England.

"That is correct," Mr. Andrews said. "His Grace and I both used to be ship's captains for Neptune Shipping."

Malcolm found that incredibly odd, a duke serving as a ship's captain, especially since it was for a rival line.

Lady Euphemia spoke up, pride on her face as she said, "James loves Sophie so very much that he insisted that she maintain ownership of Neptune Shipping. Their marriage contracts specified this, and Sophie continues to have an active role in Neptune Shipping. Of course, since she has given birth to George and Ida, she has turned over more of the day-to-day running to the captain."

Mr. Andrews chuckled. "My girls insist upon calling me the captain."

"Your girls?" Mama asked pointedly.

"All my wife's girls," the man said, now beaming. "I look upon her four daughters and two nieces as my own flesh and blood. The men who court my Effie will have not only me to answer to—but Seaton, as well."

Lady Euphemia chuckled. "The captain is all bark and little bite," she shared. "He and James pretend they will chase off men who try to court me, but the fact is I will probably chase off most of them myself."

Her statement intrigued Malcolm. "How so, my lady?"

"I am quite finicky, Your Grace. Actually, I suppose I am the only girl making my come-out this Season who is not seeking a husband."

"Not wishing for a husband?" Mama asked, her shock evident.

"No, Your Grace," Lady Euphemia said. "I lead a very full life at Shadowcrest, our family's country estate in Kent. I have a great many animals I care for, and I also assist my cousin Caleb. He is steward of the estate."

Now, Malcolm was the one who tried to hide his own shock as Mrs. Andrews smiled fondly at her daughter.

"Effie is known for bringing home all kinds of strays and injured animals and caring for them. She is under no compunction to make a match this Season or any other."

Mr. Andrews slipped his hand around his wife's, their fingers intertwining, causing Malcolm to be stunned by the public display of affection.

"This family is known for making love matches," Mr. Andrews explained. "Effie knows that. She has seen her brother, along with all her sisters and cousins, also make love matches. If her heart is not whispering to her to give a certain gentleman proper consideration, then she will simply wait until she is moved by her heart in the right direction."

"I am greatly relieved because of this," Lady Euphemia said. "This way, I can go into the Season and simply enjoy it for what it is—a time to be with loved ones—as well as make new friends." She grinned at Ada. "I was so pleased to meet Lady Ada at Madame's yesterday. Mama has promised that she will take us on a few outings together before the Season starts. I am quite familiar with places in town because I came here every year when my parents did each spring. I have several places I wish to show Lady Ada. Mama will chaperone us, of course, and James and Sophie will be happy to do so once they arrive in town next week."

"That is quite unnecessary," his mother said cooly. "My daughter and I have a crowded calendar leading up to the Season. Perhaps you will be able to visit at those social events when the time comes, Lady Euphemia."

He saw how Mama's words crushed Lady Euphemia, and his heart went out to her, as well as his sister. Glancing to Ada, he saw her sitting stiffly, trying to hold in her emotions, a blank stare upon her face.

Though Mama would make certain Malcolm regretted it, he said, "I am certain at least some time might be carved out for an outing or two, Lady Euphemia. What did you have in mind?"

She gazed at him, tears glistening in her eyes, making her look both fragile and appealing at the same time. "I had wanted us to ride and walk in Hyde Park. Do a bit of shopping for ribbons and new bonnets. See the British Museum." She swallowed. "And most definitely go to Gunter's."

He frowned. "Gunter's? I am unfamiliar with that."

Lady Euphemia brightened. "It is simply the best place to go in town," she declared. "They serve the most marvelous ices."

"I have never heard of such a thing," he said, baffled by the term.

"Then you must accompany us to Gunter's, Your Grace," the young lady said. "You will fall in love with it. And then you can take a woman you might court to eat there. It is the only place in town where a gentleman may escort an unchaperoned lady."

Her hands flew to her mouth, her eyes growing large. "I am sorry, Your Grace. I am being presumptuous. You mentioned being a widower yesterday. I assumed with you being a duke, you would wish to wed again so that you might have your heir."

"I will be looking for a bride on the Marriage Mart this Season," he confirmed.

But Malcolm now knew Lady Euphemia Strong would make for a most unsuitable duchess. She was far too talkative, and despite being the daughter of a duke, her family was certainly questionable. He would strike her from his list of possibilities.

"At least come to Gunter's with us," she said. "Could we go tomorrow, Mama?"

"I have appointments throughout the day, Effie. Perhaps the day after?"

Malcolm saw the disappointment flash across his sister's face. He knew how hard his mother was on Ada. How little time she devoted to her only daughter, despite this being her come-out Season. More than anything, he wanted his sister to be happy.

But he even surprised himself when he said, "If it is all right with you, Mrs. Andrews, I will take my sister and Lady Euphemia to Gunter's tomorrow in your stead."

Chapter Five

"Perhaps I should accompany you to Gunter's," Mama said.

Malcolm looked up from the newspaper he read at the breakfast table, his gaze connecting with that of Ada's. For a moment, he saw the panic in them. Then Ada swallowed, and he saw resolve instead.

"If you would like to accompany us, Mama, I think it a lovely idea," his sister said calmly.

He knew that was the last thing Ada wanted—and yet she was agreeing to Mama's suggestion. He started to protest and then decided to let it play out as he watched his mother contemplating her daughter's response.

Finally, Mama said, "I actually have other things to do, Ada. Waterbury will be chaperone enough for you. Although I must voice again that I am not entirely comfortable with this new friendship of yours and ask that you limit your time with Lady Euphemia."

Though Malcolm thought forming a connection with his family and Lady Euphemia's undesirable, he couldn't see the harm with Ada seeing the girl a few times before the Season's start, and came to his sister's rescue.

"I know you said you had qualms, Mama, but Mrs. Andrews comported herself with such grace and dignity at tea yesterday. It is obvious she is the daughter of a gentleman and her many years of being the Duchess of Seaton is evident in both her speech and actions. She also seems quite happy in her second marriage with Mr. Andrews."

Mama clucked her tongue. "It is hard for me to understand how His Grace allows everything to go on that he does. Then again, Seaton has done some questionable things himself."

Malcolm knew exactly what she meant, but he played along in order to soothe her. "What upsets you, Mama? What are you concerns about Ada's new friendship with Lady Euphemia?"

"Obviously, I do not know these people personally, but I do recall what a scandal it was when Seaton wed the Grant widow several years ago. Why, *everyone* knows that a lady does not own anything. That when she weds, everything in its entirety goes to her husband. The fact that the duke specifically wished for his wife to maintain ownership of a large company—much less soil her hands by running it? It simply isn't the done thing, Waterbury."

Ada finally spoke up. "I think it is a good opportunity for the duke's children."

"What do you mean, Ada?" Mama asked sharply.

Meekly, his sister continued, saying, "If the heir apparent is to take on Strong Shipping as his legacy, it only makes sense that his brothers would be able to do the same at Neptune Shipping. It must be very hard to be a second, third, or even fourth son and not have a true role to play within your family or in Polite Society. This way, His Grace's other children have a true place and can contribute."

Mama sniffed. "Second sons are destined for the military, Ada," she said brusquely. "Third sons almost always go into the church and God's service. As to others, they either earn their own living or get by thanks to the largesse of the brother who holds the title in the family."

"I think it a good thing they are keeping both shipping empires within their family," he said. "It makes good business sense. I have read a bit about both these companies in the newspapers. How in recent years, they are not truly competitors but voyaging along different trade routes and bringing back varying items which the other does not. The thoughtfulness and planning which went into that idea, each company moving along trade routes in different parts of the world, is brilliant."

His mother shrugged. "I know nothing about business affairs, and you should not pursue this line of discussion, Ada. Do not encourage her in these matters, Waterbury," she said sharply. "As for today? No talk of business at Gunter's," she instructed. "You may discuss your come-outs. That is all."

"Yes, Mama," Ada said submissively.

But Malcolm caught the fire in her eyes before she lowered her gaze and continued eating.

They left at a quarter past noon. It had been arranged to call for Lady Euphemia at half-past twelve so that they might arrive at Gunter's by one o'clock or shortly afterward.

The moment they were in the carriage, Ada let out a huge sigh.

Malcolm praised her. "You handled Mama beautifully. When you asked her to accompany us today, I do not know who was more surprised—Mama or me."

Ada grinned shamelessly. "It was Lady Effie's idea. She told me as we walked out to the carriage yesterday that Mama would most likely decide to come along and that I should not react adversely when she suggested doing so. She told me to smile sweetly and agree that it was a lovely idea for all of us to be at Gunter's—and then most likely, Mama would choose not to come along with us."

"You two are quite the conspirators," he noted. "Mama is right, though, Ada. We do not know much about these Strongs. Or at least what we do know, Mama is not pleased with, despite the fact Lady Euphemia is the daughter of a duke."

When Ada frowned, he added, "I am not saying you cannot continue this new friendship. You simply need to make friends with other girls, as well." He paused. "But I do like this new you."

She frowned. "What do you mean, Waterbury?"

"You have always been so quiet. So reserved. I know that Mama is quite strong in her opinions, and that probably has stifled you at times. You are growing up, though, Ada. It is time to think for yourself, and I believe you are beginning to do so."

"I do want to be more like Lady Effie," she admitted. "Oh, not that I could ever truly be her, but Lady Effie is not shy around anyone. She speaks her mind without even being asked to do so."

She most certainly did. Malcolm recalled how the girl had discussed how she wasn't truly interested in finding a husband this Season and if she did, she and her family all expected it to be a love match. He did not want to clip Ada's wings, nor did he want her to think the idea of a love match was usual.

"I do hope you are interested in finding a husband this Season, unlike Lady Euphemia."

"Oh, I simply must find a husband, Waterbury," she said passionately. Then, smiling shyly, she added, "I am ready to be out from under Mama's thumb." Her face softened, and she quietly said, "Yes, I have felt stifled all these years. *Yes, Mama. No, Mama, Of course, Mama. Whatever you say, Mama.*"

Malcolm was amazed how quickly she slipped into both docile posture and tone, so it didn't surprise him when she became the new, fiery Ada in the next moment.

"I want to start a new life, Waterbury. My *own* life. I certainly want to run my own household, and I am looking forward to having children."

Ada gazed out the window a long moment and then turned back to him. "Do you believe Mama even wanted children?" she asked. "I know it was expected because she had to provide an heir for Papa. It was the only thing he married her for, and I know she was happy to have had a son that first time so that she had done her duty to the

Ware family."

She shrugged. "But I have always seemed like an afterthought, Waterbury. I realize females are not valued in Polite Society, and Mama has treated me not with loathing... but indifference. I almost think I would rather have had her hate me than be indifferent to me."

Resolve filled his sister's eyes. "That is why I am determined to find my husband this Season. I want to leave your household and go to my own. I will always love you, Waterbury. You know that. You have constantly looked out for me, and I appreciate that more than I can ever convey to you. But it is time for me to stop being smothered by Mama. Time for me to begin anew. I vow I will never treat my children the way she has treated me.

"Look at Mrs. Andrews and Lady Effie and see how close they are. Not only mother and daughter, but they seem to be true friends and enjoy one another's company immensely. Though I have yet to see Mrs. Andrews with her other children, she seems most loving and protective toward them. That is what I want," Ada declared. "I simply wish to love my children unconditionally."

Malcolm had to ask. "What of your husband, Ada? Do you intend to love him?"

The question seemed to startle her. "Why, I suppose I will respect him. It would be nice to actually like him." She shook her head. "Love, however? I have never assumed I would love my husband, Waterbury. I know the topic was mentioned at tea yesterday. How Strongs wed for love." She smiled ruefully. "Apparently, Wares do not—as do most of Polite Society. I realize you did not love Imogen. That Mama picked your bride because Imogen was beautiful and would not challenge you—or Mama. Let's face it, Waterbury. Imogen was never mistress of your household. Mama was the entire time the two of you were wed. I liked Imogen. I liked spending time with her simply because it was someone new to be around, but she had to be the most dull person I have ever encountered."

He couldn't help but laugh aloud. "I would agree wholeheartedly with you about that, Ada. Imogen was lovely to look at, but she had no substance to her. No depth."

"I hope you will not let Mama select your next wife, Waterbury. You are a grown man of eight and twenty. A duke, for goodness' sake. Of all the things you do in your life, choosing your duchess is, without a doubt, the most important decision you will ever make."

Malcolm had never thought of it in those terms. He understood that he wished for a woman who would be suited to become a duchess. He wanted one he might converse with. It would be marvelous if he actually liked her, as Ada had mentioned when speaking about other future husband.

"It will be our secret for now, but I will be selecting my own wife," he told her. "I was not pleased the first time with Mama's choice, and I had already determined I would be making this decision on my own, with no help from her."

"I am delighted to hear that," his sister said, rewarding him with one of her sweet smiles. "I do hope you might share with me if you are interested in a particular lady. I would like to get to know her, see if the two of you might suit. Why, she might tell me things she would never tell you," Ada declared.

He laughed. "Then we will agree to you helping me shop for a bride on the Marriage Mart, and I shall see if I can find you a proper husband. I will get to know the bachelors in town for this Season and see if they are worthy of my beloved little sister."

They arrived at the Seaton townhouse, and Malcolm said, "Wait here. I will collect Lady Euphemia and return shortly."

He stepped from the vehicle and went to the front door, again being greeted by the butler. What surprised Malcolm, though, was that Lady Euphemia was already in the foyer without being summoned.

She smiled brightly at him. "Good morning, Your Grace. Or I

suppose I should say good afternoon now that it is after noon," she said, laughing. "What? You seem surprised to see me? Do you not recall I was to come on this outing with you and Lady Ada to Gunter's?" she teased. "After all, you have shown up here at the proper time."

He was certainly not used to being teased by anyone and found he rather liked it.

"I was merely surprised to see you ready and waiting, lady Euphemia. When escorting my mother and sister anywhere, I used to linger in the foyer many minutes before either arrived. Frankly, I finally figured out not to show up until a quarter-hour after our designated departure time—and then I still am the first one in the foyer."

She laughed, a deep, rich laugh. One which sounded genuine. He recalled the false titters of women of the *ton* from the Season he had attended, deciding he liked this woman as a friend for his sister, despite his previous misgivings.

"I think you will be good for Ada," he told her. "For your punctuality alone." Offering her his arm, he added, "Shall we go?"

Lady Euphemia slipped her hand through the crook of his arm, and a warm, glowing feeling settled over Malcolm. He told himself to ignore it because he had already decided that Lady Euphemia Strong would not be a candidate to become his duchess. Still, he was growing to like her more by the minute.

In the carriage, Lady Euphemia immediately sat next to Ada, and the two women embraced enthusiastically. Malcolm sat across from them and did not have to contribute anything to the conversation. He observed how alive Ada came in this woman's presence, and he thought the change a good one. Lady Euphemia brought out the best in his sister, and that would be apparent to other gentlemen when the Season began. He promised himself that he would not let Mama dictate to Ada as to who her husband would be. Malcolm would make certain he had several, long discussions with Ada and would insist her wedding the man of her choice.

Not Mama's.

"The unique thing about Gunter's is that you may dine indoors or outside," Lady Euphemia told them.

Ada's eyes grew round with surprise. "Dine outside? I have never heard of such a thing beyond a picnic, and I have never been on one of those."

"It is too brisk for us to eat outdoors today, and usually it is only ices and sorbets they serve outside, not a full meal," Lady Euphemia explained. "There is a place on Berkeley Square in which you may pull up your carriage. It is shaded by numerous trees, which makes it comfortable to sit under during the heat of summer. Someone who works from across the street at Gunter's comes out to greet you, dodging traffic along the way. He will write down what you request to have and then return with it minutes later."

"I am so interested in these ices," Ada said. "Might we try one even though we will dine inside today?"

"It would not be a trip to Gunter's if we did not consume an ice," Lady Euphemia declared. "Mama always took us to Gunter's when we came to town. It is the place we all adore."

Lady Euphemia told them about various flavors of ices and sorbets, and he found himself growing hungry.

"We must return another time when the weather is warmer so we can pull in and eat from our carriage."

She turned to Malcolm. "Might you have a barouche in your mews, Your Grace?"

Startled to be address by her so suddenly, he said, "Um . . . yes. I do."

"Excellent," she declared. "That is the best way to go to Gunter's. Sitting in a barouche, you can see all the others who come to eat their ices. You can even converse with them from your carriage. It is ever so much fun. Perhaps we can bring Mama and the captain with us the next time we come. Mama has a sweet tooth, and the captain is sweet on her. He would be happy to bring her here."

"They seem... very much in love," Ada remarked.

"They are," Lady Euphemia said, her smile radiant. "It is lovely to see Mama so very happy. She was my father's second wife for many years. He was much older. He did not get the sons off her which he desired, but Mama was a wonderful mother and hostess. I can recall so many events held at our house during the Season. Even simple dinners changed under Mama's elegant hand into lavish affairs."

"You said that Strongs wed for love," Ada said. "Is it true that all your sisters are in love with their husbands?"

Lady Euphemia nodded enthusiastically. "It started with James and Sophie. I cannot wait for you to meet them. Here they were, the heads of rival companies, and yet they fell madly in love with one another. Ever since then, everyone in our family has wed for love."

Malcolm listened intently as she ran through a list of her sisters and cousins and the circumstances in which they had met their future spouses, and how one set of twins even became betrothed at a house party held at Shadowcrest in their honor.

"A house party sounds like ever so much fun," Ada said. "I wonder if I will ever be invited to one."

"I think you would enjoy attending one," Lady Euphemia said. "You go for rides and walks in the country. Boating, if you have a lake nearby. There are outdoor teas and pantomimes. All kinds of lawn games, from archery to bowling. In our family, music plays a tremendous role. Georgie and Mirella are incredible pianists, and my brother-in-law Silas has the most marvelous voice. When we get together, music is a focal point, and we all enjoy singing along while Mirella or Georgie take turns playing the pianoforte for us. We had the most wonderful house party of family only this past August and September. Pippa and Seth had returned from their honeymoon. They had been gone for well over eighteen months. During the time they traveled the globe, all my other sisters and female cousins had wed, with most already having children. So it made for a very happy time together for our family."

"Then I look forward to attending a house party someday, "Ada declared.

The carriage slowed, and Lady Euphemia pointed out an area, saying, "This is where you would have our coachman pull into if we were simply stopping for ices outdoors, particularly after driving through Hyde Park during the fashionable hour."

Lady Euphemia took Ada's hand and squeezed it. "I am so glad you were able to come today, Lady Ada."

"Mama almost joined us," his sister confided. "I did exactly as you suggested, though, Lady Effie. "I pretended as if I had not a care in the world and seconded what a good idea that would be." She grinned. "Mama decided Waterbury was chaperone enough for us."

Looking to him, Lady Euphemia said, "Thank you, Your Grace. For being our chaperone. I hope you, too, might enjoy this trip to Gunter's."

Malcolm knew he would enjoy this outing today.

And Lady Euphemia's company.

CHAPTER SIX

As they approached the tearoom, Lady Euphemia pointed to the sign above it, saying, "Gunter's was once called The Pot and the Pineapple. It started as a confectionery store. They have kept the pineapple sign as an homage to their roots."

Malcolm opened the door for them, and the ladies entered first. As he stepped inside, he heard Lady Euphemia already being greeted by name.

"Ah, Lady Effie. What a pleasure to see you again. You did not come to Gunter's last Season," a woman said.

"I was enjoying a bit of freedom, Mrs. Taylor. I am making my come-out this year and wanted to spend a final, blissful summer at Shadowcrest with my animals. How is Priscilla doing?"

"Fit as a fiddle, my lady," Mrs. Taylor replied. She looked to him and Ada. "Lady Effie found a litter of kittens and convinced me to take one a few years ago. Then poor Priscilla broke one of her legs, and Lady Effie took the cat in herself and nursed my Priscilla back to good health."

Lady Euphemia smiled fondly at the memory. "It was hard to give her back, truth be told. Not only did I fall in love with Priscilla, but Daffy did, as well."

"Who is Daffy?" Ada inquired.

"My cat. Mama made Daffy stay in my bedchamber when you

came to tea yesterday. Usually, Daffy is given run of the house and enjoys coming to tea and begging for bits of sandwiches or sweets. We are all immune to her. Except for the captain. He has a soft spot for Daffy and will slip her food throughout tea You must come again so you can meet her."

Malcolm could only imagine how his mother would have reacted if a cat had come strolling into the drawing room during tea yesterday. Frankly, he would not have been comfortable with the idea himself. Animals did not belong in a house.

"This is His Grace, the Duke of Waterbury, Mrs. Taylor. And his sister, Lady Ada. Mrs. Taylor has worked at Gunter's for many years."

The woman smiled. "Longer than you have been in existence, my lady," she teased.

He was amazed at how comfortable the two seemed with one another. They came from such different worlds, and yet it would not have surprised him if Lady Euphemia asked *this* woman to tea the next day. Malcolm also noted how the women had not addressed her as Euphemia but Effie. He believed allowing such familiarity with those outside her class was a mistake on Lady Euphemia's part. Or that of her mother, who had allowed for it to take place in the first place. Malcolm deepened his resolve not to be taken in by her charm.

"It is a pleasure to meet the both of you, Your Grace. My lady. Come, let me seat you."

"Is Billie here?" asked Lady Euphemia. "I would like her to wait on us if possible."

"She is working today, my lady. I will make certain to let her know you are here."

Mrs. Taylor led them to a round table which seated four. Malcolm held out Lady Euphemia's chair for her before seating his sister.

"You know these workers by name," Ada marveled.

"We have come here frequently over the years," Lady Euphemia said. "It would be wrong to patronize an establishment and not form a personal connection with them. Mama taught us to be friendly to everyone and treat others as we wished to be treated. I would hope others might be interested in me, and I am always interested in them."

A woman in her mid-thirties approached them, with dark hair and a huge smile. "Lady Effie. It is so good you have come back to town. Mrs. Taylor tells me it is your come-out Season. How did that happen? It seems only yesterday when you were eight years of age and begging to learn the history of Gunter's from Mr. Gunter himself."

"It is lovely to see you again, Billie. Since it is my come-out, I am thinking of having the cake to be served at the ball given in my honor made here at Gunter's."

"We would be delighted to bake it for you, my lady. Anything for you and your lovely mother," Billie replied. "Shall I tell you about our menu?"

"Please do so," Ada said, her eyes bright with interest.

They made their selections, with recommendations from Billie. Lady Euphemia asked that their ices be held until they had finished their light luncheon.

When Billie left, Ada asked, "What do you know about this place?"

"I told you it started as a confectionery. Mr. Negri, an Italian pastry chef, opened it a little over fifty years ago. He produced wet and dry sweetmeats. You may not know much about confections, but they require time and precision, as well as talent. I believe confectioners are artists working with food. They have all kinds of specialized pans and also use many kinds of molds to create shapes for their ices, jellied fruits, and candies."

Lady Effie smiled. "Mr. Gunter became Mr. Negri's business partner and later the sole owner. I have met his son Robert, and he is responsible for making many of the confections and ices which are served these days. Robert is desperate to travel to Paris and live there so he can learn all about French baking. He plans to do so once this terrible war with Bonaparte ends."

Malcolm said little because he was a bit overwhelmed by Lady Euphemia's ebullient nature and knowledge. At the same time, he also thought her a breath of fresh air. As she and Ada talked, he worried that it was dangerous being around her. It was important for him to select the right kind of woman as his duchess, and a marriage of convenience was the only one he would consider. He could not afford to admit to his growing interest in her. After all, he had declared to himself that she was not duchess material.

So why did he seem to hang on every word that came from her tempting mouth?

Their food arrived, a plate of delicious sandwiches, accompanied by fruit and salads. As they ate, Lady Euphemia told them a little more about Gunter's catering business.

"Several hostesses in town use Gunter's to cater the food for their balls. Cook would be hurt if we did so with the ball James and Sophie will hold in my honor, but even she will not mind if my cake comes from Gunter's. It will help the kitchen staff concentrate on other items which will be served."

He couldn't help but think Lady Euphemia might be the only girl making her come-out that worried about her household's kitchens being overworked. Who thought of such things?

This woman.

"When will your ball be held?" Ada asked.

"I am not certain," Lady Euphemia admitted. "I have not even thought to ask. As I told you yesterday, I am not hunting for a husband. I am only doing my come-out because Mama has looked forward to me making it. Since I am the last of her girls, I did not want to deny her this pleasure. What about you? When will your mother hold your come-out ball, Lady Ada?"

Ada bit her lip. "I do not know. Mama has not mentioned this to me. I was not aware this was a custom."

"Not every family hosts one," Lady Euphemia said, trying to be helpful.

Malcolm hated to see his sister looking hurt and immediately volunteered, "If Mama has not already planned one for you, Ada, then I will host it," he proclaimed. "The ball *will* happen."

"You would do that for me, Waterbury?" Ada asked, tears glistening in her eyes. "Oh, thank you so much!"

"What are big brothers for?" he said, trying to lighten the mood.

Billie approached their table again. "Are you ready for your ices? You are in for a real treat, my lady," she said to Ada, who beamed at the woman.

"We are ready, Billie," his sister replied. "And very much looking forward to what you bring us."

Again, Malcolm was amazed at his sister. She was responding to others and not hanging her head, avoiding contact. She was initiating conversation. She was not the quiet wallflower he had anticipated she would be during the upcoming Season. Instead, she was like a caterpillar, gnawing its way from the cocoon which had protected it, spreading her wings to become the beautiful butterfly she always had been.

Pride filled him as he continued to watch her. Listen to her as she talked with Lady Euphemia. This relationship of a few days had already changed his sister in ways too immeasurable to count. His worries of Ada not being able to attract a gentleman—much less a decent one who would treat her kindly—now evaporated.

While they waited for their ices to arrive, Lady Euphemia told them of some of the extravagant sweets the tearoom sold—cakes, pastries, and various confections. She even told of being adventuresome and trying some of the ices with meats inside them.

Ada frowned. "That does not sound good at all."

Her friend laughed. "They weren't. Mama told me they wouldn't be, but Pippa and I had to try it. We never did after that initial time. Mama said we had ordered it and must finish our dish. Everyone else had lovely ices of vanilla, white coffee, or pistachio. It was one of the only times my sisters did not offer to share with me."

Billie arrived with their ices, which were in small dishes. He had chosen bergamot, while Ada had been intrigued by pineapple. Lady Euphemia had gone with a mix of chocolate and vanilla. It had not been one of the menu items recited by Billie, but he supposed a longtime customer would be awarded special favors.

Ada took one bite and sighed. "Oh, it is even better than I imagined it could taste."

Malcolm dipped his spoon into his selection and relished the cold pop of flavor in his mouth. "This is very good. *Very* good."

"I am glad you both are enjoying the flavors you selected. You must come back and try the lavender. Or maple. Or elderflower. They are also favorites of mine."

"We can do that, Waterbury, can't we?" his sister pleaded.

He swallowed his bite. "We will definitely return to Gunter's, Ada," he confirmed, causing both girls to giggle.

"You simply must try this chocolate, Lady Ada," Lady Euphemia insisted.

His sister dipped her spoon into her friend's dish and sampled a bite. "Oh, that is heavenly."

Lady Euphemia looked to him. "You, too, Your Grace. I am happy to share with you. I think I have sampled every flavor Gunter's has to offer over the years. Their chocolate is unbelievable. I am a fiend when it comes to chocolate," she confided, her eyes dancing with mischief.

"I have never had chocolate," he told her, seeing the look of astonishment on her face.

"No . . . chocolate. Ever?" she asked, a quizzical look on her face.

"Never."

She smiled broadly. "Then this will definitely be a treat."

Scooping her spoon into her ice, she brought up a bite of chocolate to his mouth. A shot of lust shot through him as he opened his mouth, accepting it.

In that moment, it all mixed together. Chocolate. Desire.

And Lady Euphemia . . .

The sweetness melted in his mouth, but it did nothing to cool his ardor. He could not have this. This woman was Ada's friend. He must look elsewhere—because this woman would only wed for love.

And Malcolm did not think he had any to give.

Oh, he did love his sister, but that was the extent of it. He had never felt much of anything for his parents. He spent so little time in his father's company, the duke had been a stranger to him. Mama fussed over him, but it was as if she did so because she was supposed to. As Ada had put it to him, Mama most likely did not like children and only went through the motions of pretending to care for her offspring.

No one had ever offered him a treat such as chocolate. No one had wanted to be his friend. Share their innermost thoughts and listen to his own. Malcolm was gifted academically and athletically. Everything came to him with ease.

Except the notion of love.

"Thank you, my lady," he said brusquely as she returned her spoon to her bowl and dipped it into the ice again, bringing it to her mouth.

The thought of the spoon sliding across her tongue nearly did him in. He wanted his tongue stroking hers.

Malcolm cursed under his breath and then found Lady Euphemia gazing at him.

She giggled.

"Did you hear that?" he asked.

"I could be polite and tell you I did not, but having used that word a time or two myself, I recognized it right away."

"You . . . have *used* it yourself?"

She shrugged. "It is a word my cousin Caleb has spoken upon

occasion when he is frustrated. The last time I heard it, he and I were repairing a fence. We *both* used it," she confided. "And it was called for, I assure you. That fence was as surly as they come."

Malcolm could not believe she cursed. Or repaired fences. Or had lips which tempted him more than he could say.

"What flavors will we try next time?" Ada asked brightly, looking up from the ice which had thankfully consumed her attention. "That is, if there is a next time," she said, hope in her eyes.

"Of course, there will be a next time," Lady Euphemia assured her. "We will have all my sisters and cousins come with us once they arrive in town. Before the Season starts. I cannot wait for you to meet them. We have ever so much fun."

"You will need an escort," he said gruffly. "I can offer you mine."

"Oh, that is not necessary, Your Grace," Lady Euphemia replied. "Why, look around you. You can see women dine here alone. It is perfectly appropriate. The same is true for a lady and gentleman. Gunter's is the only respectable public place where a couple can go in public without it causing harm to a lady's reputation. I believe I mentioned that to you before."

She laughed again, and it was as if it were music to his ears. "We might need the loan of your carriage, though, Your Grace, with so many ladies. Lady Ada and myself. My three sisters and two cousins. Mama. That is eight in all." Frowning a moment, she added, "And Her Grace, of course. We would not wish to leave your mother out from our outing."

Ada's face reddened. "I am not certain Mama would like coming here," she said quietly.

Malcolm watched Lady Euphemia contemplate Ada's words. "We can talk about this in the carriage, where we have more privacy."

They finished their ices, and he signed the bill, asking it go directly to his solicitor, who took care of such matters for him.

Billie and Mrs. Taylor thanked them for coming in and both said they looked forward to seeing the three of them again very soon.

Malcolm guided them back to his ducal carriage and gave his coachman instructions to return to the Duke of Seaton's townhouse.

Inside the vehicle, Ada burst into tears as Lady Euphemia slipped an arm about her friend and urged, "Please, tell me what is going on, Ada."

He noticed she used Ada's name without her title but did not want to correct her with his sister in distress.

"It is Mama. She is not . . . well . . . she is . . ."

"She is uncomfortable with you forming a fast friendship with my family and me," Lady Euphemia sagely said.

His sister nodded, clearly miserable. "I cannot understand why. Status is important to Mama. She . . . well, she is surprised your mother gave up her title and prestige to wed a man with neither."

Lady Euphemia stroked Ada's hair. "Mama was more interested in love and happiness than those things," she explained. "The same holds true for my entire family. You have met the captain. He worships Mama. You will not find a more loyal and intelligent man than our captain. My mother deserves all the happiness she can find after surviving a loveless first marriage. For Mama, a lofty title is unimportant. It is who you are—what your character consists of—that trumps your standing in Polite Society."

Malcolm took in all Lady Euphemia said—and wondered if he had ever been happy.

Could the right woman bring this magic into his life?

Perhaps the woman before him—who was all wrong to become his duchess—might be the right one to save him.

CHAPTER SEVEN

EFFIE COULD HARDLY contain her excitement. Both Pippa and Georgie had arrived in town and were coming to visit this afternoon. James and Sophie had come to town yesterday, bringing George, Ida, and Aunt Matty with them. Her spirits were soaring as she thought of her family and knew they would only grow higher once the others showed up for the Season.

Despite having doubts about what she would do in the month before the Season, being away from her beloved Shadowcrest, Effie had kept busy. Besides fittings for the numerous gowns being made up—and those seemed endless—she had seen Lady Ada almost daily. She couldn't help but enjoy seeing her new friend come out of her shell. Lady Ada had been a bit timid and reserved when they had first met, but now she was much more sociable and less reticent. Effie thought lady Ada grew prettier by the day and knew she would attain her goal of finding a husband once the Season began.

They had gone riding at Rotten Row several times, accompanied by the Duke of Waterbury. He was Lady Ada's shadow. His Grace had also taken them driving through Hyde Park. Even when Mama went on an outing with them, the duke insisted upon going. She supposed he did so to prevent Lady Ada's mother from accompanying them. Anytime the dowager duchess came along, Lady Ada's enthusiasm was tamped down at the constant, cutting remarks made to her by her mother.

Effie couldn't quite figure out the duke. He was very quiet, rarely contributing to their conversations. She supposed he was solemn because he was a widower and missed his wife. His Grace never brought up anything regarding his personal life, and she couldn't help but wonder what his duchess had been like. Effie had only said that her sister-in-law had died in childbirth, so Waterbury was not only mourning the loss of his spouse but that of his first child. She couldn't imagine going from having a family to suddenly losing it.

At least the duke had his sister. Though Effie estimated there was at least a decade between the pair, they seemed close. In a way, she felt sorry for him, having chosen a wife and started his life with her, only to lose her so tragically. And his mother didn't seem sympathetic in the least. The dowager duchess had mentioned a few times that her son would be taking a bride again this Season and that she would guide him in this decision.

That seemed laughable to Effie. Why would a grown man need his mother to make such an important decision for him? Unless His Grace had allowed her to do so the first time around. Knowing how opinionated and overbearing the dowager duchess was, Effie could not see her backing down and keeping silent while either of her children decided upon a spouse. She did believe the duke would look out for his sister, though, and not force her to wed a gentleman she opposed to entering into marriage with. She also assumed it had been His Grace who had allowed Lady Ada to see Effie so often, and for that, she was grateful to him.

Though Effie did not know anyone in Polite Society, her family certainly did. Perhaps she could enlist her relatives to help introduce eligible men and women to Lady Ada and His Grace.

"Oh, no!" she cried aloud.

They were coming to tea today. Mama had invited them so they might meet James and Sophie. This was before they had received word that Pippa and Georgie had reached town and would be coming to tea. While she knew Lady Ada would not mind, since she was eager to meet Effie's many relatives, she thought His Grace would be less inclined to be present with so many others. She saw him as a lone wolf, always observing.

On top of that, the Dowager Duchess of Waterbury would be thrown into the fray. Not that her family would be disorderly or some fight would break out, but she knew with so many of them, things could get quite lively. Anything above a whisper, the dowager duchess termed too boisterous.

She went to find Mama and found her in her sitting room, working on an embroidered blanket.

"Who is that for?" Effie asked, fingering the intricate threading.

"Georgina's babe," Mama replied. "I know the babe will not come until November, but once the Season starts, I will not have the luxury of time as I do now, leading up to it. I thought if I got a good start, I could pick it back up in the autumn and complete it in plenty of time." She paused. "You look worried. What is it, Effie?"

"I had forgotten that we had asked Lady Ada and her family to tea this afternoon so they might meet James and Sophie."

"Yes, I recall that." Mama hesitated. "Are you worried how the dowager duchess will react since so many others will be present?"

"I will admit it has crossed my mind. You have seen her, Mama. She is quick to judge. Haughty. I am afraid once she sees a room full of Strongs and their spouses, it will put her off so much that she will not allow Lady Ada to see me again."

"If that is the case, I will feel sorry for Lady Ada, but the Season starts in two weeks, my dearest. She cannot follow her daughter around at every event and prevent her from talking to others, especially you. Let us make the best of today. If we see the dowager duchess reacting poorly, you may have to cool your friendship with Lady Ada until the Season is in swing. Her Grace will be sitting with the matrons at balls. She will not be hovering over her daughter. Lady Ada—and you—will have more freedom than you might think."

Mama smiled to herself, causing Effie to prompt, "What? What are you not telling me, Mama?"

"I suppose it is time we have the first of a couple of talks." Mama set aside her sewing, placing it in her sewing basket and closing the lid. "We need to talk about the gentlemen you will be meeting."

She frowned. "What of them? I know I am not to speak to anyone unless we have been introduced. You will be there for most of those introductions."

"Yes, I will stay by your side when we first enter a ballroom or other event. I will happily introduce everyone who approaches us. You will be the one to decide if you wish to spend more time with any of them, whether they are gentleman or lady. I know how particular you can be and how opinionated you are, Effie. I am not saying do not speak up, but at the same time, temper your words and actions with a smile. It will go a long way."

"Yes, Mama."

"Dance with the gentlemen you find interesting. Talk with other young ladies and find out what you have in common with them. I encourage you to make friends beyond Lady Ada. While she is a lovely young woman, you want to meet as many others as you can."

"And that includes kissing a few gentlemen, Effie."

She blushed. "Mama. We have talked about this."

"No, we really have not. I require your full attention now, Euphemia."

Oh, Mama was serious if she was calling her Euphemia.

"I am listening, Mama. You have my full attention."

"There are many aspects which should be considered going into a marriage. You want to like the person you are to wed. They should be someone you enjoy being with and talking to. Hopefully, you will find you have some things in common, but you do not want to wed someone who is simply the male version of yourself. While I believe you will be drawn to those who value the same things you do—family, loyalty, honesty, respect—they may be different from you in other aspects. You are quite outgoing, Effie. As effervescent as the bubbles in champagne. You will attract men who share that same quality, but you might also draw others who wish they could be that way."

"You mean how Lady Ada used to be quieter and now she appears freer now."

"Yes. You might find a most somber gentleman grows fond of you and wishes to pursue an attachment with you because of your outgoing nature. Regardless of the gentlemen who become interested in you, you will be able to get to know them better as the Season progresses. Those who wish to pursue you will call in the afternoons and send beautiful flower arrangements to you. Use your time wisely in getting to know these suitors."

She frowned. "Where does the kissing part come in?"

"I am getting to that." Mama cleared her throat. "Besides liking a person enough to want to spend the rest of your life with them, you must have a physical attraction to them. You will understand when this occurs. You will be drawn to their looks. Their smile. Their scent. Their touch. Only with the ones you are truly considering as your husband should you take the next step. A step to see if you have that special spark between you. Kissing is a very good way to see if that is the case."

"I see you kissing the captain all the time, Mama. I know you like him—and kissing—because you would not do it so much if you didn't."

"There is a fine line you must walk, Effie," Mama continued. "You are not to be alone with a gentleman under any circumstances. If you are found alone with him, it is understood that he must extend a marriage proposal."

"This is very confusing, Mama. How am I to kiss a man if I cannot be alone with him?"

"There will be opportunities which come along, which you should use sparingly and only for the men whom you truly have an affection for. A stroll along the darkened terrace at a ball or through the gardens. A stolen moment in an alcove when you might walk a suitor to the front door from the drawing room after he has called upon you."

Mama took Effie's hands in hers. "I *want* you to take those opportunities. Just be very careful about doing so. As I mentioned, if you are caught kissing a gentleman, you are ruined for other men. He must offer for you—and you must accept."

"But what if I find I do not like his kiss and do not wish to wed him?'

"Then be honest as you let him down gently. Remember, he is kissing you to also determine whether or not you might suit. Kissing can be pure drudgery with a man you have no affection for. Or it can be the most glorious thing in the world."

"You are talking about Papa and comparing him to the captain, aren't you?" she asked.

Her mother nodded. "I had no choice but to wed Seaton. My parents were dazzled by his title and thought my life would be one of ease and status if I became a duchess. While it was nice to live in such splendor, I never felt close to your father and wished I would have had the chance to make my own choice regarding a husband."

"You and the captain love one another a great deal. That is why kissing is so pleasant. Something you wish to do often."

"Yes, we do love one another, Effie. So much that it hurts sometimes." She squeezed her daughter's hands. "I want you to have the right to choose the man you love. If one does not touch your heart, I will never force you to enter a marriage."

Mama paused. "I know you are making your come-out for me, Effie. Because you know it is important to me for you to do so. I also hope you will open your heart to the possibility of love and marriage."

"I would be a fool not to do so, Mama. I see how happy other Strongs are. I would never deliberately *not* wed out of stubbornness. But I must say, I like myself the way I am. You have raised me to think for myself. Most girls making their come-out will not think at all. They will wed for looks or a title or prestige. Then they will think as their husband tells them to do. I would never stand for that.

"So, yes—if I can find that rare man who will accept me as I am, flaws and all, then perhaps I will make a love match."

Mama kissed her cheek. "That is all I can ask of you, my little love. I am off to the nursery to see Jamie before his nap. I think I will bring him downstairs after it so that everyone can see him. I wonder if Georgina and Pippa will bring their children."

"They most certainly will," Effie predicted. "Or August and Seth will. And I fully expect James to wander into tea carrying George in one arm and Ida in his other."

Her mother laughed. "The men in our family are a bit indulgent when it comes to their children."

"Let us hope all those children will behave and not frighten the Dowager Duchess of Waterbury so much that she runs from the drawing room in terror," she joked.

"I am certain tea will go well," Mama predicted. "Her Grace will see what a loving, happy family we are."

Effie was not nearly as certain as Mama as to how this afternoon's teatime might fare.

Chapter Eight

Malcolm had been going to White's regularly for two weeks now, mostly to reacquaint himself with other men his age and inspect which ones might be suitable for Ada. Some eligible bachelors lived in town year-round, and White's was a place that they frequented. Others were just starting to arrive for the Season from their country estates. He already had a few gentlemen in mind that he wished to introduce his sister to once the social events began.

A few men he had been friendly with during his school and university years had approached him. Now that the competition of academics and athletics was behind them, they seemed to have set aside their petty jealousies. He had high hopes he might make a few good friends himself, even as he looked for a bride on the Marriage Mart.

Though he had never been a gossip, Malcolm managed on a few occasions to steer the conversation around to the Duke of Seaton and the Strong family. Opinions varied wildly regarding both. Most of the men he spoke with said Seaton was brilliant, guiding Strong Shipping into new avenues of revenue, though they said His Grace wasn't very sociable and stuck to his own family. The duke rarely made an appearance at White's, but some of his brothers-in-law did. Unfortunately, none of them were back in town, so Malcolm had yet to meet any of them.

At least today he would be introduced to the Duke and Duchess of Seaton. Mrs. Andrews had asked Mama, Ada, and him to come to tea today since the Seatons had come in from Shadowcrest. Lady Euphemia was anxious to introduce her new friend to her brother and sister-in-law, as well as her aunt, whom she spoke quite highly of.

He had made no progress with her. Absolutely none. Malcolm did not think she even saw him as anything more than a protective older brother who chaperoned his sister about town. When he was with her and Ada, the girls talked incessantly about a variety of topics. Malcolm listened and rarely interjected himself into their conversations.

But all the while, he was learning more and more about what an unusual woman Lady Euphemia Strong was.

She had definite opinions on many topics. She read the newspapers voraciously and shared her ideas regarding politics with Ada, who most likely had never picked up a newspaper in her life. Still, he saw his sister becoming interested in things outside the realm of her existence. Lady Euphemia also talked quite a bit about the animals she raised and the many ways she assisted her cousin, who was the steward of Shadowcrest, the country estate where she had grown up. Listening to her, he was astonished how much he had learned about breeding animals, gardening, and tenants' needs. In fact, he anticipated implementing a few of her ideas once he returned to Waterside.

He went to the foyer now, surprised to find Ada already waiting for him.

"My, don't you look lovely," he complimented. "Is this one of your new gowns from the modiste you have been seeing so frequently?"

"Yes," she said, smoothing her skirts. "I thought since we are meeting a duke and duchess today, I want to look my absolute best."

Mama came down the stairs, also looking quite fashionable. Whether she approved of Mr. and Mrs. Andrews or not, it was apparent she was making an effort to look stylish for their hosts at tea today.

"You look very nice, Mama," he praised, leading them outside to the waiting carriage.

"I am still on the fence, Waterbury, as far as the Seatons go," she said. "I can still recall all the gossip when His Grace wed. The fact that he allows his wife to run a company is, frankly, quite appalling."

"I believe the captain makes most of the day-to-day decisions now, Mama," Ada said. "From what Lady Effie says, Her Grace still has the final say on large decisions, but she devotes a great deal of her time now to her husband and children."

Mama sniffed. "Well, she should. That is the role she is to play in Polite Society, not filling her head with . . . business."

Malcolm watched Ada stifle a laugh, coughing and gazing out the window to cover her reaction. He had to admit that he was eager to see the kind of woman this duchess was, owning a shipping empire while being a part of the *ton*.

"I am certain you will afford Her Grace the respect she deserves, Mama," he said. "You always taught me to respect the rank of a man or woman in Polite Society."

Mama smiled at him. "We will see you claim a bride of good standing, Waterbury. As a duke, you should be conscious of wedding a woman whose parents hold not only high-ranking titles, but ones who are blemish-free from gossip. I will know more once the Season is underway and be able to select your bride for you."

Ada flashed him a concerned glance, but he shook his head. Now was not the time to quarrel with his mother. Malcolm was going to have to inform her soon, however, that he would be solely in charge of plucking a bride from the Marriage Mart. And if she knew he was even considering Lady Euphemia, it might send Mama into a fit of apoplexy. Despite being a duke's daughter and sister, his mother was still wary of Lady Effie because of her outspokenness, along with her mother's decision to wed a man of no rank. He hoped meeting the Duke and Duchess of Seaton might change Mama's mind about the

Strong family.

Because the more he was around Lady Euphemia, the more he wanted her as his wife.

Malcolm decided today was the day he needed to start making her aware of him. Not as Ada's older brother.

As a man...

He promised himself to speak up today. Enter a conversation with her with something to say. After all, he was gifted intellectually. He had thrived at public speaking in school. He could actually be quite charming when he chose to be. He just had not felt like doing so in a very long time. If he was to have a chance with Lady Euphemia, however, he needed to quit being an observer and become an active participant when she was near. If he could get her to thinking about him as a possible suitor before next week, when the inaugural ball of the Season would be held, he hoped it would give him an advantage over others.

Though he was interested in Lady Euphemia, he had not totally settled upon her, however. After all, he was a duke. He could have his pick of the litter, as far as young, eligible ladies went. He might find one much more suited to the role of duchess. One who was dignified and quiet and beautiful. One who would not challenge him at every turn and still interest him.

They arrived at the Seaton townhouse. He was surprised to see two other carriages sitting in front and wondered if Mrs. Andrews or the Duchess of Seaton had asked others to tea, as well.

Deciding he would rather be prepared than not, he asked the butler as they ventured up the stairs, "Have others come to tea this afternoon, Powell?"

For the first time since they had been visiting this household, the butler smiled. "Yes, Your Grace. Their Graces are now in residence, and two of His Grace's sisters have stopped by for a visit."

They reached the drawing room, and Powell announced them,

ushering them in.

The room was filled with men, women, and children. And a cat, who was playfully running everywhere.

A large man, several inches over six feet, with broad shoulders and eyes the color of Lady Euphemia's, carried a small boy, not even yet two, on his shoulders. The boy was squealing loudly. The man dropped swiftly to his hands and knees, and the child rode him like a pony, his little hands fisted in the man's blond hair.

"Faster, Papa!" the boys hollered.

Another man, just as tall, with black, curly hair and skin bronzed by the sun, swung another small boy in his arms up in the air and back again. The child shouted in glee each time he was lifted high into the air.

A third man, just as tall and muscular as the other two, with jet black hair and one penetrating green eye, walked behind a babe who was apparently learning to walk. He held both her hands and moved slowly behind her, encouraging her with each step. Besides the black eye patch he wore, a nasty scar sliced down his cheek, marring his good looks.

The only man he recognized, Mr. Andrews, cradled a babe in the crook of his arm, walking about the room and smiling at everyone.

The women present were chatting, seated in a grouping of chairs. Mrs. Andrews and Lady Euphemia were not holding a child, but two of the women, who looked strikingly similar, both had babes on their laps They each had the same cornflower blue eyes of Lady Euphemia. An older woman with the same cornflower blue eyes looked at him with interest. Another one, a pretty woman with warm, brown eyes and golden-brown hair, came to her feet.

"Oh, it is so lovely to meet you, Your Graces. Lady Ada. Effie has told us all about the three of you."

She moved toward them and since she did not possess the same shade of blues eyes as did the others, he assumed her to be the

Duchess of Seaton.

Mrs. Andrews sprang to her feet and joined them. "Your Graces, may I present my dear friend, Her Grace, the Duchess of Seaton. This is the Duke and Dowager Duchess of Waterbury and Lady Ada Ware."

He could feel Mama stiffen beside him, but she was polite. "Charmed to meet you, Your Grace."

"Yes, it is lovely to meet you, Your Grace," echoed Ada.

"We have heard quite a bit about you as well, Your Grace," he said. "Lady Euphemia was most excited for you to arrive in town."

"Come meet the others," the duchess said, and they followed her across the room.

Lady Euphemia leaped to her feet. "Good afternoon, Your Graces. Lady Ada. May I present to you my aunt, Lady Mathilda, and my two older sisters, who are twins. This is Viscountess Hopewell, who is holding her daughter Lady Louise, and the Marchioness of Edgethorne, who is entertaining Lady Ida, Her Grace's daughter."

Greetings were exchanged as the men in the room made their way toward them and Lady Edgethorne returned Lady Ida to her mother.

"I am Seaton," the tall blond man who had been serving as his son's pony said. He smiled at the boy in his arms. This rambunctious tyke is the Marquess of Alinwood, our son George."

Seaton indicated the scarred man who steered the walking girl toward them. "This is the Marquess of Edgethorne and Lady Evelyn, who will soon be a year old."

Lord Edgethorne smiled, and Malcolm could see he had been a handsome man at one time. His wounds, though, had disfigured him considerably. "My daughter is learning to walk. Rather, she has skipped from crawling and is trying to run. I am functioning as the man who is charged in helping her keep to a slower pace until she is a bit more steady on her feet." He laughed. "If I dare let go of her hand to shake yours, she will be off and running like a colt."

"This is my brother-in-law Viscount Hopewell," Seaton continued. "With Adam, who is eighteen months of age."

The viscount swung Adam high in the air, placing him on his shoulders, then offering his hand. "Very pleased to meet you all," he said.

Mr. Andrews joined them. "You have yet to meet our boy. This is James, whom we call Jamie, named after my closest friend, the man I call brother."

Malcolm was slightly overwhelmed by not only the sheer number of people present in the drawing room but the names which had been tossed out. Fortunately, he had an excellent memory and had been able to keep everyone straight.

"We are a very merry party for tea today," Lady Hopewell said. "I am so glad we were able to join you today. Effie says she has seen quite a bit of you since coming to town for all her gown fittings."

"Yes," Ada said brightly. "We met our first day at Madame Dumas' shop and have become fast friends."

"I am glad to hear that," Lady Edgethorne said. "My sisters and cousins have always been my best friends, but I enjoyed making my come-out and getting to know other young ladies within the *ton*. Miss Bancroft and I became particularly good friends. She attended a house party Mama gave at Shadowcrest for our cousins, Allegra and Lyric, and Miss Bancroft is now Viscountess Tillings and soon to be a mother."

"There are so many of you," his mother remarked. "Do you . . . always bring your children to . . . tea?"

"Every chance we get," Seaton said, laughing. "We are a family who values family and enjoy all the time we can get with our little ones."

Malcolm could remember only one occasion he had had tea with his parents, just before he left for university. His father's rule had been to keep children out of sight at all times and only trot them out on a special occasion—of which there had been none. He couldn't help but be a tad envious of these children present in the drawing room, knowing they were not only loved but shown love on a regular basis.

Mama's disapproval was obvious from the look on her face, but she held her tongue, obviously not wanting to alienate a duke and duchess.

They formed a large group, with the men passing off babes and moving furniture so they could all be gathered around in a circle. It surprised him when these titled lords kept hold of their children, bouncing them on their knees or placing them on their shoulders and patting them.

Several teacarts were rolled in to feed them all, and the Duchess of Seaton and Mrs. Andrews took charge of pouring out for everyone.

When Jamie began to fuss, Mr. Andrews handed his son over to his mother, saying, "I can hold a teapot and pour tea into a cup, love. I think the babe wants attention from his mother."

He tenderly brushed his lips against hers, and Malcolm noted it was not for the first time. The Andrews had been quite affectionate toward one another, making him more than a bit uncomfortable.

"How are you feeling, Georgie?" Seaton asked.

The marchioness sighed heavily. "Sick as a dog, James. August tells me I was worse with Evelyn, but I believe this time is harder on me. Mornings are the worst. I still cannot eat anything before noon. Finally, around teatime, I am able to eat several bites and almost feel like myself."

Lady Edgethorne turned to the dowager duchess. "My child is due in mid-November. We only came to town to see family for a few weeks, and then we will retreat to Edgefield. I did not want to miss the beginning of Effie's come-out."

"I see," his mother said primly, sipping her tea and making no further comment.

As they sipped their tea and talked, Malcolm was aware of how at ease these lords were holding their children. He found it odd—and yet at the same time, refreshing. His impression had always been that servants raised children, and parents saw very little of them. Yet these men were perfectly at home, holding and playing with their little ones, passing them back and forth between themselves and their wives, even taking on other babes while one of them slathered jam or clotted cream against their scone.

Something stirred within him. Envy? No, that seemed too hateful. Perhaps yearning. Yes, a longing for something very different from what he had experienced growing up. Malcolm thought back to how Imogen and he had been practically strangers when they wed, having spoken no more than half a dozen times together. How they had lived in the same house and yet led incredibly separate lives. It struck him how lonely his young wife must have been, and he had done nothing to put her at ease or even spend time with her.

Malcolm vowed his next marriage would be different. That he would make the time to get to know his wife and not abandon her as he had Imogen.

"Are we too late for tea?" a voice asked.

They all turned, and Malcolm saw an auburn haired beauty approaching, one with the same shade of eye color all these Strongs seemed to possess. Following her was a large, muscular man with dark hair and gray eyes, carrying the smallest babe of the bunch present.

"Mirella!" Mrs. Andrews cried. "And Byron. Please, come in. I will ring for more tea, but we have plenty of sandwiches and sweets."

Lady Euphemia hurried toward the pair, throwing her arms about her sister and kissing her. "I did not know you were already in town."

"We just arrived. Dropped our trunks and servants off and came here straightaway. I was hoping everyone would be gathering here."

Lady Euphemia held out her arms. "Oh, I have missed you, Daniel," she said, and the man passed the baby to her.

The Duchess of Seaton said, "We have guests. Friends of Effie's."

Her Grace introduced them to Lord and Lady Bridgewater, who lived close to Maidstone in Kent. Their babe was Daniel, a two-month-old who already had the marchioness' red hair and blue eyes.

"How are your gown fittings coming along, Effie?" Lady Bridgewater asked.

The women launched into a long discussion about gowns, leaving the men to talk amongst themselves.

"It has been good of you to squire Effie and Lady Ada about town, Your Grace," Seaton said. "Thank you for taking care of my sister in my absence."

"My sister and Lady Euphemia have grown quite close in the last few weeks," he shared. "Your sister has helped draw mine from her shell. Ada has always been shy."

"You wouldn't know it from today," Lord Hopewell said. "She has most certainly been a part of the conversation."

Malcolm worried about that, thinking Mama would severely chastise Ada once they were in the carriage for speaking so freely in such a large group of titled members of Polite Society.

Daniel, the newest arrival, began fussing, which caused a ripple effect amongst all the other children, who began fidgeting and crying.

"They are overtired," Mrs. Andrews said apologetically. "We have kept them from their naps and routine."

"It was good seeing all our grandbabes," Mr. Andrews proclaimed, striking Malcolm as odd that this man felt that relationship with all the children.

"I will ring for the nursery governess to come," the Duchess of Seaton said. "Did any of you bring yours with you today?"

"Don't bother," her husband said, standing and lifting Lady Ida from his wife's lap, even as he held his son in his other arm. "We men can run the children upstairs. It will save time and provide quiet for you ladies to talk without interruption."

Every gentleman present but Malcolm left, taking their children with them, Lord Edgethorne allowing Lady Evelyn to hold both his hands and toddle from the room. Even the cat followed the others out.

Embarrassment filled him when his mother breathed a loud sigh of relief, saying, "It is nice to reclaim the drawing room for adults. It is hard to visit without quiet."

Her statement caused a few eyebrows to shoot up, and Malcolm saw Ada wince.

Lady Euphemia spoke up. "We Strongs are not much for quiet, Your Grace. Mama always kept the six of us girls close. It is the way we learned how to comport ourselves, and it allowed us to spend more time with her than most mothers do with their children. Above all, we felt loved—then—and now."

His mother's jaw dropped. "You are quite free with your opinions, Lady Euphemia," she said sharply.

"As free as you are with yours," Lady Euphemia retorted.

Mama stood. "Well . . . I never!" she exclaimed. Looking to the Duchess of Seaton, she said, "It was nice to meet you, Your Grace." To Mrs. Andrews, she said, "Thank you for having us for tea, but we will be off now. Come along, Ada."

His sister rose as Malcolm did, and he said, "It was a lovely teatime, Your Grace, Mrs. Andrews. And it was a pleasure to meet so many members of your family."

"Waterbury!" Mama barked.

"Coming, Mama," he said, leaving the drawing room with her and Ada.

Inside the carriage, Mama shuddered. "That was a most unruly group of people. I do not care if they hold titles or not. Who in their right minds would allow children at tea? And Lady Edgethorne talking openly of increasing in front of everyone? That simply is *not* an acceptable topic of conversation."

She continued her rant the rest of the way home, disparaging the parents for allowing little ones in the drawing room when guests came calling and even the cat who had made an appearance.

"I blame it on Mrs. Andrews. Former duchess or not, she raised those girls to be this way. Why, they think nothing of breezing in without an invitation, carting unruly children along, ruining a perfectly good teatime."

"They were not unruly, Mama," Ada said gently. "They were just being children. And I thought their parents quite good with them. You can tell both the mothers and fathers have spent a great deal of time with their children because they are so comfortable with them."

"That is the problem, Ada," Mama said haughtily. "Children are never to be heard and only rarely seen. I am aghast at the lack of civility that occurred in a duke and duchess' drawing room." She paused, eyeing her daughter. "One thing I do know—you are not going to be seeing Lady Euphemia anytime soon."

"Mama!" Ada protested, her shock apparent.

"Duke's daughter or not, that girl is not a good influence upon you, Ada. Why, did you hear how she spoke to me? Her mother should have slapped some sense into her and sent her to room, keeping her on bread and water until she learns some manners."

Ada opened her mouth again, but Malcolm shook his head imperceptibly. It would make no difference what his sister said. Mama was incredibly upset, and Ada defending Lady Euphemia and the rest of the Strong family would only worsen matters.

Malcolm wondered what his mother would think when she learned that Lady Euphemia was definitely someone he planned to woo.

CHAPTER NINE

EFFIE SAT AT her dressing table as Mama's lady's maid finished styling her hair. She tried to quell the nerves roiling within her. Tonight was the opening ball at Lord and Lady Simmons' townhouse, and she was a mixture of nerves and excitement. She would be meeting so many new people this evening.

Perhaps even the man she might decide to wed.

"How does that look, my lady?" the maid asked.

Peering into the mirror, Effie was pleased with the results. She had always thought her siblings were beautiful and that she did not compare favorably with them, but in her new ball gown and her hair dressed high upon her head, she felt quite pretty.

"You have made me look like a fairy tale princess," she told the servant, bring a smile to the maid's face.

"Anything else, my lady?"

"No. Please go see if anyone else needs help getting ready. Thank you again."

After the maid left, Effie stood and practiced a few steps of the waltz, laughing as Daffy, who perched on the bed, studied her with interest. She had seen most or all of her sisters and cousins this past week, and they had emphasized how important the waltz was. She learned that it had become fashionable to make the waltz the supper dance at each ball.

Mirella had been the one to tell her to choose her supper dance partner wisely because not only would he be the gentleman she danced with, Effie would also spend the next hour or so in his company as he escorted her to the supper room. Mirella shared that it was these supper dance partners which you got to know the best during a ball and that Effie should only allow a gentleman she was truly interested in to sign her programme for that number.

It had been wonderful seeing all her relatives and playing with their children. Effie had also spent her share of time in their husbands' company, as well. She liked these men her sisters and cousins had married, and they all treated her as a little sister, equally teasing and yet being protective of her at the same time.

She had missed seeing Lady Ada, though. After the dowager duchess had stormed out of tea a week ago, Effie had not been able to see her friend. It was not for lack of trying. Both Mama and Sophie had sent notes to the Dowager Duchess of Waterbury, asking for her and Lady Ada to accompany them on outings or come to visit over tea. Each time, the older woman had replied to the invitation expressing her regret, saying they already had plans but were thankful for the kind invitation.

Mama had told Effie not to take it personally and reminded her it did not reflect the way Lady Ada thought. She had also emphasized to Effie that once the first ball began, it was very likely the two girls would get to visit with one another unless the dowager duchess had expressly forbidden it. Effie hoped that would not be the case.

She sat on the bed, stroking her cat. "I will be certain to tell you everything about this evening, Daffy, whether you are interested or not."

A knock sounded at her bedchamber's door, and she rose to answer it. Opening the door, she found her mother standing there.

"Oh, Mama, you look so lovely. The captain is going to be proud to have you on his arm this evening."

"May I come in?" her mother asked. "I have something to give you."

Effie guessed what it was. She had seen her sisters and cousins wearing a gold locket and decided that was the gift Mama brought to her now.

"Come in," she said, closing the door behind her mother.

Mama's eyes glistened with tears as she said, "With the birth of each of my girls, I purchased a locket from the same jeweler. I had the initial of your first name engraved upon it. I also snipped a lock of your baby hair to place inside it." She chuckled. "Some of you took longer than others for me to do so."

She laughed, knowing that she was in that category. Mama had told Effie that she was born completely bald, with her large Strong eyes dominating her face. It took almost a year for the baldness to leave her and her golden hair to begin to appear.

"I am here to present your locket to you tonight, my darling girl. I hope you will wear it with pride, knowing you are a Strong, which means you are a strong, capable individual who has now reached womanhood. While you will always have the support of your loving family, you now stand on your own two feet and are to make all decisions for yourself."

She knew her mother referred to whether or not Effie would choose to wed or if she did, the decision of her choice of groom would be hers alone.

"Thank you, Mama," she said, enfolding her mother in a tight embrace, thinking she was leaving her carefree girlhood behind as she embarked upon being an adult.

"Let me put it on you and see what you think."

Her mother handed Effie a small packet. She untied the ribbon and then unwrapped it, gazing upon the locket with the beautifully scripted *E* upon it. Opening the locket, she spied the lock of golden hair and thought about the journey her mother had watched as Effie had grown from a babe to a woman. In that moment, she believed she might decide to wed simply because she wanted to watch her own children make that same journey through life. Already, she was immensely enjoying time spent with her nieces and nephews. While she had not thought of birthing children of her own, she realized her own opinions were changing as she matured. She could even picture a similar moment with her future daughter receiving a locket, and this scene grew even more poignant as she thought of life as being circular, with moments playing out and repeating from mother to daughter over generations.

Love for her mother spilled from her. Tears welled in her eyes and she closed the locket and handed it to Mama. "It is so beautiful. Would you place it around my neck for me?"

Mama tried to blink away her own tears. "With pleasure."

Effie turned so that Mama could slip the chain about her neck, fastening the clasp, and turning her, brushing a kiss upon her daughter's cheek.

"The last locket for the last of my girls," Mama said, pride evident in her voice.

"I know you cannot give Jamie a locket. Have you thought of an item for him?"

Mama nodded. "Drake and I decided to purchase a gold pocket watch for your brother. It is engraved with his initials, and we will give it to him upon his eighteenth birthday."

Effie swallowed, her throat thick with emotion. "Shall we go downstairs?" she asked. "The others will be waiting for us."

Her mother slipped her arm through Effie's, and they made their way downstairs. Mama paused before they reached the last landing.

"I have let other daughters make this trip on their own. Stay here a few seconds and then you may come down. I want you to bask in this moment and shine for your family."

Mama embraced her, kissing her cheek again. "I love you so very much, Effie."

"I love you, too, Mama," she echoed.

Effie counted slowly to ten in her head and then made the turn, seeing Mama had reached the bottom of the staircase. Slowly, she made her own descent, the eyes of her loved ones upon her. She gazed out at them, their love for her shining brightly. Aunt Matty smiled at her, brushing tears from her cheeks. James and Sophie beamed with pride. The captain stepped to the stairs to wait for her, love for Effie radiating from him.

When she reached the last step, he offered his arm to her, saying, "This may be the proudest moment of my life. My baby girl making her come-out into Polite Society."

Waves of love for this man filled her. In such a short time, he had become the father to her that hers had never been. The captain freely gave his love and time to all Mama's children, and Effie believed if the time came for her to choose a husband, she would discuss her decision with him before anyone else.

He claimed Mama, leading them outside to the ducal carriage, James, Sophie, and Aunt Matty following.

"Lord and Lady Simmons are our hosts this evening," Mama told Effie once they were settled inside the vehicle. "They are on the younger side, having wed three years ago, I believe. I have found Lady Simmons to be quite charming."

Both her nerves and excitement heightened as the carriage brought them closer to their destination.

Mama took Effie's hand and squeezed it reassuringly. "You will have your entire family with you tonight, my dearest. If at any time you need one of us, we will be here for you. I will be making many of the introductions to you, along with James and Sophie."

"That is good to know, Mama. I cannot help but wonder what tonight will be like."

"Why, it will be full of dancing and new friends," Aunt Matty declared.

She only hoped she would have time to speak to Lady Ada and share some of this special night with her. Though the letter had not been delivered to the house, her friend had actually written to Effie. She had received the note yesterday when she went for another dress fitting with Madame Dumas. The modiste herself had given Effie the note, saying that Lady Ada had left it for her friend. Effie reflected on its contents. In it, Lady Ada had apologized for her mother's rude behavior and lamented the fact they had not been allowed to see one another this past week. Lady Ada said she looked forward to the opening ball of the Season and hoped that she and Effie would be able to speak there.

The carriage slowed to a crawl, and she thought it a waste to have taken it when they could have walked to the ball so much faster. Then it came to a complete halt, and everyone in the vehicle began chuckling.

"What?" she asked, wanting to be let in on what was so humorous.

Sophie announced, "This happens every year. We will need to disembark and walk the remaining way. The opening night of the Season is the best-attended event, and people are eager to see one another after so many months in the country. The crush of carriages makes it almost impossible to be dropped off in front of the townhouse where the ball is being held."

"At least we had no rain today," Mama said. "It will keep our new slippers from being muddied."

Soon, they were all outside the carriage and joining the throngs of people which moved toward Lord and Lady Simmons' townhouse. Mama called out greetings to a few others but did not have them stop for introductions at this point, saying it was important to reach the receiving line.

When they entered their destination, the receiving line already went the entire length of the staircase and wound about the large foyer. They quickly joined the end. Effie searched for Lady Ada and spied her and her brother near the top of the stairs. She had no way of gaining her friend's attention, but she saw Lady Ada also peering at the crowd. When their gazes connected, her friend's face lit up. She gave a small wave, which Effie returned.

She wondered where the Dowager Duchess of Waterbury might be. Lady Ada and His Grace were near the front of the line, but their mother was nowhere in sight. Effie thought it odd that the older woman would have gone through the receiving line before her children, especially because her daughter was making her come-out. The dowager duchess should have been eager to introduce Lady Ada to Lord and Lady Simmons.

As the line moved, Mama introduced Effie to the parties on both sides of them and then proceeded to point out others in line to her, giving her their names and sharing a bit about them. She saw two other girls on the stairs close to her age, and her mother mentioned both were making their come-outs this Season.

They finally reached and greeted Lord and Lady Simmons. Lady Simmons looked to be only a few years older than Effie, and was so gracious.

"I hope you enjoy your come-out Season as much as I did my own, Lady Euphemia," the countess told her. "It is a very special time in your life. Perhaps you and your mother might wish to come to tea some afternoon, and we can talk about things."

"I would be honored to do so, Lady Simmons," she replied.

"Have a lovely evening," the countess wished to her.

As they moved toward the ballroom's entrance, Mama said, "That is a great compliment Lady Simmons paid to you. She will only issue an invitation to tea to a handful of others this evening. You made quite a good impression upon her, Effie. She would be a good friend to make."

While she had supposed she would make friends among the other girls making their come-outs, Effie had not thought about becoming friendly with matrons. She did like Lady Simmons, though. She and Mirella had always been the best judges of character within the Strong family. She could not wait to share with Mirella about this special invitation.

Mama guided them to the left once they were inside the ballroom, and they paused, where Mama said, "This is where will we stay until the ball opens. Others will be circulating throughout the ballroom, but with your brother being a duke, guests will make their way to him."

"Do all the dukes position themselves throughout the ballroom?" she asked.

Her mother laughed. "Yes, for the most part, they do. Because of their rank in Polite Society, it is fitting for others to come to a duke."

She glanced about and spied Lady Ada standing with her brother and another couple. The Dowager Duchess of Waterbury was still missing, causing Effie's curiosity to grow. Again, she and Ada's gazes met, and this time they both grinned at one another. Effie hoped it might be possible to ask her supper dance partner if they might share the meal with Lady Ada and her partner. She could not get ahead of herself, though. She would first need to see if anyone asked her to dance before she planned supper scenarios in her head.

Quickly, they were joined by Allegra and Sterling, and Lyric and Silas.

"This is so exciting," Allegra said. "I cannot wait to dance this evening." Her cousin looked to her husband and said, "You had better not hide in the card room, Sterling."

Sterling laughed, brushing a kiss against his wife's cheek. "I will dance every dance if that is what you wish me to do, love."

Her other sisters and their spouses also joined them, making them quite a large party. Other guests made their way toward them, and Mama introduced her to each of them. A few were married couples, but several were gentlemen who appeared by themselves or in pairs, asking her for a dance this evening. Effie saw no reason to turn any of them down and so accepted each time. Once she actually knew something of a gentleman, she could decide whether or not to dance with him at future balls.

An odd feeling coursed through her, and she glanced up, seeing the Duke of Waterbury headed toward them, his sister on his arm. She found it thoughtful of His Grace to make certain she and Lady Ada had a chance to speak to one another.

"Why, Your Grace. Lady Ada," Mama said, smiling at the pair. "It is so very nice to see you this evening. Is Her Grace here?"

"Unfortunately, Mama had a headache and was unable to attend the ball this evening," the duke said.

Though he had answered quickly and smoothly, Effie knew the duke lied. Under no circumstances would the dowager duchess not have attended the opening ball of the Season unless something drastic had occurred. She could not wait to get Ada alone to discover what had happened.

She looked to her friend and smiled. "It is so very good to see you, Lady Ada. I had an idea. Perhaps we might join one another at supper this evening. We can see if our dance partners might be agreeable to do so."

Her friend's face lit up. "Oh, that would be wonderful, Lady Effie. I will certainly see if we can make that happen."

A new gentleman arrived, and Mama introduced her and Lady Ada to Viscount Ashmore. Immediately, he engaged Lady Ada in conversation.

Suddenly, the Duke of Waterbury asked, "Would you like for me to sign your dance card, Lady Euphemia?"

Immediately, Effie replied, "No, Your Grace. You should choose to dance with someone else. Not me."

Chapter Ten

Malcolm should not have let it go on this long. He cursed inwardly—and blamed his mother for avoiding him during the past week.

Ever since she had flown into a rage at the Duke of Seaton's townhouse, upset at Lady Euphemia, Mama had barely been seen. She had begun taking breakfast in her bedchamber, often not until noon, telling Ada that she was merely preparing herself for the late nights when they would not come home until dawn and suggested that her daughter do the same. Mama had made herself sparse at teatime and even a few dinners, conveying through servants that she was visiting with old friends who had just arrived in town. The few times Malcolm saw her, Ada was around, and he did not want to draw his sister into the crossfire, which was bound to occur when he told Mama that she would not be needed to find a wife for him.

She had taken Ada a few places with her as she called upon others, which he thought was good because his sister moped about, not being able to see her friend. He had hoped when they had gone to the modiste's shop for a fitting on two occasions that Ada might run into Lady Euphemia, but that had not been the case. He was certain his mother had changed appointment times so as not to allow that to occur.

Ada confessed to him that she had left a note for Lady Euphemia at

Madame Dumas' shop, pleading with the modiste to pass it along to her friend. Madame had agreed, which if discovered, would have angered Mama terribly. Malcolm supposed the dressmaker was willing to take the risk of losing the business of one client versus the entire Strong family.

He had hoped after dinner this evening that he might pull his mother aside and speak with her. Unfortunately, she had not made an appearance. When he asked Williams about her absence, the butler replied that Her Grace was dining in her rooms, wanting to have plenty of time to dress for this evening's ball.

Ada had not been affected by their mother's frequent absences. In fact, she had confessed to him that she felt a bit relieved. Malcolm had watched her leave the table to go and bathe and dress for tonight's opening ball, thinking how much he loved his sister and hoped that she would find a gentleman to her liking, one who would treat her well and bring some happiness into her life.

He retired to his own rooms, and Barker informed him that hot water was on its way. Malcolm stripped off his clothes and tossed on a banyan as he waited for it to arrive. He glanced at the evening wear laying on the bed, thinking how the last time he had worn it, he had been in search of his duchess. He pushed aside the bitterness, vowing he would not make a mess of things this time. It was a new Season. A time for new beginnings.

Hopefully, one with Lady Euphemia.

He had thought often about her during the past week, keenly feeling her absence, just as Ada had. Malcolm found himself longing to hear her opinions, even though he did not always agree with them. Lady Euphemia could be quite stubborn in her convictions, someone who always believed she was in the right. And yet it did not seem to matter to him. He yearned to see her effervescent smile. She was so curious and enthusiastic about the smallest of things. He believed he would never grow bored in her company.

But he had yet to make the impression upon her he wished to make. Malcolm wanted Lady Euphemia to see him as a person worth getting to know, not simply someone who took up a seat in the carriage or drawing room. He wanted to talk with her. Disagree with her. Tease her. Understand her.

More than anything, though, he wanted to kiss her.

Perhaps that would be what finally made her see him as a person. As a man. One interested in her, as a woman.

But how would he go about kissing her?

He had never kissed Imogen before they wed. They had only seen each other a handful of times before their betrothal was announced. Once that occurred and it was considered proper to be in a room alone with her, he had only spent a quarter-hour in her company before he tired of her and made an excuse to leave. They had wed two days after that encounter, and Malcolm knew now they never should have. They hadn't a single thing in common.

After their wedding in town, they had returned to Waterside, arriving late in the day. Imogen had appeared tired, and he had told her he would have a light supper sent up to her so that she might get some rest. He had wanted to take her around the estate the next day to show off her new home to her, but she did not ride, something he had not known. When he asked her about it, she told him horses frightened her because of their size, and she had never learned to ride one because of her fears.

He had traipsed off to the stables without her, telling her he had tenants to visit and would be out all day long, instructing his new wife to have Mrs. Calley, the housekeeper, take her around the house to familiarize her with it. When he returned, he did dine with her and then asked if he might visit her in her rooms that evening. She had agreed, not being able to meet his gaze.

The first time they had made love, she wept the entire time. Imogen was timid to begin with, and every time he touched her, she flinched. Malcolm had tried to be loving and respectful, assuring her what they did was what all married couples did in order to make a babe, but she had wept all the harder. When he had broken through her maidenhead, the tears had flowed all the more. He had finished quickly and thanked her, returning to his own room.

They had not seen one another the next day because Imogen kept to her rooms the entire time, saying she was indisposed.

Malcolm had visited her at night half a dozen times in that first month, doing his husbandly duty as his wife lay silently beneath him. When she found herself with child, she did not even have the courage to tell him to his face. Instead, his duchess had written a note and had it delivered to him, explaining that she was increasing and that it was unnecessary for him to visit her bedchamber for the foreseeable future.

That had been all the excuse he needed, and he rarely saw or thought of her after that. He did not take his marriage vows lightly, however. He kept no mistress in the nearby village, nor would he ever think to dally with one of the maids. Malcolm had become like a monk and had remained so even until now, long after Imogen and the babe's deaths.

An hour later, he was bathed and dressed, waiting downstairs for Mama and Ada. Malcolm still hadn't a clue how or where he might kiss Lady Euphemia. Hundreds of guests were present at a ball. He supposed he might ask her to walk along the terrace with him. That was a possibility, but it still wasn't private enough. It wasn't as if he could take her to a quiet, unoccupied room and talk with her. If found alone, they would be forced to wed. At any rate, he was gentleman enough not to do something of this nature and compromise her. And despite being young, Malcolm had the feeling that if she were placed in such a desperate situation, Lady Euphemia would rather leave town with her reputation in tatters and return to her beloved Shadowcrest, spending the rest of her life tending to her array of animals.

He definitely would call upon her tomorrow, as he supposed many other suitors would do. Perhaps he could create some opportunity at the Seaton townhouse in order to be able to be alone with her and kiss her. Not just a friendly touch of lips. Malcolm determined Lady Euphemia needed to be swept off her feet.

It surprised him when Mama was the first to appear, and he told her how nice she looked.

"Of course, I look my best, Waterbury," she said crisply. "After all, I am bringing out my only daughter to Polite Society this evening. Others will be looking at you and me as much as they do her. We are a reflection of Ada. Keep that in mind."

"Mama, I must address something with you that I—"

"I do not want to hear it," she said dismissively, angering him. After all, he was a duke. She *should* listen to him when he wished to speak to her.

Controlling his temper, he said, "Whether you wish to hear it or not, I am going to say it."

"Ah, Ada! Aren't you a picture of loveliness?" Mama cried.

Malcolm turned, seeing his sister float down the stairs in an elegant gown. The color complimented Ada's hair and skin, and his sister absolutely glowed.

Reaching out his hand, he took hers, leading her the remaining steps.

"You are beautiful," he said, his gaze meeting hers, seeing how pleased she was at his compliment.

"Do you truly think so? Or are you merely saying that because I am your sister and you are supposed to compliment me?"

"Once you see the number of men I have to fight to keep away from you, you will believe me," he teased, thinking he never used to tease anyone and had only begun doing so after being in Lady Euphemia's company.

"The carriage is waiting, Your Grace," Williams said. "And if I might be so bold, Mrs. Williams and I would like to wish Lady Ada the very best as she makes her debut tonight."

"Thank you, Williams," Ada said graciously.

"You've had compliments enough," Mama said, dampening the festive mood. "Too many will go to your head. Let us be off, Waterbury."

It angered him, Mama ruining this moment for Ada. Was she so jealous of her own daughter that she couldn't allow a compliment or two to be given to Ada?

Malcolm took her hand and slipped it through his arm. "You look exquisite, poppet. Do not let anyone tell you otherwise."

In the carriage, Mama began lecturing Ada on how to comport herself this evening. She was not to dance with any gentleman more than once and she must not show enthusiasm toward any particular partner. Mama emphasized avoiding gentlemen who were mere barons or viscounts, saying they were not worthy of Ada's consideration.

He interrupted. "I have met a few men at White's who hold those titles, Mama, and they are well-mannered, pleasant fellows. I do not think Ada should limit herself, especially on this opening night of the Season."

"You have paid for your sister's wardrobe, Waterbury," Mama said. "That is the extent of your involvement. It is a mother's job to make certain her daughter weds the most eligible bachelor available."

He frowned. "I thought you said I would be included in the decision regarding the man Ada wishes to be her husband."

Mama sniffed haughtily. "And I believe I have told you that it is my decision to make. Of course, I will inform you of the name of the gentleman I select, but—"

His temper flared. "No buts, Mama," he said firmly. "I do not want to appear harsh with you, but this is *Ada's* decision to make. Yes, she is free to seek your advice—or mine—but she is the one who will wed the gentleman and spend the remainder of her life living with him. We cannot force someone upon her, simply because he has a revered family name or a title that goes back for generations. I want Ada to find happiness this Season and not be miserable for a lifetime."

"Balderdash!" Mama said loudly, her cheeks growing bright red. "Happiness has nothing to do with a marriage."

"Then perhaps it should," he said, his own voice even louder than hers. "Do you know *I* have never been happy? No, you wouldn't. Because you have never really asked anything about me. You never asked who my friends were when I was growing up. What grades I earned. What sports I excelled at. If I preferred to ride or fish. You are my mother—and yet I do not believe you have the faintest idea who your son is."

"Why should I?" she challenged. "Men and women go their separate ways. My role was to birth a son and give Waterbury his heir. I did so. I was wed to him for over three decades, and I could not tell you one thing about him. We led separate lives. That is the way things should be."

"I do not want a marriage like that, Mama," Ada said earnestly. "I want to know my husband. I want to be a good partner to him. I want us to see our children every day."

Mama whirled, almost snarling. "You are a fool, Ada. That Strong girl has filled your head with impossible notions."

"That Strong girl is the best friend I will ever have," Ada retorted, not backing down. "And her family is full of love. Siblings who love one another. Spouses who love each other and are openly affectionate. Parents who love their children."

"How dare you speak to me in such a manner?" Mama said. "You are never to speak to that wicked girl—or any of her family—ever again."

Determination filled his sister's eyes. "I will speak to whomever I choose to, Mama. And I will wed the man I wish to. Waterbury said I could."

Malcolm reached for Ada's hand and squeezed it. "I support what Ada wants, Mama," he said calmly. "While I will certainly look into the man who wins her heart and make certain he is not marrying her strictly for her dowry, I will still trust her judgment. The same holds true for me. I am a grown man, a duke of eight and twenty. I do not need you to choose a bride for me. I am perfectly capable of making that decision myself."

His mother looked from him to Ada, her jaw falling open in shock. "The both of you have plotted together. You have betrayed me," she declared.

"No, Mama," he insisted. "We simply wish to decide for ourselves what will be the most important decision we ever make," he told her, echoing sentiments Ada had previously expressed to him.

"You do not want me to be a part of anything," she cried. "And I gave birth to you both!"

He and Ada exchanged a glance. Both knew Mama giving birth had been the last thing she had truly ever done for either of them. Servants, tutors, and governesses had raised them. Their parents had not shown the slightest bit of interest in either of them.

The carriage, which had barely been moving, came to a stop. The door opened, with a footman standing in the doorway.

"It's like it always is for the opening ball, Your Grace. Traffic is so heavy, we are packed in with nowhere to go. If you are to make it to the ball, you'll need to walk from here. It's only another two blocks."

"Then that is what we will do," he said.

Malcolm climbed down the steps the footman had placed and reached up a hand, taking Ada's and handing her down. When he did the same for Mama, her eyes narrowed.

"Mama?" he asked.

"I am not coming," she told him, her jaw set stubbornly.

Stunned, he climbed back into the carriage and said, "But your daughter is making her come-out. It is up to you to introduce her to the members of the *ton*."

She snorted. "You are a duke. *You* do it. I am going home."

"Mama, please, do not act in this fashion," he pleaded.

Her gaze met his, and he was taken aback. All Malcolm could see was hate filling them. He made a decision which he hoped to be the right one.

"You are right. I will take care of Ada. She does not need a venomous viper by her side this evening. I will see that she meets a good number of people and that her programme is filled. I will have the coachman take you home now."

For a moment, he caught the look of surprise in her eyes. Quickly, though, the veil was lowered, and he closed the carriage door.

"Malcolm?" Ada asked, uncertainty in her voice, and he wondered just how much of their conversation his sister might have overheard.

He took her hand and called up to the driver, "Her Grace is feeling unwell. A sudden headache has come upon her. Please see her home and then return for us."

"Yes, Your Grace," the coachman replied.

Tucking his sister's hand into the crook of his arm, they set out, following others who had also had to abandon their own carriages.

"Mama is not coming this evening?"

"No. She has chosen not to," he replied evenly, not wanting to worry Ada.

"Thank you."

He stopped and looked at her. "For what?"

"For being my big brother. For looking out for me. For sticking by my side. I know tonight will be infinitely harder without Mama to smooth the way, but I must tell you, Malcolm, I feel as if the heaviest burden has been lifted from me. It is as if I could float along this street."

Grinning, he said, "I know exactly what you mean."

An hour later, they had gone through the receiving line. He had introduced his sister to several gentlemen, all men from White's whom he had visited with over the past few weeks. Her eyes sparkled and her smile never wavered.

"You must also agree to dance with a few ladies, Waterbury," Ada admonished. "How else are you going to meet your new duchess?"

"Why don't we go and say hello to the Strongs?" he suggested. "I know you and Lady Euphemia are dying to speak with one another."

"Oh, yes. Please."

They set off to where the Strongs held court, and Lady Euphemia glowed seeing her friend. He listened to her idea of them dining together after the supper dance and decided he would see if Lady Euphemia still had that number open on her programme.

With his sister engaged in conversation with a new gentleman, Malcolm asked, "Would you like for me to sign your dance card, Lady Euphemia?"

Without a moment's hesitation, she replied, "No, Your Grace. You should choose to dance with someone else. Not me."

No? She had just told him no?

But he was a duke. No one ever told a duke no.

"I beg your pardon?" he said, hoping he had misheard her.

Smiling up at him, Lady Euphemia said, "You heard me, Your Grace. I do not wish to dance with you. Actually, I stated it poorly. I should not dance with you."

"Why not?" he boldly asked, wondering where this might be leading.

"Because you are looking for a wife," she explained. "You should be circulating through the ballroom, now that you have seen to your sister's dance card being all but filled. If I dance a set with you, it will be one less opportunity you have to meet your future duchess." Her eyes were bright with mischief. "I do not want to be blamed for that."

She leaned in, and he caught the scent of gardenias. "But at some point, you simply must share with me why Her Grace did not come with you this evening. I know she is not ill as you said."

He cocked one eyebrow.

Grinning, she nodded. "She has wanted to run your life and Lady Ada's ever since I met the two of you. Tonight, of all nights, is not an evening she would miss. Her Grace would be in her element, the puppet master pulling the strings, making the two of you dance to her tune."

"You are calling me a puppet?" he asked, his temper flaring, because what she said came too close to the truth.

Immediately, Lady Euphemia appeared contrite. "I apologize, Your Grace. I have grown too familiar with you. You have become like a brother to me these past few weeks of our acquaintance." She chuckled. "Well, at least a silent brother since you are always lurking about Ada. I admire how protective you are of her. And something tells me that you finally stood up to Her Grace—for both your and Lady Ada's sake. She is probably at home, sulking, because you and your sister wish to make your own matches without her forcing her opinions on you and making the matches herself."

"You are very clever, my lady, and you speak close to the truth. But you have one thing absolutely wrong."

She frowned. "What is that?"

He smiled his most charming smile, knowing it was devastating and that she had yet to see it.

"Dance the supper dance with me and find out."

Chapter Eleven

Malcolm watched Lady Euphemia, who hesitated a brief moment. Then her curiosity won out, and she smiled at him, causing his heart to thump against his ribs in a manner he had never experienced before.

"I would be happy to partner with you for the supper dance, Your Grace."

"Good. I am glad that is settled. I suppose I should greet those in your large family whom I have already met and be introduced to the rest who are still strangers to me."

She chuckled. "Yes, you have yet to meet Allegra and Lyric, my cousins, and their spouses."

Quickly, she led him about the circle of Strongs, and he greeted Lady Mathilda, who stood with the Duke and Duchess of Seaton. Next came Lady Euphemia's older sisters, the twins who favored one another, and their husbands.

Looking at Lord Hopewell and Lord Edgethorne, Malcolm quipped, "I almost did not recognize you, my lords. You had no children in your arms or dangling about your shoulders."

Both men laughed good-naturedly, and Lord Edgethorne said, "You should have seen me waltzing around the nursery this evening with Evelyn before we departed for this ball." A wistful look entered his eyes. "I am afraid all too soon, she will be grown and no longer dancing with her papa—but with the man who will steal her heart."

He had not spoken much to Lord and Lady Bridgewater. Lady Bridgewater's auburn hair stood out among this group, and he complimented her on its shade.

"Thank you, Your Grace. Most of the Strongs have dark hair, but my red tresses come from my grandmother, just as Effie's blond ones do from our other grandmother."

"But you all have those cornflower blue eyes," he said.

Lady Bridgewater nodded. "They are the Strong eyes. We are known for them."

"Let me introduce you to my cousins," Lady Euphemia told him, easing him around the rest of the circle. "This is His Grace, the Duke of Waterbury. Lord and Lady Carroll. And Lord and Lady Blankenship."

He greeted the two couples, vaguely recalling that both these husbands had been quite wild.

Lord Carroll said, "I see you are trying to place us, Your Grace. Lord Blankenship and I had a bit of a reputation before Allegra and Lyric tamed us. Now, we are still good friends with one another, but we are quite docile husbands."

Lady Carroll shook her head in disbelief. "Docile?" she asked, arching one brow at him. "I would say you were more hungry like a wolf, my lord," she said flirtatiously, causing them all to laugh. Only Malcolm remained silent, wondering about this family.

Lady Blankenship said, "I hear that you and Lady Ada accompanied Effie to Gunter's last week, Your Grace. I hope you enjoyed the treats you chose."

"Yes, my lady," Malcolm replied. "It was our first visit to the shop, but I promise it will not be our last."

Lady Carroll said, "We ladies would like to take your sister there again so that we might have a good, long chat and get to know her. And eat ices, of course."

Lord Carroll said, "You would go to Gunter's without the men in the family, knowing how much we all enjoy their offerings?"

Lord Blankenship added, "We would not have to be seated at the same table as you. We could sit and entertain ourselves."

Lady Blankenship swatted her fan playfully at her husband. "All of you may go to White's together. Take His Grace with you and drink coffee and gossip even more than fishwives do. We will look after Lady Ada."

Talk of his sister reminded Malcolm that Lady Euphemia had suggested they dine together this evening.

"It was lovely meeting all of you, but I must speak with my sister. Excuse me."

He guided Lady Euphemia back to Ada. She still spoke with Lord Ashmore. This was the longest she had spent with any gentleman this evening, and he asked, "Ashmore, are you dancing with my sister tonight?"

The tips of the viscount's ears pinkened. "I am, Your Grace. The supper dance."

"Then I would ask for you and my sister to join Lady Euphemia and me so that we might dine together."

Lord Ashmore smiled. "Thank you, Your Grace. That is a splendid idea."

Malcolm saw happiness written on Ada's face and wondered if this man would be the one to keep his sister happy for a lifetime.

Lady Euphemia said, "Excuse us," and guided him away from the large group of Strongs.

"It is time for you to move about the ballroom, Your Grace," she told him matter-of-factly. "Sign those programmes. You must be active in your pursuit of a bride." Her eyes twinkled. "Especially since you do not have your mother perusing the Marriage Mart for you."

She glanced over her shoulder and back to him. "My brother will take care of Lady Ada in your absence."

He bowed to her. "Until the supper dance, my lady."

Malcolm actually did as she suggested. He did not want Lady Euphemia to be the only woman he danced with. While he still had every intention to stake his claim regarding her, he did not want to be too obvious this first evening. Moving about the room, he sought out a few of the gentlemen he had renewed acquaintances with at White's, meeting their wives and those who had sisters, whose dance cards he signed.

Returning to the group of Strongs, Malcolm claimed Ada, leading her away for a private word. Her cheeks were flushed, and the dancing had yet to commence, although he saw the musicians beginning to tune their instruments.

"Did you have enough gentlemen sign your programme?" he asked.

"Oh, yes, Waterbury. Every one of them you introduced me to did so. A few others also added their names when I visited with Lady Euphemia and her family. Mrs. Andrews knows absolutely everyone in this ballroom and was able to introduce me to a good number of gentlemen. Several asked for a dance, but I had no more open spots on my card. I told them we would have to partner at the next ball two nights from now."

He had no idea what events they would be attending this week. He had depended upon his mother to keep him informed, so Malcolm was glad that Ada seemed to have a grasp on where they would be going. He also wondered if Mama would be over her tantrum and accompany them to these future events. Surely, she would not sit home the entire Season. Then again, he hadn't a clue what she would do. He had accused her of not knowing him, and the same was true regarding her. Malcolm had spent so little time in her company, he knew little about her.

Spying a gentleman coming their way, he knew the man was ready to claim Ada for the first set and said, "I will be here in the ballroom if you need me. Have your partner return you to me each time."

"You will not be in the card room at all this evening?" she questioned.

"No, I am looking for a bride, remember?" He grinned. "I do not think I will find one in the card room."

Once Ada left with her partner, Malcolm moved across the room to his own partner, and they danced the first set, a lively country dance. He felt fortunate that Lady Euphemia was in their group of eight because it gave him a chance to see her dancing. She moved with ease, laughing as she did so. He did not think he had ever seen a lady enjoy herself dancing so much as Lady Euphemia did. Then again, he was prejudiced, favoring everything about her.

He sat out the next number, standing on the sidelines, watching both his sister and the woman who had captured his attention. He would not say that Lady Euphemia had captured his heart.

Not yet.

Malcolm found himself enjoying the evening and his various partners. The only Season he had attended, he had been focused on finding a bride, but he had spent more time playing cards than dancing, allowing his mother to observe which lady he should offer for. This time, he felt more lighthearted in all he did and ascribed that to Lady Euphemia's influence. Not only was she helping to change Ada, but she was changing him, as well.

The supper dance arrived, and he went to where the group of Strongs gathered. He had seen some of the men leave for the card room, but all were present and accounted for now, ready to dance with their wives and take them into supper.

Before claiming Lady Euphemia, Malcolm made certain to speak to her mother and Mr. Andrews.

"You raised a fine group of girls, Mrs. Andrews. They all seem to be most happy in their marriages."

"Are you dancing with my Effie now?" Mr. Andrews asked pointedly.

"I am, Captain," he said, addressing Mr. Andrews by the title his family lovingly bestowed upon him.

The captain cocked an eyebrow at him. "I will be watching," he said, turning to gaze protectively at Lady Euphemia.

"I know," Malcolm replied.

He moved to her and couldn't help but think she was the most beautiful woman in this ballroom. He had thought her pretty when first introduced to her, but the more he learned about her, the more he held her in esteem.

"I hope you waltz well, Your Grace," she said as they stepped upon the dance floor. "I had my toes trampled upon twice this evening. Twice! It is a miracle I am even walking now."

Smiling at her, he said, "That does not seem to have slowed you down one bit, my lady."

"Nothing would slow me tonight, Your Grace. Mama wished for me to make the most of my come-out, and I plan to do so."

The musicians took up their bows, and Malcolm slipped his arm about her, taking her hand in his. The waltz began, and they glided across the floor together with ease, seemingly as one.

"Oh, you do dance divinely, Your Grace."

"Thank you, Lady Euphemia."

Her nose crinkled. "I wish you would stop calling me that. The only person who addresses me that way is Mama, and that is only when she is put out with me. Please, I wish you would call me Effie."

"It suits you, you know."

"Euphemia was my grandmother's name. She, too, had her family refer to her as Effie."

"Then from now on, it shall be Lady Effie," he said.

Malcolm had thought they would talk during this waltz, the only dance where a conversation was manageable. Instead, he simply gave himself over to the moment, enjoying the feel of her in his arms and the subtle scent of gardenias upon her dewy skin.

When the music ended, he was reluctant to release her and held her to him a moment longer than he should have. She looked at him quizzically, and he dropped his arms, reaching for her hand and tucking it into the crook of his arm.

"Shall we go into supper?" he asked.

They moved slowly, all the guests headed to the same destination.

"Thank you for inviting Lord Ashmore to join us at supper," she said. "He spoke with Lady Ada for a very long time. It will give her even more of a chance to get to know him even better. I assume Lord Ashmore will become one of her callers tomorrow afternoon."

It struck Malcolm that he needed to be in two places at once tomorrow afternoon. How was he to chaperone Ada with her suitors when he wanted to call upon Lady Effie? He supposed he would have to apologize to Mama and make certain she took up chaperoning duties in order to allow him the freedom to call upon Lady Effie. Until he knew of that, however, he would not speak up about his intentions to visit with her tomorrow. He did not know if surprise visits occurred from suitors, but Mrs. Andrews would be gracious enough not to turn him away.

He saw Ada, who waved at him, and Malcolm began guiding Lady Effie toward his sister and her escort. He did not know much of anything about Viscount Ashmore and would definitely spend some of this supper hour learning more about this suitor.

As they joined up, Lord Ashmore said, "I have told Lady Ada that there are two ways to go about the buffet. We can leave the ladies once we have claimed a table for ourselves, or they can go through the buffet line with us and make their own selections."

Ada immediately spoke up. "I would like to see all the food on display if you do not mind, Lady Effie. I would not wish to leave you seated alone, though."

"No, I am more than happy to have the four of us stay together. I have already promised Cook I would tell her about tonight's food displays and what Lady Simmons served. Cook is already making plans with Mama about what to prepare for my come-out ball."

Guilt raced through Malcolm. That was another of the topics he had meant to broach with his mother and had forgotten to do so. He hoped Mama would not continue to sulk, and would help plan Ada's come-out ball. If for any reasons she refused to do so, he would need assistance. He thought of Mrs. Andrews and asking for her help. The thought caused him to chuckle, thinking how upset his mother would be with that suggestion.

"What is so amusing, Your Grace?" Lady Effie asked.

"The entire evening, my lady. Come, let us head to the buffet while others are seating themselves."

When they reached the place to start, Malcolm grimaced inwardly, seeing his former father-in-law. It would be the first time they had seen one another since Imogen's funeral. The earl had been quite upset about his daughter's death and had not even returned to the house with the other mourners. Already, he could tell the older man was upset to see the man who had wed his daughter in the company of another lady.

"Good evening, Lord Bilford," he said politely.

The earl's mouth hardened, and he looked as if had swallowed something sour. "Your Grace."

Knowing he would need to introduce his companions, Malcolm said, "You may recall my younger sister, Lady Ada. And this is Lord Ashmore and Lady Euphemia Strong. Lord Bilford is Imogen's—my wife's—father."

He had reverted back to Effie's formal, given name, not feeling comfortable using it as he introduced the two. Then it struck him he had called Imogen his wife, which seemed to magnify the earl's anger. Bilford looked ready to explode, and Malcolm feared what might be unleashed. Before he could speak, though, Lady Effie took Lord

Bilford's hand.

With sympathy on her face and in her voice, she said, "It must have been so hard to lose your daughter, Lord Bilford. I suppose you never quite get over such a loss."

"You are correct, Lady Euphemia," the earl said gruffly. "Imogen was the only child we had. I lost my wife almost a decade ago. Losing my girl was heartbreaking."

Taking his arm, Lady Effie patted the older man's hand. "I doubt it is something you ever recover from, but you have those wonderful memories of her forever in your heart and can always sit and revisit them when you are feeling blue. Did you know when a ship loses her captain or any of the officers during a voyage, she flies a blue flag and has a blue band painted along her entire hull when returning to her home port?"

Malcolm noticed she began guiding the earl through the line, placing things on his plate for him, talking quietly with him about Imogen and things he remembered about his daughter. By the time they reached the end of the table, he seemed calm.

"Thank you, Lady Euphemia," Lord Bilford said. "I believe I will do as you say and recall those happy moments any time I feel sad."

"Wonderful, my lord," she said, smiling gently at him.

The earl looked to Malcolm. "Enjoy your evening, Your Grace."

Bilford moved away from them, and Malcolm shook his head. "You worked a miracle, Lady Effie."

"I agree," Lord Ashmore said. "I thought Lord Bilford was about to cause a horrific scene."

"Lady Effie knew just how to handle him," Ada said. "She is so good with people."

"You should see me with my animals," she quipped. "I have always thought myself better with them than people."

They found an empty table, and Malcolm set down the two plates he carried before seating her and then himself.

"I put a little of everything on both these plates if you would like to share, my lady," he told her. "I did not wish to interrupt your conversation with Lord Bilford to ask if you preferred sliced ham or poached chicken."

"That was thoughtful of you, Your Grace. I would not mind sharing at all. Let me know if you have a favorite among everything, and I will refrain from eating it all." Her eyes sparkled with mischief.

"I will not tell you my favorites so that you will have to merely sample some of everything and not devour what I love," he teased in return.

She picked up an olive and popped it into her mouth, chewing thoughtfully. "You are not nearly as serious tonight as you usually are, Your Grace. I rather like this side of you."

"You think me serious?"

"Very. When you are not being solemn, you act incredibly detached, as if you have no interest in what is being said. Rarely do you enter my conversations with Lady Ada. Frankly, I forget you are even present sometimes."

"I have not wanted to interrupt the two for you," he shared, again thinking he needed to make more of an impression upon her. "I do have plenty to say."

She gazed at him a long moment. "That is very good to know. Tell me something about you, then."

His gaze pinned hers. Malcolm was determined to be open and honest with this woman, something that ran contrary to the way he was raised and the example his father had set for him. More than anything, he wanted to break free of the chains of his past and become more like the men in Lady Effie's family.

"I was friendless my entire life. My father was uncaring and standoffish with me. With everyone, actually. I supposed I unconsciously modeled myself after him, especially when no one wished to be my friend at school."

Lady Effie took in his words. In her eyes, he saw no judgment. Only curiosity, mixed with concern.

"Why did you have no friends?" she asked.

And then she took his hand under the table. No one would notice because they all would be eating. But the gesture meant a great deal to him. It comforted him. It showed him she cared.

And it caused desire to shoot through him.

Malcolm turned his hand so that he could lace his fingers through hers. She cocked her head, studying him intently.

"I have been the best at everything I have ever attempted," he began. "I could run faster than other boys. Shoot better. Ride with ease. Academics came easily to me, from languages to maths. Because of that, everyone wished to compete with me. Bring me down in defeat."

He shook his head sadly. "And they never did. When they saw they couldn't best me, they isolated me. I was the most outstanding at all I did, yet I never made a single friend at school. What bothers me now is that I thought it was the way it should be. That I would one day be a duke and—like my father—remain aloof from all."

She bit her lip, causing the already-present desire to flood him. "I am so sorry, Your Grace. That must have been such a lonely life."

He shrugged. "It was. But I had my studies. And I doted on Ada when I came home from school terms. I am learning it is a bit different now. Petty schoolboy jealousies end. I have become reacquainted with a few others from my past at White's in recent weeks and hope to finally make some friends."

She squeezed his fingers. "You know the men in my family would be happy to be your friends. I will have James take you to White's. No, that might be too stuffy. We will do as Allegra suggested and all go to Gunter's."

Lady Effie smiled at him, a smile that warmed him from the inside. A smile that told him she liked him. As a person—and not a duke. He still did not believe she was conscious of him as a man, but then again, she was just now coming out into society and had never really been exposed to how a man wants a woman.

Malcolm hoped the growing feelings he was experiencing for her would soon be returned.

"Yes. A trip to Gunter's would be just the thing," he agreed. "Plan it with Ada and your siblings."

He glanced to his sister and the viscount and back to Lady Effie. "For now, I believe we should learn a bit more about Lord Ashmore, don't you?"

She nodded in agreement. "And enjoy this wonderful food as we do so." She looked to the viscount. "My lord, do you enjoy riding? Lady Ada and I have gone riding in Rotten Row since we have been in town. Might you wish to join us sometime?"

Malcolm watched as Lady Effie effortlessly steered the conversation, drawing out Lord Ashmore and including his sister, making Ada shine before the viscount.

He had made up his mind. Lady Effie Strong was the only woman for him.

And Malcolm would not rest until he had made her his.

CHAPTER TWELVE

EFFIE ENJOYED HERSELF so much during supper that it was almost over when she remembered that Waterbury was going to tell her what she had been wrong about.

Perhaps she had been wrong about him . . .

She had thought him a bit full of himself before tonight. A tad pompous simply because he was a duke. Also, a man who was much too serious. At times, she had sensed an anger within him, something he hid from the world with his cold, silent exterior.

Yet after what he had revealed to her, she couldn't help but understand him a bit more. He'd truly had no one for years, other than a younger sister whom he had not been around that much. His schooldays had been lonely. His home life—with a distant father and self-absorbed mother—had obviously been miserable. Effie had seen firsthand how shallow the Dowager Duchess of Waterbury was, and she could not imagine growing up without abundant love. It made her realize how fortunate she was to have come from the family she did. True, her own father sounded an awful lot like Waterbury's ducal father, but Mama had more than made up for his lack of attention and love.

She'd also had all her sisters and cousins, all her best friends from the time she came out of the womb. Effie could not imagine what it would be like to be excluded. Isolated. Lonely.

Waterbury had not really talked about the wife and babe he'd lost. Instinct told her he had behaved much toward them as his own father had to him, not knowing how to be close to others. She hoped he would do a better job in his next marriage. She would be on the lookout for a woman who might help His Grace live up to his full potential. Effie would also ask her brother and brothers-in-law to keep a watchful eye on the duke and befriend him.

"The dancing will start soon," Lord Ashmore said. He gazed longingly at Lady Ada. "I wish we could dance the next set."

Ada looked pleased at his remark. "Then you must ask me to dance again, my lord, at the next ball."

"I will do more than that, Lady Ada," said the viscount, his face earnest. "Might I call upon you tomorrow afternoon?"

Her friend blushed prettily. "You may."

"Shall we go to the retiring room, Lady Ada?" Effie asked.

"Oh, that is an excellent idea."

The gentlemen rose and helped them to their feet. Effie said to the duke, "I haven't forgotten that you were supposed to share something with me. I cannot recall what, but please remember for me so that you might do so later."

She laughed and saw him chuckle. She also saw his eyes darken as he looked at her. An odd feeling ran through her, and Effie shook it off.

Slipping her arm through Lady Ada's they left the supper room and went to the retiring room, which was located on the ground floor.

"What do you think of him?" her friend asked breathlessly.

"Him? Who is him?" she asked playfully before bursting into laughter. "I cannot keep a straight face. I know you mean Lord Ashmore."

"Is he not marvelous?" Lady Ada asked, her face going dreamy.

"He seems like quite the gentleman. More importantly, he likes you."

"Do you really think so?" Lady Ada asked, worry in her eyes.

"I most certainly do. He hung on your every word at supper. He has asked to call upon you. I think you make for a wonderful pair. But do not rush into any commitment with him," Effie cautioned. "Continue to get to know him."

Lady Ada sighed. "It seems as if I have always known him."

Effie recalled Sophie saying something similar about James and believed her friend might have already fallen in love.

They freshened up and then primped, Effie securing a stray lock of Lady Ada's with a hairpin.

"I am so glad we were able to sup together," her friend said. "It was kind of you to dance with Waterbury."

"I only did so in order that we might spend the supper hour together. I have encouraged him to mingle more and dance as much as he can. It is the only way he will be able to determine who his next duchess might be."

Lady Ada's brow creased. "What if... what if my brother is... interested in *you*?"

Effie laughed heartily. "That would never be the case. We are as opposite as night and day. Besides, I look more upon him as a brother, not a soulmate who makes my heart quicken like I believe Lord Ashmore may do yours."

Lady Ada's face turned bright red. "I know I should not already feel this way, but there is just so much to like about Lord Ashmore. Do I love him? I am not certain what love is." She smiled. "To understand it, I should probably spend more time with your family. They are most loving, Lady Effie. Even your mama and the captain give each other such heated looks—and think of how old they are."

"Mama missed out on love the first time around. I am happy she has found it with the captain."

Lady Ada grew contemplative. "Waterbury did not love Imogen. They barely knew one another before they wed, and they spent so little time together after their marriage. She was quite ill the entire time she was increasing and took to her rooms, avoiding him."

"I am sorry to hear that. Hopefully, His Grace will make a much better second marriage than he did his first."

"Mama chose Imogen for him because she was beautiful and her family name was respected." Lady Ada hesitated. "Mama did not have a headache as Waterbury said. We quarreled with her in the carriage on the way to the ball."

"Over her involvement in choosing your mates?"

"Yes," Lady Ada said. "Waterbury said it was up to us whom we would wed. That Mama could contribute her opinion, but he and I would make our own decisions regarding our spouses."

"I can see that did not sit well with her."

Lady Ada giggled. "That is certainly one way to put it."

"We should return to the ballroom," Effie suggested.

When they left the retiring room, there were a good two dozen others milling around outside it.

Including Waterbury and Lord Ashmore.

"There is still a bit of time before the musicians take up their instruments again," the viscount said. "I was hoping you might wish to share a glass of ratafia with me before you dance your next set, Lady Ada."

Her friend glowed with happiness. "I would be delighted to, my lord."

They left together, leaving her with the duke.

"I could use a bit of air," he said. "Would you care to accompany me for a stroll along the terrace, Lady Effie?"

If he had called her Euphemia, she would have said no. Since he didn't, she agreed to do so.

Placing her hand on his sleeve, she said, "Lead the way, Your Grace."

The ventured outside through a set of French doors. Effie saw a handful of other couples strolling along leisurely. A few lanterns had been placed on the terrace, but it was only dimly lit. The cool night air felt good, however, after the crowded ballroom and supper room.

As they slowly walked the length of the terrace, she asked, "What are you looking for in a wife, Your Grace? I would like to do my best to help you find your duchess."

"You would do that for me?" he asked softly.

"Your sister is my friend. She loves you a great deal. Because of that, I am happy to help you in any way I can."

"Are you impressed that I am a duke, Lady Effie?"

His question surprised her, but she said, "If I am being honest—and I always am—no. Not one whit."

"Why not? So many women of the *ton* seek a man with a title, the higher his rank in Polite Society, the better. I would think it would help me attract women."

"It most likely does, but as you may have noticed, Your Grace, I am not most women. Why, I do not even like wearing this gown. I go about Shadowcrest in a pair of breeches simply because it is easier to ride and do the work on the estate."

Effie felt him stiffen beneath her fingertips.

"You wear . . . breeches?"

"I most certainly do. I am not a typical girl making her come-out, Your Grace. Titles mean nothing to me. My own brother is a duke, rich and powerful. Yet he is merely a man and my brother. His title does not make him any more special than the next man. Neither does his wealth. It is his manners and how he comports himself. His intelligence. His fierceness in caring for his family and his loyalty which make him James."

She shrugged. "So, no, your title means little to me. Now, it will mean a great deal to most men and women of the *ton*. You will attract women to you simply because of the title, not to mention your wealth and good looks."

"You think me handsome?"

"I had not really thought about it at all, but you are striking in appearance. Your tall, athletic frame is quite appealing. Your face is handsome. Your dark hair quite thick. And your green eyes? They are mesmerizing. I do believe you have looks and charm going for you."

They had reached the end of the terrace, and she lifted her hand from his sleeve. Propping her elbows along the terrace wall, she rested her face in her hands and stared out into the dark.

Then Effie sensed his warmth behind her. His arms came about her waist, pulling her against him. Though the night was cool, the duke radiated heat.

"Your Grace?" she asked, uncertain as to what he was doing.

His lips grazed her neck, bringing a rush of heat through her. She placed her hands atop his forearms, thinking to pry them away from her, but resting them there instead. The kisses moved along her neck, to her nape, and she felt the graze of his teeth against her skin, bringing a hot rush between her legs. He moved to her ear, his lips and teeth teasing the lobe, causing her core to pound violently.

The duke slowly turned her so that Effie faced him. She couldn't read the look in his eyes because his face was mostly in shadow. His large hands held fast to her waist.

"I am going to kiss you, Effie. Not for too long—and not the way I wish to. But I wanted you to see what a kiss could be like. You haven't been kissed before, have you?"

"No," she answered reluctantly, her thoughts so jumbled that nothing else came from her.

He bent, his warm breath caressing her as his mouth touched hers.

Oh!

Waterbury softly pressed his lips against hers, moving them back and forth as if they were a paintbrush gliding across a canvas. She could smell the spice of his cologne. Feel his body heat. She swallowed, afraid to relax, not knowing what to do.

His lips stopped moving and pressed harder against hers, causing a pleasant tingling to pour through her.

Then he lifted his head, breaking the kiss. Effie thought he was smiling but could not be certain.

As if nothing unusual had taken place between them, the duke placed her hand upon his sleeve again, and they strolled the length of the terrace again, where he walked them through the doors they had come through only minutes earlier.

When she had yet to be kissed.

Blinking, trying to acclimate herself to her surroundings again, Effie said, "Thank you for the fresh air, Your Grace."

She caught the mirth in his eyes as he replied, "Thank you for accompanying me, my lady."

Without another word, he guided her back to the ballroom and her mother and the captain.

"Here she is, Captain. Safe and sound," Waterbury said to her stepfather.

The captain harumphed.

"Please remember to organize the outing to Gunter's for us, Lady Effie," the duke reminded her. "I will see you tomorrow."

Desperate to find her voice, she cleared her throat and said, "Yes. Tomorrow, Your Grace."

She watched him saunter away as if he hadn't a care in the world.

"Effie?"

She turned, seeing Mama looking at her quizzically. "Yes, Mama?"

"Are you enjoying your first ball?"

If her mother had asked that question ten minutes earlier, Effie would have immediately responded with a yes. After kissing the duke, however, she was bemused.

"It has been wonderful, Mama," she said, trying to gain control of the multitude of unfamiliar emotions running through her. "I quite enjoyed all the dancing, and I cannot wait to share with Cook what was served on the buffet."

"Did you get any ideas for your own come-out ball?" her mother asked.

"Yes. I will sit with you and Cook and discuss them. I see my next partner arriving now."

Smiling, she greeted the rather nice-looking earl who said, "I believe we are to dance this set, Lady Effie."

"Yes, my lord. I eagerly look forward to doing so with you."

The rest of the evening, Effie had to use every bit of concentration she had to not make a false step as she danced. When the final number of the evening was played and she found it to be a waltz, disappointment ran through her.

Because she would not be partnering with the Duke of Waterbury.

Why was she taken with him after kissing him?

And more importantly, why had he not kissed her the way he wanted to? Was there another way to kiss? If so, what did it involve?

Effie hoped to have answers from Waterbury the next time they saw one another.

Chapter Thirteen

She hadn't known how to kiss. She certainly hadn't kissed him back. Then again, Malcolm had not expected her to.

Lady Effie was still the woman he wanted, however. He had felt a spark between them and wanted to explore it further. Nothing physical had ever moved him with Imogen, despite her great beauty. He had merely done his duty by her. But with Lady Effie, he felt the strongest urge to teach her about the mysteries of lovemaking. She was curious by nature, and he believed once she unleashed the sensual side of her, she would make for a wonderful bed partner.

The only thing he worried about was whether or not she would fall in love with him. He knew it was important to her to make a love match. He also knew he didn't have it in him to love a wife, but he already cared for her more than anyone but Ada. Malcolm wondered if that would be enough for her. If she could learn to love him without him returning her love.

Physically, he thought they would be well matched. Intellectually, as well. In fact, from listening to conversations she and Ada had held, he realized she knew even more than he did about estate management, and he was willing to learn from her. Eager to break away from the miserableness of his existence and begin to thrive. To be happy.

To be like a Strong . . .

Starting this morning, he would take charge of his life as he never had before. No more being passive and isolating himself intentionally. First and foremost, that meant putting Mama in her place.

Barker prepared Malcolm for the day, and he said to the valet, "Stop by Her Grace's rooms. Inform her lady's maid that I wish to see my mother at breakfast today."

"Yes, Your Grace."

He went downstairs to the breakfast room, finding Ada already present. The servants had been notified of breakfast being moved back several hours because of the Season. Ada had told him the Strong household adjusted based upon the event the previous evening. Since most members of the *ton* did not return to their homes until dawn when a ball was held, Malcolm had asked for breakfast to be at noon on those days. Any other morning, it would be served between ten and ten-thirty.

Ada smiled brightly at him. "Did you sleep well, Waterbury?" she inquired.

"I did," he responded, nodding at the footman who poured his morning coffee for him. "Mama will be joining us for breakfast," he added.

He saw her bite her lip and said, "Do not worry, Ada. Everything will be fine."

"You will be in the drawing room with me this afternoon, won't you, Waterbury? Lord Ashmore said he would call. Others will, too. I know you have said you wish to wed this Season, but I—"

"I will be present for part of the time visitors call," he assured her. "Mama will be for the entire afternoon."

Turning to the post sitting beside his plate, Malcolm began going through it as he ate. Ada talked about last night, mentioning other gentlemen whom she believed would visit her today. Frustration built within him when his mother did not make an appearance at the table.

Finally, he motioned to Williams, who stepped toward him. "Yes, Your Grace?"

"I had asked that Her Grace join us this morning," he told the butler. "Go now and fetch her."

William's eyes widened slightly at the task he had been charged with, but the butler nodded. "Of course, Your Grace."

Ten minutes passed before Mama appeared in the breakfast room. Malcolm had already dismissed all the footmen present after they had placed her breakfast on the table and poured a fresh cup of tea. By now, the meal and beverage were cold.

He did not care.

The butler seated her, and Malcolm nodded dismissively.

Mama picked up her fork without acknowledging his or Ada's presence and pushed the eggs around her plate before taking a bite. Frowning, she said, "Cold." She took a sip of tea and set down the cup. "I will require a new breakfast at once."

"You will eat what is before you—or you will wait until the next meal is served," he said, causing her mouth to fall open. "And when you are summoned by me, you are to appear promptly."

She stared at him. "I did not realize it was a summons, Waterbury," she said stiffly. "I thought you *requested* my presence at breakfast this morning."

"Plan to dine with us every morning and evening, Mama," he informed her. "And from this moment forth, you are to take up your duties and not neglect them—or Ada—further."

She shrugged. "What would you have me do?"

Their gazes met, and he stared at her a long time. Until she flinched and looked away.

"I cannot ask you to love Ada, but I can tell you to be the mother she needs this Season during her come-out. That means accompanying her to the rest of her gown fittings. Being present in the drawing room every afternoon while suitors call upon her. Attending all social events with us and introducing her around."

She started to say something, but Malcolm held up a hand to silence her.

"I am the Duke of Waterbury, Mama. You are merely the dowager duchess. I am the leader of this family. No longer the nominal head, tossing off my responsibilities to you. You will do what I say. When I say. And you will do it with civility to all. Do I make myself clear?"

"Perfectly," she said neutrally.

"As you know, I would like to find a wife by Season's end. That will entail me courting a lady—and that means I must call upon her in the afternoons. I plan to stay with you today for the first hour callers arrive, then you will be Ada's sole chaperone the rest of the time."

He looked to his sister, who had remained silent during the conversation between Mama and him. "Tell Mama about some of the gentlemen who will visit this afternoon," he encouraged.

Ada's eyes held nothing but admiration in them for him, and she smiled. "Of course, Waterbury." She turned to her mother. "I think you will like several of them, Mama. There are three whom I have a particular interest in, most notably Viscount Ashmore."

Malcolm turned back to looking over the post, listening as Ada talked about the gentlemen she had encountered last night and the ones she knew would call upon her today. She went into great detail about Lord Ashmore, explaining he had been her partner for the supper dance, and how she had quite a bit of time with him. Ada even mentioned that her brother had supped with them last night.

"You were missed last night, Mama," Ada continued. "Mrs. Andrews, in particular, asked about your health."

"You spoke with Mrs. Andrews?"

"Yes. She and the captain were in attendance with the Duke and Duchess of Seaton. I also met His Grace's two cousins, Lady Blankenship and Lady Carroll, and their husbands. They are eager for us to visit Gunter's again and would like to include you in the outing."

Mama turned to Malcolm. "Is it necessary for me to go to Gunter's with these people?" she demanded.

Knowing his mother would likely spoil the outing for Ada and the others, he shook his head. "No, Mama. I enjoyed Gunter's enough that I am happy to accompany Ada on this particular outing. Of course, when we were there, I did see other ladies dining on their own. Even Lady Effie mentioned to us that it was an acceptable place, so although Ada does not necessarily need my escort, she will have it."

He had watched Mama's face and saw the reaction when he referred to Lady Effie by her nickname. Mama had not been able to hide her response. Malcolm was done hiding his own feelings, but he had stirred the hornet's nest enough today. He would not mention which young ladies he might be calling upon this afternoon.

He should have known his mother would press the issue, however.

"Will you be calling on Lady Euphemia?" she asked casually.

Answering truthfully, he said, "Yes, Mama. She is one of the calls I plan to make."

Malcolm simply did not mention she would be only call he made. He wanted it known amongst the *ton* that he was pursuing Lady Effie Strong. As a duke, other suitors would make note of his choice and fall by the wayside without challenging him.

But would Lady Effie accept that—or him?

That remained to be seen.

He stood and reminded his mother, "Ada's suitors will be arriving in an hour. I will see you in the drawing room."

As he left the breakfast room, he winked at his sister, who giggled.

Malcolm tried to work on some correspondence but found himself too distracted to do so. He sat behind his desk, allowing his thoughts to meander, thinking about what a life with Lady Effie might entail. One thing he knew was that she would wish to know everything about Waterside. He envisioned them riding out together, visiting with their tenants, who would adore her. She was always so curious about everyone and everything surrounding her, and he believed meeting the people at Waterside would be no exception.

He pondered on their life in the country. Lady Effie was definitely a woman who would not be ignored in the way he had done Imogen. Malcolm had made so many mistakes in his first marriage, but he would not let regret swallow him whole. He had been given the opportunity for a fresh start, and he was determined to make the most of it. He pictured them visiting the nursery, playing with their children in the ways he had witnessed her relatives do with their own offspring. Every single man had worn a contented look upon his face, and it was obvious they were not strangers to their children from their play and how easily they handled them.

Malcolm could not recall a single time his parents had ventured to the nursery, much less either of them playing with him. It was something foreign to him, and yet he was excited by the prospect of spending time with his future children. Reading to them. Playing with toy soldiers or blocks. Taking walks outside. He believed Lady Effie had quite a bit to teach him, along with her Strong relatives. Being around them as a group had allowed him to see just how much he and Ada had missed out on.

He would not let that happen with this next generation of Wares.

A footman came to tell him it was almost time for morning calls to take place, and so Malcolm left his study and headed to the drawing room. Ada wore one of her new gowns, a pale green.

"You look so lovely, Ada. I like how the shade of this gown brings out the green of your eyes."

"Do you think Lord Ashmore will like it?" she asked anxiously.

He could see in all likelihood, there would be no other gentleman for his sister this Season.

Smiling, he took her hands in his. "Lord Ashmore likes *you*. That means he will like whatever you are wearing, poppet. I know you are taken with the viscount, Ada, and I am not saying that is a bad thing. I will ask that you do not ignore your other suitors, however."

"Oh, Waterbury, I would never be so rude as to do that. I also understand that the Season is in its infancy. I may meet someone else whom I like even more than Lord Ashmore." She grinned. "But, so far, the viscount is at the top of my list."

He squeezed her hands and leaned in to kiss her brow. "Then make the most of your time with him this afternoon," he advised. "I know you enjoyed his company at supper last night. I found him to be a most pleasant fellow myself."

"He liked you, too, Waterbury," she confided. "He was a bit nervous being around a duke but said you were quite a regular fellow."

Malcolm gave her a haughty look, trying to look as ducal as possible. "Well, I should have intimidated him more."

She giggled, and he loved the sound of it. He loved her. As much as he wanted to find happiness for himself, his first priority would be making certain Ada made a good match for herself. He had worried in her effort to escape Mama's grasp that she would latch on to the first gentleman she took to, but his sister had grown up without him realizing it. She had a good head on her shoulders, and Ada would make the right decision regarding a husband. Be it Ashmore or someone else, Malcolm knew he would approve her choice.

Mama entered the drawing room, gazing at the numerous floral arrangements scattered about it. She went from one bouquet to the next, reading the cards which had accompanied the flowers.

Coming to them, she said, "I see you have a good number of admirers who will visit you today, Ada. Lord Ashmore's arrangement, in particular, is quite nice."

Ada beamed. "I thought so, too, Mama. He is very thoughtful. I cannot wait for you to meet him and hear your opinion of him."

He saw his mother relax slightly.

"You wish for my opinion, Ada?" Mama asked in disbelief.

"Certainly, I do, Mama. I want to talk over everything about the

Season with you. After all, you are my mother. We are to share this special time together. While Waterbury has told me it is my decision as to the husband I take, I still need to hear what you think of these various gentlemen and give me any advice you believe I should hear."

A small smile appeared on Mama's face, and Malcolm hoped things had been smoothed over.

The door opened, and Williams announced the names of two gentlemen. One of them was Lord Ashmore, and his sister's eyes lit up.

For the next hour, Malcolm played his role of older brother and head of the family, greeting the various callers and trying to learn something about each one. Of all who came, he did like Lord Ashmore the best. Perhaps he had been influenced by Ada's favoring the viscount, but he also had enjoyed the man's company last night at supper.

Lord Ashmore told Ada and Mama goodbye, and then he motioned to Malcolm, who met the viscount at the door.

"I simply wanted to thank you again for inviting me to sup with you and Lady Effie last night, Your Grace." He swallowed nervously. "I also wanted to declare my intentions to you to court Lady Ada. She is a remarkable lady, and I hope to be seeing quite a bit of her."

"I see," Malcolm said, thinking highly of this man for making his intentions known.

The viscount smiled bashfully. "She has already promised to sit with me at tonight's musicale. If that is acceptable to you, Your Grace."

"It is, my lord. Might I join the two of you?"

Lord Ashmore smiled broadly. "I would be honored if you did so, Your Grace. Until this evening."

The viscount took his leave, and Malcolm caught his mother's eye. She nodded at him in understanding, and he slipped from the drawing

THE DUKE'S GUIDE TO WINNING A LADY

room. He had not asked for his carriage to be readied, thinking he would merely walk the few blocks to the Seaton townhouse.

He found himself eager to see Lady Effie again as he approached the door and knocked.

Chapter Fourteen

Effie allowed Mama to lead her about the drawing room. They looked at the gorgeous bouquets which had been sent by gentlemen she had met at last night's ball. The array of colors brightened the room, and the sweet smells of hyacinths, peonies, and freesias filled the air.

"How often do gentlemen send flowers to a lady?" she asked, bending down and scooping up Daffy, who had followed her to the drawing room.

"Daily if they are interested in you," Aunt Matty said, looking up from her needlepoint. "And the larger the arrangement, the more interest they have in you."

She snorted as she scratched the cat's head. "It seems like a waste of cut flowers to me. Why, look at how many arrangements are here. I will need Powell to distribute these throughout the house once visiting hours end. No sense in leaving them all here. Let the servants also have them, too. They might enjoy a fresh bouquet in their rooms."

"That is thoughtful of you," Sophie said, entering the room with James and catching the last of the conversation. "Remember, floral shops in London earn the majority of their funds during the Season, Effie, so it is not necessarily a waste."

"What are those?" James asked, pointing to an arrangement they had yet to reach. "The white ones which are drooping. I can't say I've ever seen those blooms before."

"Snowdrops," Mama said. "Along with tulips. A most unusual combination."

"I like it," Effie said, moving quickly along, not recognizing all the names from the cards. Hopefully, she would be able to match names to faces if all these gentlemen called upon her this afternoon.

When they reached the bouquet James had pointed out, she lifted the card.

Thank you for a memorable waltz and supper.

Waterbury

Effie felt her cheeks heat and quickly set down the card. She couldn't help but recall the kiss the duke had given her. She had decided that he had guessed she had never been kissed and thought to give her one so that she would know what to expect when a gentleman did kiss her. If only she had known how to respond. She hadn't known what to do with her hands. If she should lean in and press her lips back against his. Although Mama—and her siblings—had highly recommended kissing, she needed more practice at it before she would be able to say if she liked it or not.

But not with the Duke of Waterbury. Anyone but him.

"Who is that bouquet from?" Aunt Matty asked.

"His Grace. Waterbury," Effie said, trying to sound nonchalant.

James cocked an eyebrow. "*Waterbury* sent you flowers?"

"I think it rather sweet of him," Sophie said. "After all, he did dance the supper dance with our Effie, and he allowed her to dine with Lady Ada and her escort. Who knew Waterbury was so thoughtful? He always seems so quiet."

The captain strode into the room, glancing about and taking in all the flowers. Once he had, he came straight to her.

"Any of these fellows you have a fondness for?" he asked gruffly.

"No one as of yet stands out to me, Captain."

"I see."

He walked the room, reading the names on each card, nodding to himself as he did so. Effie thought it amusing and could never imagine her own father being interested enough to do so.

Looking about the room, she said, "All five of you do not have to be here. I know I need a chaperone, but I am perfectly happy for you to take turns. I do not want to keep James, Sophie, or the captain away from your shipping offices."

Her stepfather's brow furrowed. "This is the first day suitors will call upon you. We will all stay," he said firmly.

"Perhaps as the Season goes on, we can take turns," Sophie added. "I, for one, am happy to be here and meet the gentlemen interested in winning your heart, Effie."

James fisted one hand and punched it into the palm of his other. "And I most definitely want to see the type of man who believes he is good enough for my baby sister."

Horrified, she said, "Please, do not ever call me that again, James."

Everyone else laughed. Mama slipped her arm about Effie's waist. "This is the last time we will be doing this for many years, my dearest. James needs to practice for when it is Ida's turn to make her come-out."

"Ida will become a nun," her brother announced. "It is hard enough to watch men fawning over Effie. I cannot imagine them doing so over my sweet babe."

Powell entered the drawing room and smiled at the group. "The first of your suitors have arrived, Lady Effie. Shall I show them in?"

"Yes, Powell," she replied. "We might as well get it over with."

Mama said, "Remember, keep an open mind. You were not certain you would enjoy last night's ball, but you did. This will be same. Your callers will only stay a quarter-hour or so and then leave, so make the most of your time with each of them."

"Yes, Mama," she said dutifully.

Her mother was right. It was nice seeing many of the people she had met last night, and she understood they came here strictly to see her. Naturally, a few were probably interested in her connection to a duke or were curious about the size of her dowry, but for the most part, Effie felt these gentlemen truly wanted to get to know her better. She only wished they were more intriguing. While most of them seemed quite nice, she found the lot of them rather dull and their conversation boring.

The afternoon passed quickly, though, and she was happy she could place most of the names from the cards to the actual gentlemen.

Then Powell announced a name she had not been expecting.

The Duke of Waterbury.

Effie composed herself, wondering why she suddenly felt nervous around a man she had seen almost daily for several weeks. It was just in the last week she had not, when the dowager duchess had cooled the relationship between her family and the Strongs.

He did not make his way to her. It was probably a good thing he didn't because she was talking with two other gentlemen, one a baron and one an earl, and she wanted to give her full attention to them. Still, she watched the duke make his way around the room to each of the five chaperoning her this afternoon. She heard Sophie laugh at something Waterbury said, while Aunt Matty batted her eyelashes coquettishly at him.

Finally, once her other two visitors left, he made his way toward her. Her heart sped up, skipping a beat, and she told herself to quit acting like some schoolgirl. Yes, he was a duke, but that did not impress her.

Then why were her insides seemingly melting?

He reached her, smiling for only the second time since she had known him. It was a powerful smile, meant to draw a person in. She reminded herself he was not truly a suitor and had called simply to be considerate.

"Your Grace," she said, offering him her hand.

"Lady Effie," he replied, taking it and brushing his lips against her fingers, reminding her of how those same lips had been against hers only twelve hours ago.

"You did not have to call upon me today," she told him. "You went out of your way last night to dance with me and allow Lady Ada and me to sup together at our first ball. I truly appreciate your kindness, but it is not as if you are courting me."

"I am not?" he asked, cocking his head and studying her.

"Of course not," she said, brushing the thought aside. "I told you that I look upon you as yet another brother. You need not waste time in my company when you are seeking to find your duchess. Please do not feel the need to call upon me again when your time is better spent visiting with regal beauties whom Polite Society would view as the perfect duchess."

She felt Daffy brush against her legs and bent to pick up the cat. She caught disapproval in the duke's eyes as she stroked her pet.

"Do you not like cats, Your Grace?"

"Not in a house. They belong in a barn, chasing away the mice."

Effie held Daffy so they were almost nose-to-nose. "Do you hear that, Daffy? His Grace does not think you belong in the house." She smiled playfully. "What would the duke think if he knew you slept in my bed?"

"In your bed?" he asked, clearly astonished, his displeasure at the idea causing him to shake his head. "Animals are outdoor creatures, my lady."

"True. For the most part," she told him. "But I often take in ones which need extra love and care. Daffy here had been sorely mistreated. I nursed her back to health, and we are attached forever now. Where I go, she will go. If you do not like cats, Your Grace, do you favor dogs?"

"Hunting dogs are necessary," he said crisply. "But no animal should be treated as a pet, my lady."

"Then we have found something we disagree on, for you will never change my mind and I certainly will not change yours." She smiled playfully. "But Daffy is ever so warm on a cold night. She will climb under the covers and nestle against my feet, keeping them warmer than any hot water bottle ever would."

He looked aghast at the idea of a cat sleeping under the covers and abruptly said, "It was nice to see you again, my lady."

"And it was quite thoughtful of you to send the lovely tulips and snowdrops, Your Grace. Thank you for stopping by."

Effie looked about, seeing Powell at the door. The butler announced new visitors. "Excuse me," she said, leaving the duke with his jaw dropped. She supposed no one truly spoke his or her mind with a duke. At least most dukes and others in Polite Society. James was a different kettle of fish, having not been raised in this household and not even knowing he was destined to be a duke until he was an adult.

Perhaps that was the kind of man she could fall in love with. Both Pippa and Sophie had wed sea captains who had left the sea when they inherited their titles. She was not impressed by fancy titles or clothes. A rough-and-tumble man would be more to her liking. Unless some gentleman changed her mind, which she doubted, Effie would finish out this Season and return to Shadowcrest. She might find a country gentleman with no title, one who had good manners and was interesting and not opposed to dirtying his hands. An estate steward, such as Caleb would be more to her liking. Why, if she wed a steward, perhaps they could run an estate together. And then she could have the children she was growing to want, more and more.

Her new guests came to speak with her, and Effie saw the Duke of Waterbury taking his leave. James walked with him, an arm slung about Waterbury's shoulder. Hopefully, her brother would have some good advice for how to find a wife for Lady Ada's brother.

THE DUKE OF Seaton led Malcolm into his study. "Sit," he ordered.

Malcolm did as instructed and accepted the brandy snifter the duke pushed into his hand. Seaton poured a drink for himself and sat opposite Malcolm.

"Talk."

"About what?" he asked, deliberately draining the expensive French brandy and slamming the snifter onto the nearby table.

Seaton merely reached for the crystal decanter again and poured three more fingers for Malcolm. This time, he sipped it, letting the burn slowly travel down his throat to his belly, which was now warmed by the liquid.

"You asked Effie to dance. You supped with her last night. You sent her a thoughtful bouquet. Now, you have turned up to see her." The duke paused. "Are you courting my sister?"

"No," he said flatly, sipping on the brandy again. "Because she won't let me."

Seaton's brows shot up. "This is getting interesting, Waterbury. "Unburden yourself. I promise what you say will not go beyond these walls."

Slowly, he blew out a frustrated breath. "Your sister is the woman I want as my duchess," he confessed, waiting to see how the duke took that before he continued.

"Go on."

"I do want to court her. She is the only woman who remotely interests me, one who possesses both a great spirit and heart. I already knew it would be an uphill battle because she has spoken plainly about not being a lady who seeks marriage. She has a full life at Shadowcrest, one which makes her happy."

He drained the snifter again and placed it gently on the table this time before raking both hands through his hair in frustration.

"She sees me as a brother. Compared me to all the men her sisters and cousins have wed."

"Then you need to kiss her."

"I did."

Seaton arched one brow. "Then you need to kiss her so that she understands how you feel."

Malcolm nodded. "I only kissed her briefly. Our lips barely touched. I did not want to frighten her and guessed she had no experience." He paused. "I was right. She had no idea how to respond. I do not wish to force myself upon her, Seaton, but she is driving me mad."

A slow smile crossed the duke's handsome face. "That is definitely our Effie."

He grew quiet, and Malcolm knew the duke contemplated the situation.

"I will call a meeting. Of all the men in the family. Together, we will help you achieve your goal."

"You would do that, Your Grace? Why?" he questioned.

"I myself have dealt with a stubborn woman. So have several of the men who have wed Strongs. If we unite, I believe we can solve your problem."

"When?" he asked eagerly. "I will do whatever you ask of me."

The duke nodded approvingly. "I like that you want to make this happen. But I cannot guarantee even after we help you that Effie will accept your offer, Waterbury. She alone is in charge of deciding her future. If she wants you in it, that will be your success. If she does not?" Seaton shrugged. "Then you will have to find yourself another woman to be your duchess."

Within five minutes, the duke had rung for his butler, requesting four footmen be sent to each of his brothers-in-law's residences, with the request they come immediately to Lord Edgethorne's townhouse.

"I will go to Edgethorne's myself now so that he knows to expect everyone," Seaton told the servants. To his butler, he said, "Ask the captain to join us in my study."

"Yes, Your Grace," the butler said, sending the footmen off with his verbal message.

"Why are you summoning all of them?" Malcolm asked. "What good will that do?"

"It will provide a united front. Also, they will tell their wives, who will no doubt support your suit."

"Will they tell—"

"I will make it clear that Effie is not to be told."

"Told what?"

He looked up and saw Mr. Andrews in the doorway.

Seaton rose, so Malcolm did the same.

"We are going across the street to see August and the rest of the men in the family. His Grace here has a problem—and we are going to try and help him solve it."

Chapter Fifteen

A MERE HOUR later, Malcolm sat in the drawing room of the Marquess of Edgethorne, whose townhouse was located across the square from the Seaton townhouse. Tea had been brought in for those gathered, and Lord Edgethorne poured out, passing along saucers while the men of the family filled their plates with sandwiches and sweets.

Every man had responded to the Duke of Seaton's call to action. Not a one sent word that he could not come or that he would be delayed. Seaton had needed his family—and they had rallied for the head of the Strong family.

He glanced about the room, thankful his memory was good and he had a talent for matching faces with names. Besides the duke and Mr. Andrews, five other men were present. Two were viscounts—Hopewell, who had been the first to wed a Strong sibling—Pippa—and Blankenship, who had met his wife Lyric at a house party held at Shadowcrest. Two more were marquesses—Edgethorne, their host, who was wed to Pippa's twin, Georgie, and Bridgewater, who had been the last of this group to enter the family, wedding Mirella. Carroll was the lone earl, wed to Allegra, whom he had met at the same house party.

"What is the emergency?" asked Hopewell. "It must dire since you have brought all of together quickly, James.

"You haven't guessed?" asked Bridgewater, looking amused. "His Grace needs our help with Effie. He is the only man here not related by marriage. James' message to us said immediate action was required." The marquess paused. "What could be more urgent than the need to assist Waterbury here with Effie?"

"Georgie and I did note that the two of you partnered for the supper dance last night," Edgethorne said.

"That was all Allegra and Lyric could talk about in the carriage on the way home," revealed Carroll. "Both my countess and her sister thought the two of you danced together splendidly and seemed to be getting on rather well during supper."

"And Effie came back from the terrace with flushed cheeks," noted Blankenship. He shrugged. "I did not notice, but Lyric most certainly did." The viscount turned to Malcolm. Did you kiss her?"

He bristled. "A gentleman does not kiss and tell."

"His Grace did kiss Effie," the duke said. He looked at Malcolm. "It is important they have all the facts. Tell them. They are here to help you, Waterbury."

Having the attention of all seven men caused his heart to pound rapidly. He relied on his schooldays, letting his natural confidence take over.

"Let me preface things by saying that I am a widower. I wed three years ago. My wife died in childbirth two years ago, along with the babe. I did not attend last Season, so this is the first time I have been in Polite Society since Imogen's death."

"Did you love her?" the captain asked.

"No. Not at all," he freely admitted. "In fact, I did not even choose her as my wife. My mother selected Imogen for me."

Several of the men nodded, taking in his words.

"We were ill-suited from the start. Frankly, we had barely spoken to one another before our marriage ceremony took place. Afterward, I found us to have nothing in common. My duchess was very beautiful, but that cushion on the settee has more personality than Imogen possessed. More brains, as well."

More nods followed.

"I came to town this year ready to start anew. I wanted to find a woman who was not cowed by my being a duke. One who was intelligent, thoughtful, and caring."

"That's our Effie," Hopewell said. "And you should see her with Adam and Louise. She has all the nurturing instincts a mother needs."

Hearing that caused Malcolm's eyes to mist, and he blinked rapidly several times before continuing.

"Lady Effie and my sister became friends from the moment they met at the modiste's shop. I have squired them about town. Listened to their conversations. Learned a great deal about Lady Effie. She is more than the proverbial diamond of the first water." He paused. "She is the most genuine, unique, sincere, candid person I have ever met. As more events of the Season take place and other gentlemen discover her, they will admire her authenticity."

"And you greatly admire Effie?" asked Bridgewater.

"Very much so. The trouble is, she does not see me as a viable suitor."

"Why not?" interjected Blankenship.

"I have been a serious soul my entire life. Reserved. No, aloof. I have said very little around Lady Effie, merely wishing for her and Ada to enjoy their time together. I thought being a duke, with its power and wealth, would be enough to convince any woman of my worth."

"Not Effie," the captain said. "Your title is meaningless, Your Grace. Effie does not think like other women in Polite Society. She thinks for herself. She has been given a great deal of freedom at Shadowcrest. She speaks her mind freely. She pursues her own interests. And if you've kept quiet, she most likely believes you have no conversation. To Effie, talking about everything means the world to her."

"It is even worse than that," Malcolm said glumly. "She told me . . . that she looks upon me as she does all of you. She thinks of me as an older brother. An extension of Ada. How can I convince her to consider me in a new light?"

"Did kissing her not work?" asked Carroll. "If she did not enjoy your kiss, then I say it is a lost cause, Your Grace. The Strong women have strong physical and emotional reactions to being kissed." He shook his head dismissively. "As a former rogue, I can tell you now you have already lost this battle. Much as you hold Effie in regard, you must move on to someone else if that spark is not there."

"But if he already loves her, he cannot simply *do* that," protested Blankenship.

He started to interrupt and explain that he did not love Effie.

When it struck him—that he did.

"Have you kissed her properly?" Bridgewater asked. "The way a man should kiss a woman he loves?"

"No. I have not. I did not want to scare her away and supposed she had limited or no experience in kissing. I gave her a very chaste kiss last night on the terrace. As I suspected, she did not have an inkling how to react."

Edgethorne laughed. "Well, there's your answer, Your Grace. You simply need to have the time and privacy to kiss Effie properly. Your actions will first convey your feelings for her."

"And then you must affirm those actions with the words all women wish to hear," seconded Hopewell.

Frustrated, Malcolm asked, "How can I get her to kiss me again when she feels it is like kissing her brother? I cannot force her. That would drive her away, stubborn creature that she is."

"He's right about that," the duke said. "Which is why I called this meeting. We need to help Waterbury in wooing Effie. The floor is open for suggestions."

Immediately, they all began talking at once. He sat there, looking from one to another, confused.

"Calm down!" said the captain, his voice sharp, his authority unquestionable. Malcolm assumed it was his sea captain's voice, and it did the trick because the room fell silent.

"It is already hard enough on the poor duke here, having to say all he has," the captain told the group. "Now, go one at a time and give him solid advice. It can be in regard to his actions—or his words—but we must try to help the man win Effie's heart." He paused. "That is, if you believe this duke worthy of our girl."

"How will your second marriage be different from your first?" asked Blankenship.

He organized his thoughts a moment before speaking. "Most important will be the dialogue between us," he began. "If we cannot communicate well, all is lost. I spoke little to Imogen because she meant little to me. This time, I am choosing the woman I wish to be by my side, not simply a broodmare to get my heir and spare. I want a partner to share the good and the bad. I will not only love my wife—but I will also like her. And respect her."

Blankenship nodded. "I am satisfied. The first thing I would tell you is that you must be patient as you woo Effie. Take part in the usual courting rituals. Send her flowers. Compliment her. But the compliments should be unusual, not the usual which men spout to women."

"Proximity counts," Carroll told him. "Be first to greet her at a ball and sign her programme. Bring her refreshments. Lead your conversation with a compliment, as Silas recommended. A genuine one. Not that her gown is pretty or that she is fair of face. Something with more depth that would touch her and have meaning for her."

"Never be distracted when the two of you speak," James added. "That means being a good listener. Give her your full attention, and for goodness' sakes, do not interrupt her. Too many men give a woman only divided attention. I'm saying ask her thoughtful questions and truly listen to her responses. Look her in the eye. Make her feel as if she is the only person in the world. And then reply to what she has said in a thoughtful way so she understands you have truly heard her."

The captain spoke up. "I say treat her as your equal. Respect her. And watch out for other men lurking about her. You are attracted to Effie. Others will also find her attractive. Do not let your guard down, Your Grace, or someone might slip past you and sweep her off her feet."

Edgethorne said, "Be a friend first before trying to become a lover. See what you have in common. Debate the things you don't. Effie needs to see that you like her and like spending time with her. I am not saying you should ignore physical touch. A casual brush of your hands or your hand against her arm is called for. Smooth her hair. Lead up to a kiss. And give that kiss your everything when it does take place."

"I would say be confident but not arrogant," Hopewell added. "Give her an unusual gift. Not flowers. It does not have to be expensive. Surprise her with some trinket that would have meaning only for her."

"Write a poem for her if you have that kind of thing within you," suggested Carroll. "If not, share your essence with her, your deepest and most personal thoughts. Ask for her thoughts—then take her advice on some issue and let her know it proved successful. Because you listened to her."

"Be creative. Take her somewhere out of the ordinary," Bridgewater advised. "I gave Mirella a tour of Grasmere when we were both visiting the Lake District. We hiked to the top of Helm Crag and stood there, looking out at its beauty. *That* is where I kissed her for the first time. It is a kiss we will never forget sharing."

Malcolm was overwhelmed. Not merely by the large number of suggestions these men had made as they tried to help him capture Effie's heart. No, what had struck him like a thunderbolt was the fact he had been lying to himself all along. He *was* capable of love. He needed love. He deserved love.

He needed Effie.

With Effie in his life, everything would be possible. He had only been existing up until this point. Now, he had the chance to reach his full potential—and aid Effie in reaching her own, as well.

Dazed by what he had discovered about himself, he gazed out at the group of seven men in this drawing room and meekly asked, "Is there a way you might write all of this down for me? My head is swimming with your suggestions."

Viscount Blankenship enthusiastically said, "We most certainly will, Waterbury. Why, I can see the name now." He held a hand in the air, moving it from left to right as if he read a title, saying, *"The Duke's Guide to Winning a Lady's Hand."*

"Here-here," Carroll said. "Why, you fox, you." He grinned at Blankenship. "We should have done something like this years ago. Back in our days when we were the two biggest rakes in all of London. We should have written the ultimate guide on how to be a rake and seduce a lady. It would have sold incredibly well, especially if other gentlemen had known we were behind it." He grinned. "And I am certain a few ladies would have purchased it as well."

The earl paused and met Malcolm's gaze. "Silas and I have found, Your Grace, that being loyal, loving husbands is far more satisfying than the rakehells we once were. Together, we cut a swath through Polite Society, bedding every widow or willing wife who even gave us a smile, charming our way into their beds. We are reformed rakes now, though, and steadfast husbands. Silas and I will write down everything which was suggested to you, and anything else we might be inclined to think of. We will go home and do so now, and we can present it to you sometime tomorrow."

"Weren't we supposed to go to Gunter's together?" asked Hopewell. "Pippa said something about it to me. Some group outing."

"Georgie said the same to me, as well," Edgethorne piped up.

"Why don't we ask the ladies in our lives if tomorrow afternoon would be suitable?" He looked to Malcolm. "Your Grace, it would really depend upon your sister. Since she is making her come-out this Season, she will be having suitors at your doorstep every afternoon."

"I will simply tell Ada that I have made other plans for us. If those suitors are truly interested in her, then they will be that much more eager to stop by the following afternoon."

"The good thing is, we should have Gunter's to ourselves," noted Seaton. "Because all the ladies who usually patronize the place will be at home for those calls or making morning calls of their own. Shall we say meet at Gunter's at one o'clock? I can send a message alerting them to our rather large party wishing to dine upon their ices and more."

The group agreed to the time, and they decided they needed to part ways.

"Are any of you going to tonight's musicale?" the duke asked. "Sophie and I, along with Drake and Dinah, will be taking Effie, and I know His Grace is to be there."

"Georgie and I will be attending," Edgethorne said.

"So will Mirella and I, James," Bridgewater said. He chuckled. "It is music, after all. You know how Mirella and Georgie are mad for playing their pianofortes."

Seaton looked around the group. "That is it then? Very well. Then it will be Drake, August, and Byron, along with myself. Do the rest of you have other engagements this evening?"

"None," Blankenship and Carroll said in unison, while Hopewell said, "No. We are staying home this evening. We will be hard at work on His Grace's guidebook."

"Then see it is completed and have it delivered to his townhouse by tomorrow morning," Seaton instructed.

Malcolm looked about the room and said, "None of you are my friends, yet you are coming to my aid. You have said you will support my efforts in trying to win Lady Effie's hand. I cannot begin to express my deep gratitude toward each of you."

Seaton offered his hand, and Malcolm took it, shaking it. "We will do our best to see that you become one of us," the duke promised. "Even if Effie decides to wed another or chooses not to marry at all, you have a friend in me."

"And me," Bridgewater said.

The others all repeated the sentiment. "And me."

He turned toward the captain. "You are her stepfather, Sir. What say you?"

"I say if Effie chooses any man at all, it better be you, Waterbury."

He walked out with Carroll, who told Malcolm, "It was rough going between Allegra and me. The same with Silas and Lyric. I have not asked how the others came together, but just know, Your Grace, that sometimes the road to love and lasting happiness is filled with a few bumps along the way. You learn to negotiate those bumps. You go around them. You smooth some over. But if it is the road you are set to travel, take it with confidence."

"Thank you, my lord. I look forward to receiving my guidelines." He grinned. "And any other ideas you might think to jot down."

"We shall take care of you, Waterbury," Carroll promised.

As Malcolm walked across the square and turned to head toward his townhouse, he knew he had come to the turning point in the road. He was taking the path for the life journey he was meant to go on.

He only hoped Lady Effie would join him.

Chapter Sixteen

Effie came downstairs and found only James waiting in the foyer. Even though he wore his black evening dress, she still saw him more as the sea captain who had blazed into the life of the Strongs and not the duke he was. She moved toward him.

"How was your emergency?" she asked. "I am sorry you and the captain had to miss teatime with us today."

"Drake and I solved the issue for the most part. It will still take time until we know if things will be a success. Thank you for asking."

"I have not been to visit either Strong or Neptune Shipping since I came to town this spring. I would like to do so sometime."

The captain appeared. "I am glad you are taking an interest in the businesses, Effie. You're more than welcome to come with me to the office any day you choose." He grinned. "Then again, you are busy with the Season. I saw all those gentlemen in our drawing room today and the bouquets they sent. Are you leaning toward a certain admirer?"

"If you are asking if I have fallen in love at first sight with anyone, Captain, the answer is a resounding no."

"It does not have to be love at first sight," James told her. "Sometimes, you find that love grows from a friendship."

"Then the only love that has struck me has been my deep, abiding affection for Lady Ada," she said saucily. "We simply took to one another from the moment we met. I already look upon her as a sister."

"Speaking of that," James began, "I know you had wanted to have another outing to Gunter's with all the female Strongs and Lady Ada. I have arranged for that to take place tomorrow afternoon at one o'clock."

She squealed and hugged him. "You do not know how happy that makes me. It means one less time I have to sit in a drawing room and smile politely at guests. Well, suitors. I always enjoy guests that come to visit us, but I must be honest, James. Most of these eligible bachelors haven't much of anything to say."

Effie glanced up and saw Mama and Sophie descending the stairs.

"We are a complete party," Mama announced. "Aunt Matty has decided to stay home this evening. She has already claimed Daffy for company, and they are curled up in bed together with a book for company."

As they got into the carriage, she knew not all her sisters and cousins would attend tonight's musicale. From what she understood, it would only be Mirella and Georgie who did so. The evening featured two musical acts, one being a pianist, and the other an opera singer. The two sisters coming tonight both practiced their pianofortes daily, something Effie had abandoned long ago. She hoped she would not be bored this evening and if she were, she wanted to hide her boredom from their host.

"There will be no receiving line tonight," Mama explained to her. "A musicale is a smaller, more informal event. Sometimes, it is so intimate that it is held in a drawing room, with only fifty to sixty guests invited. Other times, it will take place in a ballroom, with chairs placed about the musician or singer."

With both a pianist and singer performing this evening, Effie thought a larger guest list might be expected, and she turned out to be correct in her assumption. They were ushered to the ballroom on the first floor, and she saw several rows of chairs surrounding three sides of a dais, which held a pianoforte and chairs for the musicians who would accompany the opera singer. She quickly estimated the chairs would hold eighty or so for the performance. She spied Lady Ada, who stood with her brother and Lord Ashmore.

Mama introduced Effie to a few people she had yet to meet and then smiled, saying, "Go see your friends. Enjoy tonight, my dearest."

She made her way over to Lady Ada, who greeted her with enthusiasm. "You remember Lord Ashmore?" her friend asked.

Offering her hand to the viscount, she said, "I most certainly do. How good to see you again, my lord."

"The pleasure is all mine," he replied.

She turned to the Duke of Waterbury, who smiled warmly at her. That smile made her cheeks heat slightly, as she once again recalled the brief kiss between them. He took her hand and kissed her gloved fingers, causing her heart to speed up.

"Lady Effie," he said. "I see there are not nearly as many Strongs present tonight as were in the ballroom last night."

She laughed. "Georgie and Mirella are the accomplished musicians in our family."

"Do you play the pianoforte or another instrument?"

"All the Strong women were given lessons on the pianoforte," she replied diplomatically.

A slow smile appeared on his lips, lips which she had not noticed before but could not look away from now.

"You either do not enjoy playing—or you do not play well."

She sucked in a quick breath, thinking him quite perceptive. "Why would you say so, Your Grace?"

"It was the way you stated it, my lady. I believe you do not have the passion for music which your other sisters do."

"It is true. I did take lessons. I can play." She paused. "Abysmally, that is," she revealed.

He laughed, and Effie was drawn in by it. This man did not

smile—or laugh—often, but when he did? It caused a person to sit up and take notice.

"Might I say how much I admire your locket? I noticed you have worn it these past two nights. The *E* is beautifully engraved. The locket represents you, my lady. Simple, yet elegant."

Every man who had complimented her last night had talked of her cornflower Strong eyes or how pretty her gown was. Or how pretty *she* was. No one had noticed anything else about her. Again, the duke had surprised her.

"You think me elegant?" she asked, not quite believing it.

"I do." He gazed at her a long moment, causing Effie to warm under that gaze. "You move with a natural grace, Lady Effie. And a confidence which most women simply do not possess. You never try to be someone you are not. You are comfortable with who you are and the way you live your life. I think it must be your unusual upbringing."

"Unusual?" she asked, although she was discovering just how different the Strongs were from others in Polite Society.

"I like how you can talk about more than fashion or the weather," he said. "You have to remember, I have been present as you and Ada have spoken many times these past few weeks. You have a good understanding of politics and economics, as well as how an estate should be run. In fact, I would like to speak with you about that very topic someday. I have heard some of your ideas and would like to tell you a bit about Waterside, my country estate in Kent. I have a few matters I would like to share with you and get your advice on."

Effie couldn't help but glow. This was the first man of the *ton* who was seeing the true her.

"I would be happy to discuss that with you, Your Grace."

"I am hoping a musicale does not last nearly as long as a ball," he said, glancing about to see if anyone had overheard his comment.

She chuckled. "Sophie has assured me it doesn't. It should start promptly at nine o'clock, where the pianist will play for up to three-quarters of an hour. Then the guests will be provided with a light snack for half an hour or so. The second part of the program will then commence. I hear tonight it is an opera singer from Italy. Sophie said we should be done by eleven o'clock or so."

"Thank goodness for small favors," he quipped, causing her to laugh again. Then he asked, "Would you care to go riding tomorrow morning in Rotten Row, my lady? I feel the need to be on horseback. The earlier, the better."

She found she did want to ride. With him.

"I would be delighted to do so, Your Grace."

"How early would you care to go?" he asked.

"Seven is not too soon for me," she replied. "I prefer getting up early. Country hours suit me much better than city ones, especially city hours during the Season. If we go that early, it should not be crowded at all then. In fact, we may have all of Rotten Row to ourselves."

He nodded thoughtfully. "I shall ride over to Seaton's and collect you at seven. We can go straight to Hyde Park."

"Yes," she agreed, looking forward to the ride and talking more with him. "That would be lovely."

She looked up and saw that they had been joined by three other gentlemen who were speaking with Lady Ada. Lord Ashmore had not left her friend's side, however, and Effie believed she was witnessing a romance in the making.

"He is quite smitten with her, isn't he?" the duke said quietly to her.

"Yes, he is. I think it a good thing. Lord Ashmore seems very nice."

"He asked me this afternoon if he might sit with Ada at this event. Naturally, I told him I would sit with them. Would you care to join us?"

Effie hated to take up more of his time than she already had, knowing Waterbury needed to circulate in order to find a woman who appealed to him. Still, it was only the second night of the Season, and the duke had plenty of time to find a bride.

Selfishly, she replied, "Yes, I would enjoy joining the three of you."

"Then I shall gently pry Ada away from the others."

Waterbury entered the conversation, speaking to all three gentlemen, and then he said to his sister, "Ada, we should be taking our seats since it looks as if the evening is about to begin."

Turning to the viscount, the duke added, "Ashmore, why don't you join us?"

"I would be honored to do so, Your Grace."

That led the others to fall away, and the four of them went to where the chairs were arranged.

"The farther near the back, the happier I will be," Waterbury told them.

Ada smiled indulgently at her brother. "My brother is not one for music," she explained. "While we will be listening to the pianist, he will be doing something in that head of his."

"Probably conjugating Latin verbs," the duke said breezily. "*Amō. Amās. Amat.* While I recognize and even appreciate the talent it takes to play a musical instrument or sing an aria, I have no interest in it. I do not play any instrument, but I do enjoy singing, though. Some of the old folk songs. My nursery governess used to sing them to me, and I still recall many of them."

Spontaneously, Effie said, "Then you should come some evening when all the Strongs gather to sing. Georgie and Mirella play for us, and Silas leads us in all manner of songs. James and the captain have taught us several sea ditties. They are not appropriate for Polite Society's ears, which is most likely why we enjoy singing them so loudly."

His eyes gleamed. "I may have a greater appreciation for music than I thought. I will happily accept such an invitation to learn a few naughty verses, my lady."

They seated themselves in the back row of one of the sections. Mirella and Byron stopped to visit with them before they moved to the very front row, where they sat next to Georgie and August.

"I see your sisters and their husbands have claimed prime seats," the duke said.

"Most likely, they will play every note in their laps that tonight's featured pianist hits on his keyboard. I will tell you now—before he even touches a key—either of my sisters would outshine him. It is a shame women cannot have musical careers, because Georgie and Mirella are immensely talented."

"I look forward to hearing both play, as well as learning a few wicked songs."

The final guests took their seats, and their host announced the pianist. As he played, Effie knew she was correct in her assessment. Both Mirella and Georgie played these same pieces with more passion and skill than this man would ever possess.

They applauded when the first part of the evening concluded, and Waterbury waited until her sisters and their husbands reached them. He rose and greeted the two couples, asking if his foursome might join them in the light refreshments being offered.

"We would be happy to have you do so," Byron said. "I know Lady Ada, but I do not recognize your companion."

The duke introduced Lord Ashmore to the others, and they went to the far side of the ballroom, where small tables had been placed. August and Byron said the men should retrieve food and drink, so the duke and viscount joined them, heading to one of several buffet tables set out.

Mirella said, "I hear we are to go to Gunter's tomorrow. I am so looking forward to my first visit of the spring there. How did you find it, Lady Ada? Effie said it was your first time at the establishment."

Her friend spoke enthusiastically, saying, "It was marvelous. My brother told me of our visit tomorrow." She hesitated a moment. "Would you mind if I asked Lord Ashmore to join us?"

"I think that is a splendid idea," Georgie proclaimed, smiling at Lady Ada. "Although I do believe it will be all the ladies seated at one table, while the gentlemen are at another one."

"Oh, I am certain Lord Ashmore would not mind," Lady Ada said quickly.

"Perhaps you could invite him to your brother's townhouse and the three of you could travel in the ducal carriage together," Georgie suggested.

Lady Ada's cheeks pinkened. "That is exactly what I will do, Lady Edgethorne. Thank you for the suggestion."

The men returned, bearing plates of cake and cups of punch. Effie heard Lady Ada ask Lord Ashmore to go on tomorrow's outing and saw the tips of his ears redden slightly.

She turned to the duke. "Lord Ashmore will be joining us tomorrow at Gunter's. My sister suggested, for ease, that the viscount travel in your carriage to Berkeley Square."

He looked from his sister to the viscount. "I see a little matchmaking occurred in my brief absence."

She smiled fondly at her friend, telling the duke, "Sometimes, a little matchmaking might be a good thing. It will give them a chance in the carriage to further know one another. In her chaperone's presence, of course. I hope Lord Ashmore is comfortable with you being present, so that he might open up more to Lady Ada."

"She told me he was intimidated meeting me, simply because I was a duke."

"Most of the time, others are intimidated by a man bearing such a lofty title, Your Grace."

"I have not mixed enough in Polite Society to be aware of that. I only attended one Season and a limited number of events, at that. This is the first time I am taking advantage of the full slate of affairs offered.

For Ada's sake."

"And to find a bride of your own," Effie reminded him.

"Yes, that is true."

She knew it to be so, but suddenly, the idea of helping this man find his duchess did not sit well with her. She needed to shrug off such odd feelings if she and her family were to help him find a woman appropriate for the rank of duchess. One who would understand his past and support him. Effie saw Waterbury had the potential to be a leading member of the *ton* for decades to come, and he would need for his duchess to possess an equal amount of confidence and leadership. It was too bad Georgie was already so happily wed to August because her sister was the exact type of woman the duke needed to find.

Effie decided she must start paying better attention to the eligible ladies of the Season. Waterbury seemed to respect her opinion, which flattered her. If she could advise him on selecting the right bride, he could make a successful marriage.

Again, it disturbed her that the thought of him wedding bothered her. She warned herself of growing too close to him. He was slowly becoming a friend, just as Lady Ada was. She could not think of him in any other manner and promised herself to keep the duke at a distance.

After tomorrow's ride in Rotten Row.

She would appear churlish if she canceled the outing after having just agreed to it, and he did appear anxious to ride. Yes, riding would do the both of them good.

Then she would have a talk with him and make certain she pointed him in the right direction so that he might find his duchess.

Because Effie knew of all the women in London, she was the last person who should take on that role.

CHAPTER SEVENTEEN

MALCOLM AWOKE, FEELING refreshed and invigorated. Everything in his life seemed to be falling into place.

Though the Season was still at the beginning, he already believed his little sister had found the man she would call husband one day in the near future. That had been his biggest concern coming to town this spring, especially after the conversation he'd had with Ada and how she'd expressed such a strong desire to escape from Mama's grasp. Naturally, he would watch the progression of the relationship between Lord Ashmore and his sister, but Malcolm fully believed the day would come when the viscount would ask to speak with him and make his full intention known. He had a proper sense regarding others and believed Lord Ashmore would treat Ada well. Still, he wanted to learn more about the viscount and would spend some time alone with the man at White's. That would be the easiest place to get Ashmore to open up without being constantly interrupted by others.

As for friendship, Malcolm could not believe how the men who had married into the Strong family and the Duke of Seaton himself had rallied to his cause yesterday. They had been supportive and friendly, and when he had arrived home from the musicale last night, the promised guide awaited him. He chuckled to himself, thinking of Lord Carroll and Viscount Blankenship laboring over the pages. Though he wasn't one to listen to gossip, he knew enough from his brief foray in

Polite Society previously to know of their reputations. They had been two of the biggest rakehells in London. To see how these men had been tamed by two Strong women—and how they even bragged about that taming—let him know good things could occur in a marriage.

Especially to a Strong woman.

That led Malcolm to the last item which had brought happiness to him. God only knew how it had eluded him up until now. He had never thought it would take another person to make him feel complete, but that is what Lady Effie was doing. He had feared he was so cold and distant, unfeeling like his father, that he might make the same mistakes in his second marriage that he had in his first. Yet being around Lady Effie and her affectionate, rambunctious family let him know there was another way of life. One which allowed him to celebrate himself—and her.

She was going to take some convincing, however. After all, this was the woman who had announced she was not looking for a husband and liked her life exactly the way it was. He would have to offer her more than marriage. He would need to offer her companionship. Passion.

Freedom . . .

As a duke, he held sway over other members of Polite Society, and if he wished Lady Effie Strong as his wife, he would have her. The *ton* might disapprove of the match because of her candor and unusual ways, but dukes had far greater leeway and were not judged as harshly as other titled peers.

He wanted Effie to see they were a perfect match. Or perhaps an imperfect one. He wished to teach her. Learn from her. Love her.

Malcolm consulted the guide written out by his new friends. At last night's affair, he had hit upon several of the points listed. He had kept his proximity to Lady Effie throughout the evening without forcing himself into her company. He had complimented her in a way he believed pleased her. They had had a very nice conversation, and he did not have to pretend to listen to her. He *wanted* to listen to her because he found her fascinating, unlike any woman he had ever encountered.

He had also asked to see her again, dangling the outing in Rotten Row before her. Malcolm had escorted Ada and her to Rotten Row twice before the Season began and had seen what an incredible horsewoman she was. He could imagine riding out from Waterside's stables with her, the day spent in the saddle as they toured their country estate and met with their tenants regarding their needs.

He believed they were becoming friends. The Duke of Seaton had mentioned that, forming a foundation of friendship and letting love grow from it. Already, Malcolm held strong feelings for Lady Effie. He would need to be patient and give her time to hopefully catch up to his own feelings. His gut told him Effie was not a woman to be rushed about anything, least of all love and marriage.

Consulting the list once again, he looked at the items he had yet to accomplish in this guide. It was much too soon to write to her of his feelings and saw it noted in the margin—by Lord Carroll—that the earl actually composed a bit of poetry every now and then and would be happy to assist Malcolm in writing a poem to Lady Effie. He would keep that in mind for later in the Season. It could help him stand out from her suitors, of which she had many, considering the number of flower arrangements he had spied in the Strong drawing room yesterday.

One guideline said he should surprise her with a gift. Something no one else might give her. That would take some thought. Another of these so-called rules required him to take her to a place that would astound her. Malcolm had no idea how he would accomplish something such as this. He could call upon her in Seaton's drawing room and see her at events held throughout the Season. He might ask her to go for a drive with him in Hyde Park during the fashionable hour.

Other than that, Polite Society ensured young ladies were protected from men, and he hadn't a clue how to get her alone, much less where he might take her if he did so. Again, that would call for thought on his part.

He rose and dressed without assistance from his valet, not bothering to shave. He would do so once he returned from his ride this morning, as well as bathe to wash the scent of horse from him. Leaving his rooms, he headed for the stables, and a groom saddled a horse for him. Malcolm rode it the few blocks to Seaton's townhouse, turning as Lady Effie had requested so he might meet her at the duke's mews behind the family's residence.

When he arrived, he spied her already atop her horse.

In a man's shirt and breeches.

He wondered if she appeared so to get a rise from him or if she were simply more comfortable riding in such an ensemble—and more comfortable with him seeing her dressed in this fashion. She had mentioned to him that she wore breeches when in the country, and he had let her remark slip past him, not giving it much consideration.

If this were a test, Malcolm intended to pass.

Trotting his horse to her, he pulled up beside her. "Good morning, Lady Effie. I hope you do not mind a bit of cool this early in the morning, but I think it a fine time for a ride."

She pursed her lips a moment in thought and then awarded him with one of her radiant smiles. Malcolm knew he had to be in love because that smile alone nearly brought him to his knees.

"I am ready if you are, Your Grace."

They trotted their horses from the yard, chatting briefly as they went about last night's musicale. She insisted the pianist had no more talent than her two older sisters who played so well, and she lamented on how she had not understood a word the opera singer sang.

"You are not one for languages, my lady?" he asked.

"Miss Feathers did teach me French, and I can speak it fairly well. I actually read it better, though, but operas always seem to be in Italian or German. Do you speak other languages, Your Grace?"

"I do not wish to boast, but I found languages came rather easily to me. I know French, Spanish, and Italian, and I also have passable understanding of German."

"Well, you said you were academically gifted. I suppose if you know all those languages, you must be quite intelligent. What of those Latin verbs you were conjugating last night?"

"I do read and write Latin and Greek," he admitted, having originally omitted those so she would not think him overly arrogant. "I simply enjoyed all academics. Have you ever been good at something, truly good? So much that it brings you joy? That is what school was like for me and the learning in the classes I attended. Of course, I also enjoyed sports a great deal."

"I am like that about riding," she told him. "I feel free in the saddle, especially when I gallop. The wind in my hair. Feeling one with my horse." She paused. "I miss Juno."

Confusion filled him. "Who is Juno?"

"She is my horse at Shadowcrest," she explained. "I have had her for seven years now, but I have never brought her to town. You know how limiting space is here. In fact, so many others rent horses to ride. I feel fortunate we have a few mounts here in town which are available to us."

Looking at his horse, she said, "That is a fine horse you are riding, Your Grace. What is his or her name?"

Malcolm shrugged. "I haven't the foggiest notion."

She frowned severely. "How can you not know the name of your horse? That's blasphemy! Why, this is Marigold," she said, indicating her own horse. "I never would have climbed atop her without learning that very thing."

"I, unlike you, have never made pets of my animals. A horse is to be ridden. A dog helps to hunt. A cat is a mouser in the barn. Animals all have roles to play."

"We are very different in that respect, Your Grace," Lady Effie said stiffly.

Wanting to win her favor, as well as change himself, he said, "Perhaps you could teach me a bit about animals. I have only thought of them in regard to the service which they provide to me, where you seem to have a relationship with them."

She seemed mollified and said, "You can start by learning the name of this horse. And you could be kinder to my Daffy when you call the next time."

"You seem to truly love that cat."

"You should have seen her, Your Grace. Daffy was so thin. You could count every rib on her. Her fur was matted and dull. One leg was broken. Her eyes were filled with such hopelessness when I found her. She looked at me as if to say, 'Go away. Leave me to die.' I could not do that. I took her in. Bathed her tenderly and worked the knots from her coat. Fed her with an eye dropper at first and then by hand. Slowly, she began to trust me. The bond we have formed is greater than any I have done with any other animal."

They had entered the park and were almost at Rotten Row.

"What kind of animals have you helped?" he asked her.

She began talking about owls with broken wings. Foxes. Geese. Goats. Horses.

"What is your favorite animal?"

A smiled played about her lips. Lips he longed to kiss the proper way. "Besides Daffy?" she asked, mischief in her eyes. "I would have to say horses. They are easy to build an affinity with, especially if you are there from their birth."

"You have seen a horse being born?" he exclaimed.

"I have helped birth numerous foals, Your Grace," she said matter-of-factly. "It is one of the many pleasures I have witnessed. Sometimes, I have had to step in to help the mare, especially if it is a breech birth."

The mention of the kind of birth which had killed Imogen and Eunice disconcerted him. He would not be asking Lady Effie for any details.

She looked up. "We are here. Fortunately, we have the place to ourselves. I thought we might, coming so early."

Knowing her as he did, Malcolm asked, "Would you care to race?"

Her eyes danced in delight. "I thought you might never ask."

Then with an imperceptible nudge of her thighs, Lady Effie and Marigold took off like the wind. Malcolm reacted quickly, though, encouraging his own mount. He almost caught up to her as they raced the entire length of Rotten Row, but she crossed the end two seconds before he did.

She slowed from a gallop to a canter and then a trot, and he followed suit until once more they walked their horses side-by-side.

"If I were not a gentleman, my lady, I would accuse you of cheating," he said, grinning at her.

"Oh?" she asked innocently.

"Give my horse a minute to recover, and I will challenge you again. This time, however, I will win," he boldly proclaimed.

"Just because you are a duke does not mean everything goes your way, Your Grace. I am afraid you will suffer a second defeat to me if you choose to race again."

Her confidence was playing into his next statement. "Shall we place a wager on the outcome?"

He already had in mind what he would ask for.

"If you win," he said, "I will have to buy you any book of your choosing."

Her eyes learned with interest. "*Any* book? Any book at all? Hmm." She grew contemplative. "I might like a new atlas from you. They are terribly expensive."

"They are," he agreed. "Why an atlas?"

"The one at Shadowcrest not only became worn and tattered—it is now gone. Pippa used it so much over the years. She was always interested in traveling far from England. That is why Seth is such a good match for her. As a former ship's captain, he had traveled the Seven Seas and was the perfect guide to take Pippa exploring. They spent their honeymoon sailing around the world, coming home with tales of far lands." She chuckled. "And Adam."

"He is a fine, sturdy boy," Malcolm remarked. "Their babe is a pretty one, resembling his mother quite a bit."

"Pippa took that beloved atlas with her to Hopewood when she and Seth settled there. It is the estate adjacent to Shadowcrest, so I see her often. Of all my sisters and cousins, I am closest to Pippa. We are what others refer to as tomboys. Pippa taught me to ride. To hunt and fish. To even swim."

"So, if you win our race, you wish for me to replace the atlas."

She eyed him. "There is no *if* to the win, Waterbury. I am confident of your downfall and my victory. Again."

"If you were a man, I would deem you arrogant, Lady Effie," he teased. "Don't you wish to hear what prize I will claim when *I* win?"

"You may name whatever you wish, but victory will not be yours. Besides, I am not like other girls. Or matrons. I do not have pin money. I never really ask James for anything. Mama is the one who engineered this entire wardrobe for my come-out Season." She indicated her outfit. "You are seeing me in what I am most comfortable wearing. I hope you had no objections to my wearing breeches this morning."

"Not one whit, my lady. I knew you wanted to enjoy your ride. If that meant wearing your usual attire when doing so, I am happy to see the smile this ride put on your face." He paused. "Since you have no funds to buy me a prize, I will have to ask for something which only you can provide to me."

She crinkled her nose. "What might that be?" Then she brightened. "Oh, I see. You would ask for a dance with me. That is easy enough for me to award to you. Not that I will need to do so."

His gaze pinned hers. "I would be happy to dance with you anytime, Lady Effie, but it is not a dance I seek." He paused. "It is a kiss."

She gasped. "A kiss? Why, we have already exchanged one of those, Your Grace," she said hastily. "I would think you would wish for something else other than a kiss."

He reached and took one of her hands, obviously surprising her by the look on her face.

"It is exactly what I want from you, Effie," he said huskily. "And not the kind of kiss we shared before. A different kind."

Her eyes were large. "Different?" she echoed.

"Yes. *Very* different. One I think you should experience. If you are going to contemplate wedding a man, kissing is an important part of marriage. I am certain your sisters have told you so."

She visibly swallowed. "Yes." The word came out a whisper.

"Then I will show you a proper kiss, Effie. That will be the prize I claim."

He released her hand, and she cleared her throat. "Then shall we line up again, Your Grace?" she asked confidently.

She had recovered quickly from having her confidence shaken. This was one magnificent woman.

And he would do whatever it took to claim her as his.

"Show me the starting point," he said, and she turned Marigold, trotting to a point and stopping.

"Here."

"What will be the signal to begin?" he asked as he brought his horse to stand beside hers.

"We look at one another. We count aloud to three and then take off."

"Fair enough," he said, gazing at her intently.

Together, they said in unison, "One, two, three!"

Then they both took off, and Malcolm urged his mount on, promising himself he would ask the name of this horse and all the others in his stables if he could only win this race.

They were neck and neck the entire length of Rotten Row until the final few seconds, when he pulled away slightly. He crossed the finish line first and kept riding, slowing his horse at increments.

Wheeling the horse so that he faced her, he rode back to her. She wore a dazed expression on her face, as if she could not believe she had actually lost to him.

Or had she?

Malcolm had to wonder if Effie had eased up slightly at the end.

Just so she could see what a true kiss was like.

CHAPTER EIGHTEEN

EFFIE COULD NOT believe she had thrown the contest. She hadn't meant to do so. She wanted to win. To show him she could. Yet some hidden part of her was tempted by what she would gain—if she lost to him. Her curiosity won out.

She decided to take the kiss.

At the last moment, she had slowed Marigold ever so slightly. Then she had thought better of it and tried to push the horse. But she had waited too late, and the duke had sailed across the finish line.

"A valiant effort, Lady Effie," he told her.

She noted he used her title with her given name again. Twice, he had not. Waterbury had called her Effie, her name sounding different coming from his lips than any other man's. Part of her fought the growing attraction she felt for him, while the other half was jubilant that she would be allowed to experience a kiss.

"Thank you, Your Grace." She cleared her throat, a habit she was not fond of but seemed to keep doing around him. "When would you like to claim your reward?"

Just saying those words to him caused her insides to flutter madly.

He grew thoughtful. "We will need time. And privacy."

"Time? It did not take ten seconds for you to kiss before," she pointed out.

His eyes darkened. "Ah, but that was one kind of kiss. This one is entirely different. It takes much longer than ten seconds."

"Longer?" she asked, doubt in her voice.

"I would say we need at least ten minutes."

"For a *kiss*? Surely, you jest, Waterbury."

But the intensity of his gaze told her he was perfectly serious.

"I know tonight's affair is another ball."

"We cannot kiss on the terrace for ten minutes, Your Grace," she huffed. "Why, a large crowd would gather to watch—and then we would be forced to wed."

"Would that be such a bad thing, Effie?"

Oh, dear. He was back to calling her Effie. That was not a good sign.

"It is Lady Effie," she said primly. "You seem to have forgotten that."

"After we have kissed the way I wish, we will be on more intimate terms. Perhaps Effie would be more appropriate."

"No," she said firmly. "I am sorry I lost the race to you. I will pay my debt, but then kissing between us will be over and done."

"If you say so," he said airily.

She wanted to slap the smug look from his handsome face. Wait. When had she begun to think of him as handsome? He was. There was no doubt about that. Yet she had not truly noticed the fine figure he cut. His midnight hair and green eyes were an interesting combination. His cheekbones were sharp. His lips sensual. She tried to imagine kissing this man for ten minutes. No, she would wind up giggling. That was probably best. He would break the contact between them and be a gentleman about it, assuring her she had paid her debt.

Or would he?"

"Why don't you offer to show me the gardens at Seaton's townhouse? Do you know anything about them? Or perhaps his conservatory. Does he have one here in town?"

"He does," she said hesitantly. "You wish to see it?"

He smiled, looking as sleek as a cat with those bold, green eyes. "If it offers us the privacy we require."

"Come to tea then tomorrow, Your Grace. Bring it up in the conversation and ask to see it. I will volunteer to show it to you."

His fingers captured her chin. Leaning over, he softly brushed a brief kiss against her lips before releasing her. Quickly, she glanced about them. No one in sight.

"I will be happy to come to tea, Effie," he said, his eyes laughing as she bristled at hearing her name again.

"You'd better hope I do not box your ears when we are alone, Waterbury," she warned.

"I would like to see you try," he said softly. Taking up his reins again, he said, "I should see you back to your brother's residence."

They returned to James' mews and Effie politely said, "Thank you for taking me riding this morning, Your Grace."

"Thank you for accompanying me, my lady. We will see you at Gunter's this afternoon."

He tipped his hat to her and rode away, leaving Effie in the dark as to his motives.

MALCOLM STOOD IN his drawing room, observing the gentlemen who had come to call upon Ada. She had danced every set at last night's ball and was growing in popularity. While she had promised him she would be open to getting to know other gentlemen, he knew Lord Ashmore was the one who held her heart.

He liked Ashmore, even more so after yesterday. The viscount had ridden with them to Gunter's and had been open and charming. Mama had chosen not to go, and Malcolm was glad of it. By the time they arrived at Gunter's, a lightness filled him. He would claim that kiss from Effie this afternoon. Hopefully, that would move their courtship along in the right direction.

They had been the only party in Gunter's, and Lord Hopewell had told him Seaton had rented out the entire place so that it would only be their large party present. They had started out in tables divided by male and female, but as the next few hours continued, there had been constant movement between tables and wonderful conversations to be had. He had sat with all of Effie's sisters and cousins at one point, liking them all immensely, as well as getting to know the men of the family better. Lord Edgethorne had asked Malcolm to accompany him to Gentleman Jack's, while Lord Bridgewater had offered to take him to Angelo's Fencing Academy.

It was as if his whole life he'd had a weight pressing upon him, so heavy he could not breathe. Now, being around Effie and her family, the weight had lifted. For the first time, Malcolm enjoyed the company of others and believed they felt the same way about him.

After they returned from Gunter's, he had asked Lord Ashmore to come to his study for a brandy and talk. The viscount had eagerly accepted his invitation, and the two men spoke about their country estates. Ashmore's was in Suffolk, near Ipswich. He had two younger brothers, both in university, while his mother had remained in the country this Season, preferring it to town. Ashmore had lost his father about eighteen months ago, and he shared with Malcolm that while his parents had an arranged marriage, they quickly grew to love one another. He doubted his mother would attend another Season again, for she had no plans to ever wed again. Lady Ashmore had encouraged her oldest son to do so, however, and the viscount shared how he wanted the kind of marriage his parents had had.

Left unsaid was that Lord Ashmore wished for his countess to be Ada.

Malcolm almost told the younger man to go ahead and offer for Ada, but he knew the viscount would do so in his own time.

For himself, Malcolm hoped after he and Effie kissed that she would realize they were meant to be together. It still amazed him how he already loved her and hoped her head would not be turned by another gentleman, for he could see himself with no one but her.

"She has drawn quite the number of suitors," Mama said, joining him. "Frankly, it surprises me. Ada was always such a quiet thing."

"That has been the benefit of her relationship with Lady Effie," he said. "It is obvious she has brought out the best in our Ada. All these gentlemen are seeing Ada at her best."

"I do not see Viscount Ashmore here today," Mama noted.

"That is because Ada has asked him to tea today. He will be among the last group who calls upon her and will simply stay once the others leave. As for myself, I am leaving now."

"Calls of your own to make?" she asked.

"Yes," he replied, not elaborating on his plans. "I will see you this evening."

Malcolm had asked that his carriage be readied instead of walking to the Seaton townhouse. He was hoping he might convince Effie to drive with him through Hyde Park. It wouldn't hurt for the two of them to be seen together and their names coupled by the gossips.

On the way, he thought about the guidelines drawn up for him. He had yet to think of an unusual gift to give her, but he already had the place he wished to take her. This morning, Malcolm had been among the men present when Tattersall's opened. During the Season, the establishment was opened on Mondays and Thursdays. He had sought out Mr. Tattersall himself, asking that he be allowed to return tomorrow morning to look at horses. Being a duke, his request was instantly granted, and he told the proprietor that he would also be bringing the Duke of Seaton's sister with him, explaining that Lady Effie was quite knowledgeable about horses and he valued her opinion in purchasing them. Tattersall's did not allow females, yet Malcolm knew an exception would be made simply because he held a ducal title—and he was right.

He thought Effie would enjoy going to the famed place, seeing its horseflesh, and experiencing something other women never had. Since she also knew so much about horses, he was happy to listen to her suggestions regarding those they saw.

His carriage pulled up at the Seaton residence, and he climbed from the vehicle, noting several other carriages parked along the square.

Powell admitted him and led Malcolm to the drawing room, where he counted half a dozen suitors present. Effie spied him and acknowledged him with a smile. He moved to where Mrs. Andrews sat with her husband, not seeing either the duke or duchess in the room.

Greeting the pair, Mrs. Andrews asked if he wished to sit with them, and he complied.

"Effie said you were coming to tea this afternoon, Your Grace," Mrs. Andrews said.

He noted how the couple sat closely together, their hands joined. At first, this kind of open affection had bothered him, having never seen it before, but now he realized how it was a natural extension of a couple's love. He only hoped that he and Effie might one day be as open as her mother and stepfather were.

"You are becoming quite a regular around here," the captain said.

"If Lady Effie did not want me here, I would not keeping turning up," he said. "I am interested in her. A great deal," he told the couple.

The captain nodded knowingly. "I thought so. "She likes you—or she would have chased you away by now. Effie is simply being kind to all these other fellows."

"When they are gone, I will always be the one who stays," he declared. "You know what is in my heart, Captain. I only hope I can convey that to your daughter."

They spoke for a few more minutes, and then the other gentlemen departed, leaving him as the only guest. By now, the duke and duchess had arrived, the duke holding a child in each arm.

"They wanted to see their grandparents," Seaton said, passing Ida to Mrs. Andrews and George to the captain.

Effie came to him, and Malcolm rose as she said, "It is good of you to join us for tea today, Your Grace."

"Thank you for your invitation, my lady," he responded. "Where is your aunt? We had a lively conversation at Gunter's yesterday. I was looking forward to seeing her again."

"Aunt Matty is with a friend today, waiting with her until her grandchild is born."

"Lady Mathilda is generous with her time," he said. "She was telling me about how much she travels now, going from household to household to see all her nieces and their babes."

"Aunt Matty never married. She has dedicated her life to the Strong family. Mama has said she could not have raised the six of us girls without Aunt Matty by her side."

After a few minutes, the nursery governess appeared and claimed the two Strong children. Malcolm noticed Effie's cat entered the room as the three left and began wandering about the drawing room.

"I must apologize for being so churlish in regard to your cat. I know she means a great deal to you."

"Thank you," she said, leaning down, her hand fisted.

The golden cat casually strolled over to her mistress and rubbed her face against Effie's fist several times, beginning to purr loudly. She stroked the cat the length of her body and then sat up.

Then, startling him, the cat leaped, landing in Malcolm's lap. He froze, not knowing what to do as the creature balanced on his legs.

"Oh, this is interesting," Effie said, amusement in her voice. "Daffy doesn't often take to a someone. She must be curious about you, Your Grace."

"What . . . do I do?"

"Scratch between her ears," she recommended, so he did so.

The cat's purr intensified and he kept scratching, noticing the contented look on the animal's face.

Chuckling, she said, "I think you have made a new friend, Your Grace. Whether you wanted to or not."

He stroked the cat, feeling her silky coat. After doing that several times, the cat curled up in his lap.

"My, Your Grace," the duchess exclaimed. "Daffy does not take to others outside our family." Her eyes sparkled. "She must see something in you that appeals to her."

"I have never owned a cat. Or any kind of pet," he said, caressing the sleek fur.

Mrs. Andrews laughed. "Effie has had nothing *but* pets at Shadowcrest. They have been her constant companions, and she has found homes for many of the strays and injured animals she has fostered. Shadowcrest is something of a menagerie."

"I have often said I prefer the company of animals to people," Effie told him. "They are open with their affection and do not judge. Animals are always excited to see you and never speak ill of you."

Two maids rolled in the teacart, and the duchess poured out for the group.

"Should I put Daffy back on the ground?" Malcolm asked Effie.

"She looks so comfortable where she is. I would not disturb her."

He spent the entire teatime holding his saucer in his hand instead of resting it upon his knee. Malcolm mentioned how he had learned more about Lord Ashmore and his estate, hoping to bring the conversation around to what he and Effie had previously arranged as their excuse to leave the others.

"Lord Ashmore spoke highly of his conservatory, saying it was one of his favorite places. While I have one at Waterside, it is a bit neglected. Might you have a conservatory at Shadowcrest—or even here, Your Grace?"

"Both places," the duke replied. "But I know nothing about it or what grows there."

"I could show you the conservatory here if you wish, Your Grace," Effie volunteered seamlessly. "You could see how it compares to yours and the one Lord Ashmore spoke of."

"Yes, I would like that. You must show it to me sometime."

"Why not now?" she asked breezily. "We could do so after tea if you are free to stay longer."

"I would be happy to do so, my lady," he replied, his heart racing, knowing he would soon be alone with her.

And kissing her.

Ten minutes later, he had set aside saucer and cat, and he and Effie were headed to the conservatory.

"You played that smoothly," he told her. "As an actress who knew her lines."

"I am not going to renege on my debt," she said. "I wish to see it paid in full and be done with it."

Malcolm stopped, taking her elbow and turning her so she faced him.

"I do not want you to think of this as some chore, Effie," he chided. "An obligation you need to get out of the way."

Those Strong eyes searched his own, as if she sought unspoken answers.

"I will not rush things," she said. "I will allow you to give me the kiss that you wish."

"Thank you," he said, releasing her arm, and they continued to their destination.

The conservatory was at the rear of the house, and the moment he opened its door for her, he could feel the warmth and humidity. They entered and he closed it. She led him deep into the room until they were surrounded by what seemed like an inside garden.

"I do not come here often," she told him. "It can be much too humid for me. Instead, I prefer strolling the gardens outside. "This was the only place I could think of where no servants were likely to be, though. Even the gardens outside have gardeners working in them at this time of day."

He gazed about and said, "Point out a few of the different blooms to me then. In case anyone thinks to ask of what I saw while we were here."

She did so, elaborating on three or four, and he memorized what she said. Malcolm did not think anyone would ask, especially because others knew of his great interest in her. He assumed that the men in the family, who loved their wives a great deal, had shared with them not only his interest in Effie but the guidelines he was trying to follow in order to win her over. He hoped he had their approval because he knew that would be important to Effie. He was astute enough to realize that if they did wed, he would not only be marrying her. He would be marrying the entire family, as well.

Effie finished speaking and licked her lips nervously, causing a frisson of desire to race through him. He planned to lick that full, bottom lip soon enough.

"I suppose we should get on with it now," she said, a bit breathlessly.

"Effie, this is not some unpleasant task which you are trying to rush through. A kiss is to be savored. Unhurried."

She fidgeted, wringing her hands. "Well, you did say it might take up to ten minutes. We should not be gone much longer than that. Go ahead then. Start."

Malcolm was going to take his time. He started by clasping her hands and bringing them to his lips, brushing a kiss upon her knuckles. She shivered, already pleasing him.

Releasing her hands, he framed her face, studying her a moment. Her pupils were large, her breathing already erratic.

"I will stop if you ask," he said softly. "I only hope you do not."

She gave him a quizzical look, and he leaned in, deciding to start by kissing the crease between her brows. He could tell the place he started surprised her.

Good.

He wanted to surprise her. Delight her. Make her want more.

Lifting his head, he smiled. "Shall we begin?"

Chapter Nineteen

Nerves rippled through Effie. She felt a mixture of curiosity and fear. Yes, she wanted to know more about kissing. No, she was not certain she wanted to be taught that lesson by Waterbury. The duke, who had been a figure on the sidelines for the first few weeks she had known Ada, now loomed large in her life. He had grown from a silent, older brother to a man she was incredibly interested in. She had thought him nice-looking until he had begun opening up to her. Now, she found him appealing. Vulnerable. Devastatingly handsome. And intriguing.

That combination frightened her.

She had entered this Season with the intention of experiencing some of the things her relatives had. Effie had hoped to make a few friends outside her family. Have some interesting discussions. But in no way had she supposed she would come to want a man. A deep yearning invaded her soul. She craved to know everything about this duke. Her thirst for knowledge had always been great, and both Mama and Miss Feathers had allowed her to pursue interests that appealed to her. She had held back this Season, not wanting to pine for anyone, let alone a duke.

Yet here she found herself, ready to engage in a kiss with one. Effie didn't want to want a duke. They were the pillars of Polite Society, a group of people she found ridiculous. All these odd customs of a girl making her come-out and the unnecessary waste of gowns to be worn once and never again made her head spin. She knew herself. What she wanted was to be back in the country, surrounded by its tranquility, tending to her animals and helping Caleb with the estate.

Since she was stuck in town for the next few months, she might as well make the most of it. Learn what a kiss involved with a devastatingly handsome man. Who cared if he was a duke? As long as he made the kiss pleasurable, it would be something new to learn about and would help her understand her family more since they all seemed to be mad for kissing.

Gazing up at Waterbury, pretending to have a confidence she suddenly found sorely lacking, Effie said, "I am ready if you are, Your Grace."

His thumbs caressed her cheeks, causing her pulse to quicken. His mesmerizing green eyes seemed to penetrate to her soul, as if he knew everything about her.

Slowly, he lowered his head, his lips meeting hers.

This time, the kiss felt different from the beginning. The previous time he kissed her, he had brushed his lips softly against hers. He began again the same way, but her heart seemed to pound so hard it might burst from her chest. Her breath quickened. Her hands gripped his shoulders so she might steady herself. She felt his smile against her mouth.

Then he was kissing her. Short, hard kisses that drew her in. The fluttering in her belly increased, and Effie's grip tightened on his shoulders. She refused to grow weak-kneed and be the kind of lady who fainted. She was here to learn, not swoon.

His hands, large and a bit rough, slid to her neck, holding it a moment, his thumbs now stroking her. He softened the kisses, brushing his firm lips against hers. Then the tip of his tongue touched her bottom lip, sweeping back and forth, startling her. She started to protest but decided it felt good. One of his hands moved to her nape, cradling it, while the other went to her back, stroking the length of it, up and down, hypnotizing her.

She moved closer to him instinctively, her breasts touching his chest, and the hand on her back stopped. His fingers splayed against it, and he held her in place, stepping even closer, her breasts crushed against him. They had come to life, the nipples sensitive, and they seemed heavy and full to her.

He used his tongue to outline the shape of her mouth, drawing shivers from her. Then he ran it along the seam of her mouth, teasing it open. His tongue suddenly touched hers, stroking it, causing chills to race through her. Effie heard a whimper—and realized it came from her.

She kept still, getting used to the new, delicious sensations pouring through her as his tongue continued to explore her mouth. She could taste the lemon from the teacake he had eaten and wondered if he experienced the same. Waterbury took his time, investigating her thoroughly.

He broke the kiss, but his lips continued to search, moving along her cheek to her ear. Suddenly, his teeth pulled on her lobe, sending a bolt of fire through her.

"Ah, you like that," he said, his voice low and rough, causing another chill to race along her spine.

He tugged on the lobe, teasing it, then his tongue outlined the shell of her ear. Effie had never given her ears a single thought. Until this moment. Who knew they could be so sensitive and bring such a depth of feeling?

His lips were on the move again, and she could not wait to see their next stop. It was her pulse point, and he nibbled at it, causing another whimper to escape. Then his tongue circled it, causing her breathing to go shallow. He nipped at it, then soothed the place with his tongue. Her hands moved to his nape, her fingers playing with his hair, tugging on it. He growled as Daffy might when the cat was on the prowl, and Effie almost laughed.

She had no time, though, because his mouth was on hers again, hard and demanding, his kisses almost punishing. This time when she granted him entrance, she was an active participant in the kiss, her tongue gliding along his, learning its texture and shape.

He broke the kiss, and she opened her eyes, seeing his green ones on fire, knowing that was desire.

"You learn quickly, Effie. I knew you would."

Before she could reply, he was kissing her again, demanding more of her. She wanted to give him everything he asked for. He began breaking the kiss and moving in again, on the hunt. She matched him, her fingers pushing into his hair, pulling him close, the feel of his body against hers causing her own to heat considerably. Her bones seemed to dissolve and she clung to him.

He seemed to understand her legs might give out, and he scooped her into his arms. Dazed, she looked up at him as he turned his head, moving through the conservatory, looking for something. She wanted to ask what, but speech seemed beyond her.

"Not a bloody chair in sight," he said, his frustration obvious. "The floor will have to do."

Confused, she watched as he headed to a wall, placing his back against it and sliding to the ground, with her still in his arms. Now, she was seated in his lap, and Effie looped her arms about his neck, pulling him to her, greedy for more kisses.

They kissed a long time, one kiss melting into another, his arms holding her steady. In them, she felt safer than she ever had. The world ceased to exist. It was only the two of them, in this moment, and she would happily stay here forever.

As he kissed her, his hand moved to her breast, and he began kneading it. She had not known she required his touch there, but the moment his hand touched her, she knew she could not live without it. He continued kissing her, caressing her breast, the heat now pouring through her. Her core began throbbing almost painfully, and a wicked thought occurred to her.

She wanted his hand there. Touching her where no one else had.

Breaking the kiss, her gaze met his. Effie hiked up her skirts and then took his hand, bringing it under them. Wordlessly, she told him what she needed.

And he understood.

His hand ran up her thigh and back down again several times, moving to the inside of her thigh, higher and higher, until he reached where she needed him to be. All the while, they merely gazed at one another.

"May I touch you here?" he asked roughly.

"Please," she said breathlessly.

Effie thought he might kiss her again, but he refrained from doing so. Their gazes locked on one another as his fingers stroked the seam of her sex. She whimpered but held his gaze.

"You will like this," he said, his voice low and tender.

"I know," she replied, somehow knowing she would like anything he did to her.

Waterbury's fingers danced back and forth, toying with her, her core continuing to pound violently. Then he pushed a finger inside her. Her eyes grew large and her lips parted, but she kept silent.

Then the magic began. His finger pushed deeper, caressing her intimately. She mewled softly, wriggling her bottom against him, her fingers digging into his shoulders.

"You are wet for me," he told her. "It means you want me."

She bit her lip and saw his eyes darken. Suddenly, Effie sensed a power within her, a feminine power that told her how much he did want her. How he controlled himself because he was a gentleman. It made her want to tease him.

And make him want her even more.

A second finger entered her, and she arched her back, something starting to build inside her. Still, their gazes were focused upon one another.

"I want to see you come. Hear you cry my name."

She frowned, not quite understanding what he said, but putting her trust in him.

"Show me what to do."

He smiled, a smile that drew her in. "Your body will know what to do. It will show you the way. With my help."

"I feel something inside," she said. "I cannot explain it. It feels like something is going to happen."

"You will know when it does. I promise you that."

He kissed her once, swiftly, and then broke the kiss again. "I want to see your face when it happens."

His fingers continued to caress her, and her body was on edge. It tingled. It anticipated something. She was on a precipice—and she now needed to take a leap of faith.

He pushed her to the edge.

And then over it.

Suddenly, the intense pressure exploded within her. It was like warm sunshine radiating through her, with wave after wave of the purest joy she had ever felt. It came, again and again, and crested, causing her heart to beat so fast, she thought she might die. She babbled nonsense, not understanding what happened to her. And not wanting it to ever end.

When it subsided, she felt utterly spent. His hand had stilled, but his fingers remained in her. She blinked several times, her entire body limp.

"I thought I might die," she told him, her arms so heavy they fell from his neck.

"The call it *la petite mort*. The little death."

"What I felt?" she asked curiously. "It has a name?"

He chuckled, stroking her cheek. "It is called orgasm. It is when you hit your peak of arousal. Personally, I think the French words encompass it better."

"*La petite mort*," she echoed. Grinning, she added, "That was not something Miss Feathers taught me about."

His hands framed her face. "No. I am the one to have done so," he said possessively, kissing her long and hard.

Effie felt different. Reborn.

All because of this man.

Did she love him?

She couldn't say. She was starting to like him. She certainly liked his kiss. How did a person know if they were in love?

It wasn't as if she could ask her mother about it. And if she talked to any of her sisters or cousins, they would assume she did love Waterbury.

Did she? Could she? How could she remain Effie—and yet belong to someone else totally?

She would have to figure it out on her own.

"We should leave the conservatory," he said.

Scrambling off him, she sprang to her feet. He did the same. Then he pulled her to him for a last, searing kiss.

"No one will be in the drawing room by now," he said. "Walk me to the front door."

He took her hand and tucked it into the crook of his arm. They strolled leisurely to the foyer. Effie did not want to part from him and only reluctantly pulled her hand away.

"What event are you attending this evening?" he asked.

"A rout. I cannot recall the name of its hosts."

He frowned. "We are to go to a card party."

Disappointment filled her.

"I have somewhere to take you tomorrow morning," he said, surprising her.

"Where?" she asked.

"It is a place you will enjoy going. May I call for you at ten o'clock?"

"We cannot go alone," she pointed out. "Should I bring Mama? Or perhaps I—"

"Bring the captain," he told her. "Or your brother if he is available."

"You aren't going to tell me where we are going, are you?"

He smiled charmingly. "And ruin the surprise? No, my lady. You will see when we get there."

"Very well. Ten o'clock, Your Grace," Effie confirmed. "I hope you enjoy your card party this evening."

The duke held her gaze a long moment. "Until tomorrow, my lady."

He moved to the door, and the footman on duty saw him out. Effie went to her bedchamber to think. About their kisses. About the way he had touched her.

And suddenly, she knew.

She *did* love him.

Georgie and Lyric had both told her separately that they knew they were in love when they realized they wanted to spend all their time with August and Silas. Effie felt the same way now. The Duke of Waterbury intrigued her. He challenged her. He made her feel strong and confident and able to do anything. His kiss had awakened something within her, and she wanted to explore these sensual feelings. Being with him seemed the most natural thing in the world.

The problem was that Effie did not ever wish to become a duchess.

Chapter Twenty

Effie had chosen to wear a gown which the duke had not yet seen. It was a soft rose color and flattered her skin and hair, as well as bringing out her Strong eyes. She had asked the captain if he would serve as her chaperone for the planned outing with Waterbury, and he had graciously accepted, teasing her a bit since she could not tell him where they would be going. He did tell her that he would need to go into Neptune Shipping for a couple of hours this morning, but he would return by the time the duke arrived at the Seaton townhouse.

She went downstairs now, ten minutes early, and was surprised Waterbury was already waiting in the foyer. He stood with his hands behind his back, studying a portrait of her great-grandfather. She could not help but admire the figure he cut. The duke was long and lean and moved with a grace which exuded confidence. She imagined him being the first chosen in schoolboy games, everyone vying for him to compete on their team.

He must have sensed her presence, for he turned, his gaze meeting hers. Effie went warm all over under his scrutiny, recalling their time in the conservatory yesterday afternoon.

She did not want to encourage his attention, yet she craved it at the same time. Knowing he was looking for his duchess and that he had spent an inordinate amount of time with her, showing how much he was interested in her, Effie felt she must speak up and tell him she could not wed him in case he planned to offer for her.

It wasn't that she did not wish to marry him. She yearned to do so now, having admitted to herself the strong feelings she had for him. He was a duke, however, and the woman who became his duchess would always have the eyes of Polite Society trained upon her. The *ton* would find her an unacceptable wife for a duke. She was not remotely interested in the activities the *ton* deemed appropriate for women, in general, and a duchess, in particular.

If they could simply remain in the country year-round, Effie might consider marriage with him. He would need to always return to town each spring, however, whether it was to be an active participant in the House of Lords or simply to make his appearance at social events. She could recall her own father speaking about how important a duke's influence was in both politics and society and how he and Mama needed to attend as many social affairs as possible, as well as host them, during the Season.

Waterbury must wed a woman suitable to be his duchess, one who flourished in the womanly arts. Certainly not one who preferred wearing breeches to gowns and had more experience birthing foals than babes.

She would make all this clear to him today, discouraging him from further contact with her. Effie knew she should have spoken up after his kisses yesterday, not wanting to lead him on, but she had been dazed by what had taken place between them. Then he had dangled the surprise outing, something which intrigued her. She would go with him and the captain to whatever place he wished her to see, then it was imperative that she ended whatever attachment was forming between them.

Effie only hoped that it would not affect her friendship with Lady Ada, but if her new friend must cut ties with her, she would understand. Her own family loyalties were strong, and if she had to choose family over friends, she would do so every time.

The duke came toward her now, his smile letting her know how pleasing her appearance was to him.

"I was not certain how I should dress this morning since you have not revealed our destination."

He chuckled as he took her hand and kissed it, holding it a tad longer than he should have before releasing it.

"It is eating you up, not knowing where we are going, isn't it?" he asked, mischief gleaming in those green eyes of his.

"I must admit that I am rather curious."

"Will the captain be accompanying us, or is he busy at his shipping offices?"

"He agreed to go with us and should be here at any moment. You are early, you know."

The duke grinned shamelessly. "I do know. I was eager to see you again. I have to admit that our time in the conservatory had me a bit addled. I had even brought my carriage yesterday and was going to ask you to drive in Hyde Park with me."

Effie was glad he had not asked her to accompany him to the park. To do so—especially during the fashionable hour, when the park was littered with carriages—would have instantly coupled their names together, something she was trying to undo.

Or at she would try to do it sometime today.

"The park is too crowded for my taste," she told him. "It is not as if you can actually enjoy a drive there. Carriages clog all the pathways, and people are constantly stopping their vehicles to talk to others. It is one of many reasons why I prefer the country," she said, beginning to lay some of the groundwork for her argument, in case he did offer for her.

"I prefer driving a cart down a country lane and only seeing the occasional passerby," she continued. "Not inching up a few feet, surrounded by so many people that I cannot enjoy the peace and beauty of the day."

"I did not realize it was so crowded, else I would never have dreamed to ask you to accompany me. I had simply thought it might be a pleasant diversion after tea." He smiled. "Then again, we had diversion enough in seeing the conservatory yesterday."

Effie felt herself blushing to her roots, thankful the footman was so far away and not able to hear their conversation.

The door opened, and the captain entered. Relief spilled through her.

"I see you are already here, Waterbury. It is still five before the hour. I like promptness in a man," he said approvingly.

"Thank you for agreeing to accompany us today, Captain. I think you will enjoy our destination."

Her stepfather cocked a brow. "Is that so? Effie said that she had no idea where we might be going."

"I will tell you about our stop along the way. Come, my carriage is waiting for us."

They went outside, where the duke handed her up. His carriage was as luxurious as that of James. Effie realized in some ways she had been immune to Waterbury being a duke because she had lived with a duke her entire life. Though she'd had little contact with her father, she had enjoyed the benefits of the trappings of a ducal lifestyle, from their large townhouse and abundant staff to amenities such as the best carriages in town.

The captain climbed into the vehicle and sat opposite her, which meant Waterbury would seat himself next to her. Effie's heart sped up considerably when he did so. Even though the seat had plenty of room, he sat close enough that their bodies touched. She glanced out the window, not wishing to see the captain's reaction to this. When she finally did turn, she noted a glint of amusement in his eyes.

Waterbury asked the captain about his duties at Neptune Shipping, and her stepfather elaborated on some of the projects he currently oversaw.

"It seems quite a lot for one man," the duke commented.

"Ah, but I have Her Grace to guide me. I will be honest, Your Grace. I had never been around women much, being at sea most of my life. Her Grace was the one who had actually promoted me to captain on one of her vessels." He paused, and Effie saw the smile tugging at the corners of his mouth.

"Then I met Effie's mother, and Cupid's arrow struck straight into my heart. I could not return to sea and leave such a lovely creature behind. Dinah held my heart and soul, and I refused to be parted from her. That's when Sophie offered me the chance to help lead Neptune Shipping. She still is active in all major decisions, but she knows because of my unique background, she can entrust me with the day-to-day running of the place. Thanks to the strategies employed by her and James, Neptune Shipping is no longer a direct competitor to Strong Shipping Lines. We have divided up the trade routes and bring different products home to be sold to the public. It has been extremely profitable to both companies."

The captain paused and then said, "The women in this family are unique, Your Grace. There isn't anything they cannot do."

Effie almost flinched hearing this. She did not need the captain singing her praises. She was trying to get rid of Waterbury, not latch on to him.

"I am beginning to learn that, Captain," the duke said. Then he cleared his throat. "I suppose it is time to let you know exactly where we are headed."

He turned to face her. "I know of your great love of animals, especially horses, so I thought it only right that you visit the most important horse dealer in London."

Her heart nearly burst from her chest. "Do you mean . . . Tattersall's?" she asked in wonder.

"I do, my lady. They are open on Mondays throughout the year and on Thursdays during the Season."

She frowned. "But today is Friday, Your Grace. And I know for a fact they do not allow women on their premises."

He smiled at her, that smile that would convince anyone to do anything. "I am a duke, Lady Effie. I spoke with Mr. Tattersall himself and explained that I needed a private tour of his facilities because I planned to buy several of his horses. Naturally, he granted my request. When I shared with him that my chief adviser regarding horseflesh was a lady—and that I wished for her to accompany me—he did not bat an eye. We are both expected."

Excitement filled her. "Oh, Your Grace, you do not know what this means to me. To visit the legendary Tattersall's. They have the best horses in all of town. Simply everyone purchases their horses from Tattersall's. And dogs, too," she added. "They breed hunting dogs, as well. You could not have given me a better present. The opportunity to see a place I have yearned to visit."

"I am happy you are so pleased, my lady."

She thought a moment. "Do you really need to purchase any horses?"

"That remains to be seen," he said. "Yes, I would like a new carriage team, but it would depend upon what they have available. And what my trusted adviser recommends. Or if you see a quality horse which you believe should not escape my notice, then I will purchase it, as well."

She had the feeling he did not need a new carriage team, but she would not call him out over this. She was getting to go where no female in town had ever been. Tattersall's reputation was sterling, and for her to be allowed to see its horses was nothing short of a miracle.

"Ah, I think we have arrived," the captain said.

Effie looked out her window and saw Tattersall's, knowing they were now at Hyde Park Corner.

Soon, they were out of the carriage and speaking with Mr. Tattersall himself. The owner of the establishment was very businesslike, and she understood while he dealt with the highest levels of English society, he would never be a part of it and had to show proper deference to his clients.

He tested her, though, and she would have less respect for him if he had not. They spoke of Waterbury's wish for new carriage horses and discussed the age and height range, type of body build, temperament, and color of the team.

Apparently, Effie passed Mr. Tattersall's test, and he said that he would allow his son to take them about, as he other business to attend to.

She liked the son very much. The younger Mr. Tattersall took them through various stables, noting the outstanding qualities of each horse. Upon her recommendation, after having led several horses from their stalls, she put together a team of blacks and asked that they be exchanged for the bays of the duke's current team of horses. She wanted to see how this group of horses performed together.

The two teams were changed out, and Waterbury asked if she would like to go along in the carriage to see how the ride went for a passenger.

"No, Your Grace. I want to sit next to your coachman," she declared. "I must see how the horses travel together with my own eyes and if they are suited to their role."

She heard the captain chuckling and saw Mr. Tattersall's eyes go wide.

"Then I will also sit atop so I might hear your comments," the duke proclaimed.

Effie was assisted up to the driving bench, and the coachman sat next to her, followed by the duke.

"Where to, my lady?" the driver asked her, and she instructed him where to go, giving him directions on which corners to turn as they went along, in order to allow the team the chance to make different turns, as well as try varying speeds.

After she had them return to Tattersall's, they were greeted by both Mr. Tattersalls, which did not surprise her.

As she was handed down, the older Mr. Tattersall asked, "What did you think, my lady? Usually, I sell teams that I have put together. Instead, you chose individual horses." He gave her a brusque nod, as if he bowed to her judgment. "It looks to me as if this is an excellent combination, however."

She went to the horses and stroked the neck of one. "I would switch this one to the left front," she told the men. "He is a natural leader and has good instincts for the road. It would be a shame to keep him back and not let him lead."

"You have a good eye, my lady," the younger Tattersall said. "I quite agree with you." Looking at Waterbury, he asked, "Will you be keeping the team you came with, Your Grace? If you choose to sell them to us, we are happy to take them off your hands."

"No, I plan to keep both teams," the duke replied. "We can leave my new horses in place, and you may return the other ones to my mews later today if it is convenient for you."

"It will be as you wish, Your Grace," the older Tattersall said. "Might we interest you in any other horses?"

Effie could appreciate the businessman wanting to sell even more horseflesh, but she spoke for the duke. "No, Mr. Tattersall. I believe this is all we found to our liking today. Thank you again for allowing me to come and advise His Grace on his purchases. I know you broke one of your longstanding rules to allow me on these grounds."

The old man shrugged nonchalantly. "It is a Friday, my lady. I see no other clients present who might spread gossip regarding your appearance. As for my staff? They will never divulge your visit here."

He took her hand and bowed to her. "I know it is thanks to you that I have sold this team to His Grace. You know your horseflesh, Lady Effie. You are welcome here anytime." He smiled. "That is, when we are closed to the public."

"I understand. Thank you, Mr. Tattersall."

They returned to the ducal carriage, Effie almost floating, so happy at having visited the renowned Tattersall's and having gained the respect of its owner.

In the carriage, the two men continued to discuss the new team of horses, leaving her to her own thoughts. She knew she could not continue to see Waterbury. It would not be fair to either of them. Already, she knew she loved him and could not imagine what it would be like to give him up. She would, though—after she did something that would allow her to always carry a piece of him with her.

Effie could not see herself wed to any man, even the handsome one now beside her. She was too free a spirit to tie herself to anyone. But what had taken place between them yesterday was, she suspected, only the tip of the iceberg. She wanted to know what coupling with a man was like. No, not any man. With Waterbury. It would satisfy her curiosity to do so.

And it would be the most incredible memory which she would take with her to her grave.

Somehow, she needed to ask him to make love with her and find a place to do so uninterrupted. She wanted to know all there was to know about him—and about physical love.

Only then would she reluctantly push him away so that he could find a woman worthy of him.

CHAPTER TWENTY-ONE

A PLOT BEGAN to form in Effie's head, the speed of the scheme so rapid that it almost frightened her. Her mother was unique in that she rotated when house servants were given time off. Effie counted upon the Dowager Duchess of Waterbury being more traditional in the schedule she followed regarding her staff.

They reached James' townhouse, and she said, "I am certain Mama would like to see you, Your Grace. Perhaps you might go and find her, Captain, and let her know we are home."

As they left the carriage, her stepfather said, "I will do that very thing, and then I plan to return to Neptune Shipping. Go to the drawing room, and I will have Dinah meet you there."

She began leading the duke up the stairs and as they turned at the first landing, Effie asked, "When are your household servants given time off?"

The question seemed to startle him, and she saw him thinking for a moment.

"Once a month, they receive the last Sunday afternoon of the month. And then every third Wednesday afternoon, as well. Why on earth do you wish to know that?"

"Because I am ready to explore more of what we did in the conservatory," she said boldly. "I want to know all of it. All of you."

The duke stopped on the stairs, looking thunderstruck. "Are you saying what I think you are saying, Effie?"

Her courage wavered, but she nodded with false confidence. "Yes. Mama has always rotated when our servants are given free time, and Sophie has kept to that routine. That means we would never have a chance to be alone here. I am asking if you would allow me to come to your townhouse instead to spend time alone with you."

Without waiting for his reply, she continued up the stairs and hurried to the drawing room. When they reached it, they went inside, Waterbury closing the door behind them, taking her hands in his.

"This is a big step, Effie. One which people make—"

"Do not speak of such things now, Your Grace," she begged. "I just want to enjoy being with you. Can you allow that?"

Hot desire flooded his eyes, and she knew he would not be able to turn down her request.

"Just because the servants will be gone, it does not mean Mama and Ada will be. They will be in the midst of morning calls, with suitors coming and going."

She smiled, having already looked at the schedule to see what she had to endure for the next week.

"Wednesday, a garden party is being held. Tell your mother a sudden business matter has arisen. One which you must tend to immediately. Your mother can take your sister to the garden party."

"And you?"

"It will be easy to convince James and Sophie to go into their respective offices. I can tell Mama I need a respite from the whirl of social activities. That will not surprise her. It will give her a chance to go and visit one of my sisters. The captain will either be with Mama or he, too, will go into the shipping offices."

"How are you to get to my townhouse?" he asked.

She thought a moment. "At the last minute, I can say that Lady Ada has begged me to go to this garden party with her. That she believes Lord Ashmore might offer for her at it, and she needs my support. Your carriage could call for me. Your mother's presence would be sufficient to protect my reputation. As it is, Mama might not even be home. You could come in and retrieve me as you have before, and our footman would assume the others are waiting in the carriage."

He leaned in and kissed her softly. "Who knew such a devious mind lurked behind such an angelic front? All right. I agree to this scheme of yours. But afterward, Effie, we must talk."

"Of course," she reassured him. She knew they would need to do so.

It simply wouldn't be the talk Waterbury expected.

THINGS HAD GONE better than Effie had hoped. James and Sophie seemed relieved when she spoke of not attending the garden party. Mama had said they could go to Pippa's instead. Several of her relatives were gathering at the Hopewell townhouse that afternoon.

That was what had hurt most this Season. Effie had been thrilled her entire family would be in town for the spring and summer, and she thought she would see them daily. Instead, her sisters and cousins only attended events sporadically. When they did, she did not get to talk hardly at all to them because she was too busy meeting others and spending her time with eligible bachelors. She had yet to sup with anyone in her family, while they continually dined with one another.

Instead of having to be home for morning calls, as she did to engage with her suitors, her family visited with one another each day. Shopping. Having tea. Holding dinner parties. She had not been excluded on purpose. They simply knew from their own experiences how busy she was and how little time she had to devote to family.

Effie agreed to go with Mama to Pippa's, and then that morning, she went and found her mother in her sitting room.

"I do not mean to interrupt your letter writing, Mama, but my plans have changed. You will need to go to Pippa's without me."

"What?" her mother asked. "Have you changed your mind about attending the garden party? If so, I am happy to accompany you to it."

"That is not necessary. You already have plans with Pippa. I simply received a note from Lady Ada a few minutes ago. She believes Lord Ashmore might offer for her this afternoon, and she would like my company. She already knew you and I was not attending the garden party this afternoon, but she said the dowager duchess is more than happy to chaperone me at the event."

She watched as her mother contemplated things, hoping Mama would not change her plans. As it was, it was already hurting her to lie to her mother, something she had never done before.

"I think it is important for you to go and support your friend, Effie. The dowager duchess is an appropriate chaperone for you. You do realize arriving at the event with her and His Grace might cause a bit of gossip, however."

She shrugged. "I know others are already linking our names together," she said neutrally.

"How do you feel about that? How do you feel about him?" Mama pressed.

"Can we speak of this later?" she pleaded. "I have some thinking I must do regarding His Grace."

"Of course," Mama said swiftly. "I do not wish for you to rush into anything."

Guilt flooded her. If only her mother knew what she was up to. Mama would be appalled at her licentious behavior. Excusing herself, she returned to her room.

At the appointment time she and Waterbury had agreed upon, Effie went downstairs and found him entering the house.

"Good afternoon, Your Grace," she said pleasantly.

"Good afternoon, Lady Effie. Thank you for agreeing to attend the garden party with my mother and sister."

For the sake of the footman standing nearby, she said, "I cannot wait to see Lady Ada's gown. She told me she is most pleased with it."

"She and Mama are waiting in the carriage for us." He offered his arm. "Shall we go?"

He escorted her to the carriage and handed her up.

Inside the vehicle, she said, "I noticed you had no footman with you. And it did not look to be your usual driver at the reins. In fact, this is not the coach you usually use."

"No, I left that driver and vehicle with Mama to use. This driver is the son of my usual coachman."

"You do not think he will say anything to his parents?"

"No. I told him that I wanted him to gain experience in driving and that he is free to take the carriage through the streets for an hour after he drops me at home."

Effie wondered if that was how long it might take. An hour for them to couple. Nerves flitted through her, and suddenly her wild hare of an idea did not seem appropriate at all. Still, they had both gone to great lengths to pull off this clandestine meeting. She would follow through, knowing she would hurt him when things ended this afternoon, but she told herself it would be for the best. Effie would make certain she broke all ties between them. The duke would be clear that he needed to find a more appropriate woman to become his duchess.

As for herself, it would hurt her to see him with others throughout the remainder of the Season. It was necessary, though, because she owed it to Mama to finish out her debut. Effie's heart told her she would never love anyone the way she did the man seated beside her. But as much as she did love him, she wanted what was best for him. It was not her.

It would never be her.

They reached his townhouse, and the carriage halted. The duke helped her down, and they entered through the front door, the coachman driving away. No one would see them. The pavement was deserted. His neighbors would all be at the garden party, the first of the Season.

Her heart beat faster and the blood rushed to her ears when they entered his ducal rooms. She began to tremble, the thought of what they were doing overwhelming her as he closed and locked the door behind them.

He turned to her, enveloping Effie in his arms. She inhaled the now-familiar spice of his cologne and gave herself over to the warmth she craved. She would miss this.

She would miss him.

Waterbury led her through the outer room and into his bedchamber, which was dominated by a large bed. The room was flooded with sunlight.

"Are you going to draw the curtains?" she asked.

He cupped her cheek, his thumb caressing it. "No, love. I want to see all of you."

Her gut twisted. She almost called the entire thing off. Then his mouth came down on hers, and she lost herself in his kiss. The kisses they exchanged were like fire. Burning her. Branding her as his.

He broke the kiss, saying, "I do not wish to rush our time together. Know that when I undress you in the future, I will take my time."

Her throat thickened with emotion. There would be no next time. No future for them. Effie blinked away the tears forming in her eyes, allowing him to quickly disrobe her. He placed each layer neatly over the back of a nearby chair.

When she stood before him, naked, she thought she might have been self-conscious, but the admiring look in his eyes once again allowed her to feel her feminine power.

"You are . . . breathtaking," he said hoarsely, kissing her again, and then moving away, quickly stripping off his own clothes until he, too, was bare.

Her eyes swept over his lean, but muscular body, so very different from hers. She reached out a hand and stroked his chest, seeing his eyes close, much as Daffy's did when Effie petted her cat. Waterbury would laugh if she compared him to Daffy, and so she kept quiet.

His arms went about her, and his hands began to roam her back, dropping to her bottom.

Squeezing it, he said, "You have the most deliciously rounded derriere, Effie Strong."

Trying to keep things light between them, she said pertly, "Why, thank you, Your Grace."

His gaze held hers. "Do not call me that again," he cautioned. "Within these walls, I am Malcolm."

She had not known his given name and thought it suited him.

"Malcolm," she echoed, liking how it sounded as she spoke it. Liking the feel of him against her. "Kiss me," she urged.

His kisses enthralled her. His touch bewitched her. All the while, his hands caressed her body lovingly. He guided her toward the bed and released her a moment, tossing back the bedclothes, and then easing her onto the mattress.

Malcolm proceeded to worship her body. He kissed every part of her. Effie never knew the inside of her elbow or the back of her knees could be so sensitive. He fondled her breasts, toying with her nipples. His tongue flicked back and forth against one nipple until it stood taut, aching. He licked and sucked her breasts until that same, wonderful feeling she had experienced in the conservatory engulfed her, shattering her.

He looked down upon her with such tenderness that her eyes misted with tears. She did not want to hurt him. She had been wrong to come here and steal such precious moments from him.

Before she could speak and bring things to a halt, he kissed her again. The magic of that kiss swept away her misgivings. His body now hovered over hers, and he broke the kiss.

"Thank you," he said softly. "For giving yourself to me."

Then he kissed her again, and she felt something hard pressing against her between her legs. He thrust into her deeply, and Effie gasped at how full she felt. How complete she was in this moment. Then he slowly withdrew and pushed into her again, the feeling wonderful.

He moved in and out of her, kissing her, caressing her breasts, stroking her hips, until she felt ready to ride the crest of the miraculous wave once again. She writhed beneath him, calling his name as he moved in and out of her, trying to commit these few moments to memory, knowing she would never experience them again with Malcolm. Or any other man.

Suddenly, he withdrew from her, turning away and reaching for a handkerchief on the bedside table. She heard him groan deeply and then understood he spilled his seed into the cloth and not her. Effie supposed she should be grateful no child had been created from this coupling, and yet she would have given anything to bear it. To have a piece of him always.

He turned toward her and kissed her again, almost reverently, and then said, "We must get you home."

Malcolm instructed her to stay where she was as he retrieved a basin and washcloth. He bathed her where they had joined together, the act tender and intimate, causing her throat to swell with unshed tears. Then he dried her and helped her rise from the bed, where he dressed her carefully.

"You might wish to secure a few of your pins," he advised, and she went to the mirror as he dressed.

Once her hair was in place, he laced his fingers through hers and led her downstairs.

"I have a gift for you," he said, taking her into his study, to his desk.

He released her hand and frowned, lifting papers and pushing them around. "It was here. I know it was." He paused. "Ada. I told her what I had gotten you. I forgot I took it to her in the drawing room. Give me a moment to retrieve it."

Malcolm strode from the study, and Effie looked about, seeing the room that he spent so much of his time in. Then she couldn't help herself. He had left a mess at his desk. Caleb had always taught her to keep a neat desk so that anything could be found easily. The least she could do would be to stack the papers he had combed through.

Coming around behind the desk, she began straightening them, placing them in neat stacks. Then the title of one page caught her eye.

The Duke's Guide to Winning a Lady's Hand.

Frowning, she lifted the page and began reading. Horror filled her.

It was as if Malcolm had followed everything written down with the time he spent with her. He had given her genuine compliments, unlike other gentlemen of the *ton*. He had kept close to her at events and asked to see her again. In their conversations, he had been an attentive listener, asking thoughtful questions and never interrupting her. He had touched her, small touches, which caused her to hunger for him. He had asked her thoughts about estate matters and told her he would follow her advice. He had even taken her to what the guide said must be somewhere creative. That had been the outing to Tattersall's yesterday.

One thing he had not checked off this list was to present an unusual gift. Even now, he was on his way to retrieve it for her. Hurt filled her, knowing he had not responded to her as himself but as these awful guidelines told him he must be. He had looked upon her as a project to complete, and she had thought all along he was so different from other gentlemen within the *ton*. Everything that had happened between them had been false. That is what hurt the most.

She came from behind the desk, the pages in hand, her anger building. Effie would confront him and be done with him.

He entered the room. "Here it is. An atlas. What I would have presented to you had you won our race in Hyde Park. Ada wished to see where Ipswich is. Ashmore's country estate is there." He paused, frowning. "Effie? What is wrong?"

"This," she said, raising the pages she had just skimmed. "Your... guide. I am surprised you did not check off each item from your bloody list as you accomplished them."

He had gone still. "Effie," he said, his voice low. "It is not what you think."

"Oh, it isn't?" she asked, her tone brittle. Glancing to the list, she began reading each item, seeing him wince as she did so.

"Stop," he begged. "They were only trying to help me. I told them what you meant to me, and I was afraid because you had said you did not wish to wed that I would never have a chance with you."

"Who is *they*?" she demanded.

He flushed. "No one."

"Tell me," she said, her voice low. "Tell me now. You owe me that much, Your Grace."

"Your brother and brothers-in-law," he said, his reluctance obvious. "They came up with suggestions and wrote them down for me to follow. But I was already doing much of what they recommended, Effie. Being with you, I—"

"My family. They are the ones who did this?" she asked, her voice rising with hysteria. Her thoughts swirled, thinking how her own family had betrayed her.

"They meant well. They want what is best for you."

"*I* decide what is best for me," she shouted at him, banging her fist against her chest. "*I* make my own choices."

Effie threw the pages at him, and they fluttered to the floor. A hurt deep inside filled her. Her own family had turned on her. Schemed to marry her off to a bloody duke.

"I never want to speak to you again," she said, meeting his gaze, seeing the hurt in his eyes.

She crossed the room and almost made it to the door. Then he grabbed her shoulders and spun her around.

"You don't mean it," he said, panic in his voice.

He tried to kiss her, but she turned her head.

"Release me, Waterbury. Now. I wish to leave."

His hands fell from her shoulders. The duke dropped to his knees and grabbed her hands, saying, "Forgive me."

"No," she said coldly. "You are like all the other men. I never wanted a Season. I only did so to please Mama and be able to come to town and see my sisters and cousins. This has been the worst time of my life. I will never come to town again."

Jerking her hands from his, she said, "Do not approach me or anyone in my family, Your Grace. I hope you can use your bloody rules to find some emptyheaded girl who will hang on your every word. Someone who longs to be a stupid duchess. It certainly is not what I want."

She hurried from the room. He caught up to her in the foyer, clasping her elbow. She shrugged him off.

"At least let me have my driver take you home, Effie."

She glared at him. "I want nothing more to do with you, Your Grace. I can walk a few blocks home by myself. The streets of Mayfair are safe. And if anyone happens to leave the garden party early and sees me out alone? I simply do not care. Polite Society can say whatever they wish about me. They can rot in hell, for all I care."

Effie opened the heavy front door and set out, wishing she wore her breeches and boots to make walking easier. She went a block and turned left. Glancing over her shoulder, she saw Malcolm following her at a distance. At least he was gentleman enough to see she arrived home safely.

When she reached James' townhouse, she went inside and told Powell she needed water heated for a bath. She wanted to wash every trace of the duke from her.

And purge him from her heart.

CHAPTER TWENTY-TWO

EFFIE SAT IN her bath, brooding. She had dismissed the maids who tried to stay and assist her. She needed to be alone.

How could her family have gone behind her back the way they had? Conspired with Waterbury? Hot tears fell down her cheeks, and she brushed them away, taking up her brush and scrubbing herself raw.

She did not know who to trust anymore. She certainly wasn't going to remain in town any longer, Season be damned.

Placing her forehead upon her knees, she wrapped her arms about her legs, struggling to make sense of everything. She had truly loved Malcolm. No, Waterbury. She must never think of him as Malcolm again. She had thought everything between them was so easy. Even though she knew she would be a spectacular failure if she attempted to be his duchess, Effie had enjoyed the time she had spent with him, so much that she had coupled with him. Relief poured through her now as she recalled him withdrawing from her so he might keep from emptying his seed into her. She would not want to have his child, especially one who looked like him and would remind her of him every day.

What of her family, though? Above everything, Effie had cherished her large, happy family. The thought of them talking about her behind her back, plotting to have the duke do and say the things that would make her fall in love with him, sickened her. She had no idea how deep the betrayal ran. He had mentioned James and her brothers-in-law. Had they told their wives? Were all her sisters and cousins also in on things?

And what of Mama and the captain?

She soaked in the tub until the water was ice-cold, her spirits lower than they ever had been. Finally, she rose and toweled off with a large bath sheet, dressing herself as best she could in one of her older gowns, one which she felt comfortable in. Effie determined never to go to another social event this Season or any beyond it. She would retreat to Shadowcrest and lick her wounds.

Since the garden party would last through teatime, she remained in her bedchamber, finally leaving it when she went downstairs for dinner at seven. She did not plan to eat.

Instead, she would confront the others.

Slipping into the dining room, she took her seat and waited until the first course was served.

Then Effie looked to Powell and said, "I need to speak to my family about an important matter. Would you please see the room cleared?"

The butler did not look to James, which she was grateful for. "Of course, my lady."

He glanced around the room, and the footmen waiting on them quickly left. Powell was the last to depart, nodding deferentially to her and closing the doors behind him.

"What is this, Effie?" Mama asked eagerly. "Did Lord Ashmore offer for Lady Ada?"

"Effie would not have the room cleared for that, my love," the captain said, his gaze meeting hers. "Did His Grace offer for you? Is that what you wish to share with us?"

"Were you a part of it?" she demanded, her gaze penetrating his. "The conspiracy?"

He did not bat an eye, nor did he flinch. "Yes," he admitted.

Bitter disappointment swept through her. "He said James knew. And the men I thought of as my brothers. But you? How could you, Captain?" Tears welled in her eyes.

"Because I could see he was in love with you," her stepfather said. "We all could. And he said you only looked upon him as you did the other men in our family. Like a brother." He paused. "Waterbury was desperate, Effie. You ignored him, thinking him merely the brother of your good friend. Meanwhile, he was trying his best to get you to notice him and think otherwise of him."

"So, you all wrote up this witty little guidebook, with rules he could follow to persuade me to accept him?"

"Actually, I think he would have done well on his own without it," James interjected. "Yes, some of our suggestions were ones I am certain he decided to follow, but the man plainly loves you, Effie. He just needed a little help opening your eyes so that you could see him for who he truly is—a good man. One who would make for an excellent husband."

"What if I do not *want* a husband? she countered. "I have mentioned it upon several occasions now. You yourself, James, led me to believe that if I did not wed, I would still have a home at Shadowcrest."

Her brother nodded. "That will always be the case."

"But you all plotted to marry me off. To a duke, no less. The exact kind of man I would *not* wish to wed even if I *did* decide to marry."

Aunt Matty finally spoke up. "What does his title have to do with any of this, Effie? It is not as if you are impressed by one."

"I am not a person who has the qualities a duchess requires," she said stubbornly.

"That is not true, Effie," Mama said swiftly. "As a former duchess myself, I believe you would easily slip into the role."

Her eyes narrowed. "It is not a role I ever wish to play, Mama," she said coldly. "Were you also in on the scheme?"

Her mother's mouth trembled. "I knew of it. Drake told me how all the men in the family had met with Waterbury. How much he wanted you as his wife. I did not push you toward him, however, Euphemia. The choice has always been yours."

Her eyes went to Sophie, knowing her sister-in-law's face would tell the truth. "I assume the rest of the family knows about this."

Sophie winced. "Yes, all the husbands told their wives, but I will echo what your mother said, Effie. No one has tried to influence your decision. No one has nudged you toward the duke. You seem to have willingly spent time with him, which means you must like him a great deal if you have done so. We all know your feelings regarding marriage and how particular you are. We would never use any kind of coercion to see you wed."

"Good," she said, rising and tossing her napkin into her chair. "Because I am not going to ever wed. I am not even going to finish out the Season. I am sorry, Mama, for the trouble you went to on my behalf. Please have Madame Dumas not make up any further gowns for me. I am going home. To Shadowcrest. I am tired of the emptiness, and I have been incredibly bored at all the events. I have only smiled and pretended to like going because I did not want to displease you."

"You will never displease me, Effie," Mama said softly. "And if you wish to go to Shadowcrest, we can leave in the morning."

"No," she said firmly, not ready to be in proximity with any of them, with nowhere to escape. It was taking everything she had to contain her fury. "I know you enjoy the Season, and the captain's work keeps him here much of the year. I can ride for several hours in a carriage by myself. I need no escort to Kent."

"I will go with you," Aunt Matty volunteered. "Most of my friends are dying off as it is. You know I am closest to Flora and Hugh, and they stayed home at Benbrook, as usual, instead of coming for the Season. I will go and see them sooner than I planned. In fact, you are welcome to accompany me if you would like to do so, Effie. I know how much they enjoyed your previous visit to Benbrook."

While the idea moderately appealed to her, Effie wanted nothing more than to sink her roots deeply into Shadowcrest.

"No, Aunt Matty. I want to be home, working with Caleb."

Her aunt nodded. "Then I will see you back to Shadowcrest and leave for Grasmere after you are settled in. I hope that is acceptable, James. We shall need your carriage tomorrow morning to do so."

"It is yours," he said, looking beseechingly at Effie. "Are you certain this is what you want? Have you spoken of this to Waterbury?"

"I have made it clear to him that I want nothing more to do with him," she said. "I long for the peace and solitude of Shadowcrest, James. I have much to think about, including how loyal I have been to this family and how hurt and disappointed I am in the way others have treated me."

Effie paused. "If you will excuse me. I will see to packing now."

"Effie, at least stay and eat," Mama begged.

"No, Mama. I have no appetite."

She left the dining room, seeing Powell and the group of footmen hovering in the corridor.

"You may go inside now," she said. "The soup course has gone cold and should be removed."

"Yes, my lady," Powell said, flicking a finger. Immediately, the footmen poured back into the dining room. The butler lingered, though. "Are you all right, my lady?"

"Not really, Powell," she admitted, glad to see someone was concerned about her. "But I will be. When I get back to Shadowcrest."

⊱⋆⊰

MALCOLM ROSE FROM his bed simply because it was expected of him. He had escorted Mama and Ada to last night's ball. Effie had not made an appearance. In fact, none of the Strongs and their spouses had been present at the event. His sister had remarked how strange it was that her friend had missed the garden party and a ball.

He didn't have the heart to tell Ada that her friendship with Effie most likely was a casualty of the mess he had created. She would learn soon enough.

His valet shaved and dressed Malcolm, and he went down to breakfast, finding only his mother present.

Taking his seat, he nodded at her and sipped the tea a footman poured for him. Another placed a plate before him. He merely looked at it and shook his head.

"Take it away," he instructed.

He opened the newspaper because he had nothing to say. His eyes skimmed over the content, not reading it, only pretending to.

"Leave!" Mama said sharply, startling him and the servants in the dining room. "Calley, have breakfast taken up to my daughter's room. She is not to enter."

"Understood, Your Grace," the butler said, ushering the footmen from the room and closing the door.

Frowning, he asked, "What is that about?"

"Why are you so glum?" she demanded.

"It doesn't matter," he said toneless, wanting to escape her scrutiny.

"It is Lady Euphemia who is causing this melancholy, isn't it?"

Anger simmered through him. "And what if it is?"

"Careful, Waterbury," she warned. "You may be a duke—but I am still your mother."

"She has rejected me," he said flatly, staring at his teacup. "You should be pleased about that. You have never liked her or her family."

He kept himself from darting from the room like an immature schoolboy.

"And you accepted being spurned?" Mama sniffed. "I would have thought a man in love would not accept no for an answer."

His gaze flew to hers. "What did you say?"

She shrugged. "You heard me. I suppose you do not love her as much as I thought you did."

"You *knew* I loved her? How? When?"

"We may not be close, Waterbury, but I did give birth to you. I have always been able to read your moods. You cared for the girl very early on."

"Then if you knew I did, why did you constantly criticize her and her family?"

"To see if you would defend her." She paused. "And you did. Whatever tiff has occurred between you, it is up to you to remedy it."

He laughed harshly. "It is no petty quarrel, Mama. She ended all contact between us. In fact, it would not surprise me if she is done with the Season. In all likelihood, Lady Euphemia has gone back to Shadowcrest."

Mama's brows knit together. "Without saying goodbye to Ada? That is cruel."

"What I did to her was unkind. She will not forgive me. Ever."

"The girl has backbone. Standing up to a duke is no easy task." Mama gazed at him intently. "I think you should go after her."

His jaw dropped. "Go . . . after her? Mama, she never wants to see me again."

"Do you love her? Does she love you?"

"I love her with all my heart. I had yet to tell her so," he said, despondency blanketing him. "And I have no idea what her feelings are toward me. I thought she loved me. For me. Not because I am a duke. In fact, she was not impressed in the least with my title or status or wealth."

"All the more reason you should find her—and tell her you love her. That girl will make for an exceptional duchess. Just as her mother and sister-in-law."

Malcolm could not believe what he was hearing. Mama had belittled the Strong women, criticizing them for every little thing.

But she was right. Effie would make for an extraordinary duchess.

His duchess . . .

He pushed to his feet. "You are right. Things ended on a poor note between us. I need to find Effie and tell her I love her. It might not make a difference to her, but at least I will have given it my best effort."

"Go to Seaton's first," his mother suggested. "She might still be there. If not, take the carriage to Kent. Convince her, Malcolm. She is a woman worthy of you. And you are worthy of your title."

Going to her, he kissed her cheek. "Thank you, Mama."

"I wish you success in your endeavors. I will say nothing to your sister until this matter is resolved, one way or the other. Ada will be told that you have been called away on business."

Malcolm rushed from the breakfast room and out the front door, not wanting to wait the time it would take to ready his carriage. He strode down the pavement, thinking on what his mother had said. She was right. Effie was the one for him. He had loved her from the start, not knowing he had because love was something foreign to him. The feeling had overcome him—eventually overwhelmed him—until his heart told him she was as essential to him as the air he breathed.

He arrived at the Duke of Seaton's townhouse seven minutes later, fear gnawing in his belly. She might have told the staff not to receive him. She might already be gone. Whatever the case, Malcolm would deal with it. Make a plan. He *would* see her. Too much had been left unresolved between them.

And he had yet to tell her he loved her.

Rapping sharply on the door, it was answered by a footman he recognized. His astonishment was obvious.

"Is Lady Euphemia home?" he asked.

The footman started to speak and then merely shrugged, looking at Malcolm helplessly.

"Did she ban me from the house?" he demanded. "I am not angry with you. Or her," he said, tempering his tone. "I simply must see her as soon as possible. It is most urgent."

"Your Grace," he heard, glancing over the footman's shoulder and spying Powell approaching.

The butler dismissed the footman with a subtle nod, stepping aside so Malcolm could enter the foyer. Surely, that was a good sign.

At least he tried to convince himself it was.

"Lady Euphemia is not here, Your Grace." The butler hesitated a moment and then continued. "She is returning to Shadowcrest this morning. She left a little more than an hour ago with Lady Mathilda."

"You did not have to share this with me, Powell, but I thank you all the same," he said earnestly. "Might I speak with Mrs. Andrews or the captain if they are here?"

"Mrs. Andrews is . . . indisposed," Powell told him. "Mr. Andrews has gone into Neptune Shipping. You may find him there. As has Her Grace. His Grace is at Strong Shipping this morning."

"I see. Might you give me an idea where Shadowcrest is located?"

The butler said, "I would be happy to share that information with you, Your Grace."

Powell walked Malcolm through how to reach Crestview, the nearest village to the estate, and explained where to go beyond that.

Clear on the instructions, he said, "Then I will be on my way, Powell. Thank you again."

Malcolm turned to go when he heard his name called. Turning, he saw Effie's mother coming down the stairs. It was obvious she had been crying, her eyes swollen and her face mottled red.

"Mrs. Andrews. It is lovely to see you."

"Did you come for her? My Effie?"

Determination filled him. "I most certainly did. I have discovered she is not here, so I must go to her and speak with her in person." He paused and spoke from his heart. "I love her. I want to marry her."

She shook her head sadly. "You have cut her to the quick, Your Grace. We all did. What we thought was merely assisting you, Effie viewed quite differently. I doubt she will see you, even if you do go to Kent."

"I cannot live without her, Mrs. Andrews. I cannot be the man I am destined to be unless Effie is by my side. She has already rejected me once, but she will have to do so to my face again. I have a thick skull, and her first message did not penetrate it."

The older woman smiled through her tears. "Good for you, Waterbury. I hope that pleading your case to my daughter in person will make a difference. If Effie did not care for you so much, she would not have reacted the way she did. Convince her. I believe the two of you are meant to be together. So do the others in our family."

She leaned up on tiptoe and brushed a kiss upon his cheek. "Godspeed."

He took her hands in his and kissed them. "Thank you. For being so welcoming to me—and supporting me in this endeavor."

With that, Malcolm hurried back to his mews, having his new team of blacks readied in order to make the run to Shadowcrest.

CHAPTER TWENTY-THREE

Effie sat in the carriage, deliberately thinking only of Shadowcrest. Of getting out on the land. Riding Juno again. Wearing her breeches and being comfortable. Not having to smile at people she did not care to know and talk about inane things that meant nothing to her. She stroked Daffy, who sat sleeping in her lap. Oh, to be a cat and have no worries.

Her only regret was leaving town without saying goodbye to Lady Ada. The one thing Effie had wanted out of a Season was to make friends beyond her family, and Lady Ada had become a close one in a short amount of time. Unfortunately, there was no way for Effie to pursue her friendship with Lady Ada because of her brother.

She wondered if she should write to her friend and tell her anything about what had occurred between Effie and Waterbury. No, that would be unfair to Lady Ada. Effie would never want her friend to pick sides and choose her against her brother. Family was too important.

She would write to Lady Ada, though, and simply tell her the truth. At least, part of the truth. That she had missed Shadowcrest and the country terribly. That it was the reason she had left the Season behind so abruptly, in order to come home. Perhaps the two could continue their friendship through a correspondence. If Lady Ada wed Lord Ashmore, which Effie believed would be the outcome at the end of this Season, she might even receive an invitation to go and visit her friend in her new home. Effie would certainly do so.

As long as the Duke of Waterbury would not be a guest at the same time.

"A penny for your thoughts," Aunt Matty said, breaking the silence between them which had existed since they left London an hour earlier.

She had been grateful that her aunt had not tried to converse with her and draw things out of her which she didn't wish to talk about. Aunt Matty was good about that, always with a willing ear to listen to Effie's problems yet shrewd enough to know when talk was not wanted. Effie loved her aunt very much and reached for the older woman's hand, squeezing it.

"Actually, I was thinking of my friendship with Lady Ada and how that came to an abrupt end with my departure from town. I am hoping that we can continue it by corresponding with one another."

"Will you ever tell her the true reason you left town and the Season behind?"

"No. she loves her brother a great deal, just as I love James." She snorted. "Even if he tried to run my life, along with all my brothers-in-law."

Aunt Matty squeezed Effie's fingers gently. "Do not be too harsh in judging them, Effie. They all love you a great deal. I think they saw how much Waterbury cared for you, and that you also had an affection for him. They were merely trying to help nudge things along."

"They were trying to manage my life," she said, new waves of anger rolling within her. "If I wanted to wed the duke, I would have. Not that he had asked me. Nor had he even told me he loved me."

She grew quiet, wondering whether the hurt inside her would ever go away or if it would be her constant companion from now on.

"Do you have feelings for him?" Aunt Matty asked gently.

Tears formed in her eyes, and Effie nodded, not wishing to lie to her aunt. "I love him. At least, I think I do. Or did. I may have fallen in love with someone who does not even exist. A man who was following a set of rules which would make me find him appealing."

"What were some of these guidelines which your family suggested he follow?"

She thought a moment. "Things such as giving me compliments which were not meaningless. Talking with me about topics which I was interested in and truly listening to me without being distracted. Asking me my advice on issues. Taking me somewhere I wished to go that no one had ever offered to bring me. In general, simply being thoughtful and engaged and present in conversations with me."

"And was His Grace that way?" her aunt prodded.

"Yes, very much so. Only because he was told to do so."

Aunt Matty clucked her tongue. "If Waterbury were a shallow man, he could not have followed those guidelines for long. Perhaps for one conversation, but I know you spoke with him a good many times. A man cannot be false to himself—or others—for an extended amount of time, Effie. I think you were seeing the true duke. Or should I say the man behind the title?"

She reflected on how Waterbury had shared with her about his past and his family. How lonely he had been at school and how unhappy he was, despite excelling in academics and sports. She pictured him at tea with her family. How well he got along with everyone. How interested he seemed and how at ease he was.

As if he had found the family he had always yearned for.

Her throat tightened as a few tears escaped. Effie brushed them away.

"Perhaps the duke was that man, and these guidelines simply reminded him what was best about him," she admitted.

"Then if you think you made a hasty retreat to the country, it is not too late. We could always turn the carriage around."

More than anything, Effie longed to do that very thing, but it did not solve the dilemma that overshadowed everything else. Waterbury would always be a duke. Marrying him would turn her into a duchess. That was the last thing she wanted for herself.

"No, Aunt. I still wish to return home. I was bored silly by all the events I had to attend. I had thought I would be able to see my sisters and cousins, along with their families, but all I did was waste my time with shallow people. I missed Shadowcrest. I missed the country. Town life—and being a duchess—are not for me."

"Very well," Aunt Matty said. "This is your decision today. It might even be the same one tomorrow. One thing maturity brings to our lives, Effie, is that we understand compromise. How to be flexible. If you change your mind at any point, I can accompany you to town again so that you might finish out the Season. You may not wish to do that. You might instead make a fresh start next Season. Or the next. The important thing is the choice is—and always has been—yours."

"I have learned just how different my family is from others in Polite Society. I do realize I am unique in that I am being given the ability to choose my own future. Mama and the captain have never pressed me to wed, nor has James. He has assured me that Shadowcrest can be my home as long as I wish."

They rode the rest of the way in silence, reaching home in a little over two hours. Since her trip had been so sudden, no messenger had been deployed, so their arrival was a surprise. Both Mr. and Miss Forrester greeted them, and footmen carried up the single trunk she had brought with her. Effie had left most of her new gowns behind, not needing ball gowns in the country. She set Daffy on the ground, and the cat scrambled off, ready to explore and see if anything had changed since they had left Kent.

The first thing she did was to go to her bedchamber and change into a shirt and breeches, slipping into her sturdy boots, before making her way downstairs to Caleb's office. She stood at his open door, seeing her cousin deep in thought as he scribbled in a ledger. How she loved him and all that he had taught her about estate management. Perhaps one day, she might even become the steward at Crestridge, Mama's country place which had been awarded to her when she became a widow. It was only about ten miles from Shadowcrest, a small estate, one which Caleb also managed since it did not take much of his time. It would be a dream to take over Caleb's responsibilities at Crestridge, and she would still be able to visit Shadowcrest often. Once she settled in here at Shadowcrest, she might see if she could go and spend a week or so at Crestridge, learning as much as she could about it. The thought excited her.

And would keep her mind off Waterbury.

Caleb must have sensed her presence because he glanced up, his surprise evident.

"Effie!" he cried, coming to his feet and hurrying to embrace her. "I suppose you are done with the Season?"

"You do not know the half of it, Caleb. Most of it was pure torture. You meet dozens of people whom you have no interest in getting to know. You discuss things which have no value or importance and try to avoid listening to gossip about people you have never heard of."

He laughed. "It does sound awful."

"Not all of it was," she told him. "The dancing was fun. You know I have always enjoyed attending the assemblies in Crestview. And I did make a wonderful friend. Lady Ada Ware. She was a delight to be around. As for the others, I will not miss any of them. What I did miss was Shadowcrest. And working with you."

"I am always happy to have your assistance, Effie. It is good to have you home."

"Do you think I have what it takes? That I might be able to run an estate someday on my own? I do not mean one as large as Shadowcrest, but I was thinking about Mama's country property. That way, you would not have to divide your attention."

Her cousin beamed at her. "Effie, you could run England if you put your mind to it. I am not teasing you in the slightest when I say so. You are intelligent. Capable. Wise beyond your years. Nurturing. Any estate would be fortunate to have you helming it."

"Unfortunately, I doubt anyone outside our family would hire a woman to do so. For now, I will simply continue to shadow you, helping in any way I can, Caleb."

"What are your plans today?" he asked.

"I want to claim Juno and ride the estate. Riding in Rotten Row is a poor substitute for galloping across fields in the country. I need to get a feel again for the land. I will report to you tomorrow."

He pressed a kiss against her brow. "I am sorry the Season did not work out for you, Effie, but I am glad you have returned home."

She made her way to the stables, asking for Juno to be saddled for her. Effie allowed the groom to toss her into the saddle, feeling like her old self in her breeches, riding astride. She giggled, wondering what the members of the *ton* would say about her if they saw her now. The gossips would have a field day.

Trotting from the yard, she was soon galloping across a meadow. Though her heart was still heavy when thinking about the duke, Effie knew the power of Shadowcrest would heal her emotional wounds.

Eventually.

***

MALCOLM ARRIVED AT Shadowcrest, thinking it a most impressive estate. He knocked at the door and was greeted by an older servant.

"I am His Grace, the Duke of Waterbury," he announced. "I have come from London to see Lady Effie. Is it possible for my team to be watered and fed?"

"I am Forrester, Your Grace. Have your driver go 'round to the stables, and your horses will be cared for. Tell him to report to the kitchens, and Cook will see he is fed."

"Thank you, Forrester," he said, going to his coachman and giving him instructions.

Then Malcolm returned to the waiting butler, who ushered him into the house, saying, "Lady Effie is out on the estate, Your Grace. You are welcome to wait in the drawing room, but it may be a while. Lady Mathilda is in residence. I can let her know you are here."

He wanted to immediately ride out to search for Effie, but he didn't think it would hurt to visit with her aunt first. She might be able to give him insight into the situation and Effie's current mood.

"Yes, thank you, Forrester. I would like to speak with Lady Mathilda if she is available."

The butler escorted Malcolm to the drawing room, a large room which was tastefully furnished and yet had a feeling of home about it, much as Seaton's drawing room in town did. He wandered about it aimlessly.

Then he felt something brush against his leg and saw it was Effie's cat, Daffy.

Bending, he fisted his hand as he had seen her do, and the cat rubbed its cheek against his knuckles. Malcolm ran his fingers along the cat's back. Immediately, Daffy began to purr.

If it could only be so easy with Effie.

Five minutes later, Lady Mathilda entered. He went to her, taking her hand and kissing it.

"Thank you for agreeing to see me, my lady."

Her sparkling Strong eyes gleamed with a bit of mischief. "Thank you for coming after our Effie, Your Grace."

"Have I made a wasted trip? Or do you believe I have a chance with Effie?"

"She and I spoke on the way here. Effie was definitely upset about these silly rules the men in her family tried to get you to follow. I pointed out to her, however, that it had to be in your nature to behave as you did because no one could follow those rules if they were not true to his character. You would not have been that attentive to her if you were not interested in her. You would not have given her sincere, genuine compliments if you did not believe them."

Lady Mathilda shook her head. "She does have feelings for you, Waterbury. Deep ones. But what stands in the way even more than that ridiculous guidebook is the fact that you are a duke."

He frowned. "I cannot shed my title for her. It is a part of me."

"Effie does not feel worthy to be your duchess, Your Grace. That much I got out of her. She is a country girl, through and through, and does not favor the eyes of Polite Society upon her as she tries to be something she is not."

Surprise filled him, because Malcolm believed Effie had all the confidence in the world. "She might believe she is not capable of holding the title of duchess, but she could not be more wrong," he said earnestly.

"Then find her. Tell her what is in your heart. And let her know she is the only woman who *can* be your duchess. A Duchess of Waterbury who will shine brightly amongst those in the *ton*."

"Thank you, Aunt Matty," he said, calling her by the name all the Strongs did. "You have given me hope when before I had none. I intend to ride out and find her now. Wish me luck."

"You do not need me to do so, Your Grace." She smiled at him. "Men such as yourself? They make their own luck."

Malcolm went to the stables and spoke to the head groom, who agreed to loan him a mount. He made certain to ask the name of this horse, learning it was called Zeus and was the Duke of Seaton's personal horse.

"Do you know where Lady Effie rode to?" he asked hopefully.

Another groom spoke up. "I saddled Juno for her myself not five minutes ago, Your Grace." He pointed. "She went that way."

"Thank you. Thank you all."

With that, Malcolm urged Zeus on, riding out to find the woman he loved.

Chapter Twenty-Four

Effie rode, the wind in her face, feeling free from all the constraints of the past few weeks. No more perfect hair or elaborate gowns. No feigning interest in people she found to be ignorant and frivolous.

But no more Malcolm.

She slowed Juno, bringing her horse to a canter and then a trot. Finally, she began walking the horse, leaning down and stroking her neck.

"I missed you," she said softly, hearing Juno nicker. Then she said, "I miss him. Malcolm."

Juno came to a stop, and Effie slid from her back. She pressed her face into the mare's neck, wrapping her arms around the horse. Hot tears coursed down Effie's cheeks.

Had she made a mistake in quitting town so abruptly?

She might not have liked the superficiality of the Season—but she had liked him. Effie thought about what Aunt Matty had said. That Malcolm might have played the role outlined for him in the guidelines her well-meaning relatives had set forth for a short while, but he would have reverted to his true nature after a few times of them being together. What she had seen was a consistency with him. A constancy which told her she had observed his true character. He had not stuck to rules outside his realm. He had been himself with her.

He had been the man she had fallen in love with.

Still, Effie told herself things could never have worked out between them. She was not suited to be a duchess. While other girls making their come-outs yearned to wed a duke and live in wealth and comfort and hold a lofty title, that had never been her goal. She did not want the attention being a duchess brought. How would a marriage ever have worked between them if she had demanded to stay in the country each year, while he spent months in town at the Season? It wouldn't have. It was better that things had ended between them when they did. It would give him the opportunity to find a wife since so much of the Season still remained. In the meantime, she would be happy here at Shadowcrest.

Perhaps not happy. But content. She would be satisfied with her life here in Kent. More importantly, she still had precious memories of her time with Malcolm. She would never forget his kiss. His touch. His passion. His tenderness. Effie was fortunate to have experienced that with him, a magical joining. No one could ever take away those treasured memories.

She heard hoofbeats and turned to look over her shoulder, wondering if Caleb had decided to join her.

Instead, she caught sight of the Duke of Waterbury atop Zeus, riding hell-bent toward her. Her heart nearly exploded in her chest as she grew dizzy. Surely, she was simply conjuring his image because she longed to see him.

No, those hoofbeats were not of her creation. Neither was the look she saw on his face as he reached her, pulling up hard on the reins, leaping from the saddle, yanking her to him. Their mouths collided.

And it was like coming home.

They kissed, both desperate for the other, as if they had been wandering in the desert for weeks and had finally come across an oasis. They drank from one another, her body heating until she thought she might burst into flames.

Malcolm broke the kiss, his eyes searching her face. Though she wanted nothing more than to be with him, she must send him away. For both their sakes.

"I love you," he said, his breathing harsh. "I love you and did not tell you. I had to find you. Let you know."

He kissed her again, hard, demanding, and she sensed the emotions roiling inside him.

Breaking the kiss, she pushed against him, trying to free herself. His arms tightened about her, letting her know she wasn't going anywhere.

"I love you, Effie. I am sorry about those stupid rules. I was desperate for you to see me as a man. Not as Ada's brother. James called a family meeting, and the men in your family couldn't have been nicer to me. They could see how conflicted I was, not knowing what to do or how to win your love. The guidelines were merely meant to help me express myself to you. I actually found I did not need them."

Malcolm smoothed her hair. "What I found was that I could be myself with you. All my life, I got what I wanted. I was the best at everything. I took every prize in school. Won every athletic contest. But I shared with you how lonely I have always been. I never truly was myself. Until my time with you."

He looked at her, anguish in his eyes. "Say you love me, too, Effie. Say you will wed me and be my duchess."

A sick feeling washed over her. She refused to tell him she loved him. If she did, he would never let her go.

"I do not want to be your duchess, Malcolm," she said, using his given name to try and soften the blow. "I do not want to be anyone's duchess. I do not wish to belong to any man."

Hurt filled his face, but she saw determination in his eyes. She knew his argument would be strong. She would have to stay immune to it. And his kiss.

"You know, without realizing it, I modeled myself after my father.

He thought a duke above the masses, and he remained detached from everyone his entire life. You thought me cool, arrogant, and dispassionate. You were right. But I changed *because* of you, Effie. I am not the stiff-necked duke I was when I met you."

He took a deep breath. "You are everything I had missed out on in life. You have taught me to be my true self. I love you. I want the world to know that."

She looked at him, sadness permeating her soul. "Sometimes, love is not enough, Malcolm."

His grip tightened on her. "Do you love me? Answer the question, Effie. Quit avoiding it."

"Yes," she admitted. "But we are so different. I do not wish to be a part of the superficial world of the *ton*. You are a duke, a man who leads Polite Society. Your duchess should be by your side, also a leader." She swallowed. "I have no interest in that role."

The tenderness in his gaze almost undid her. "Can you not see that, as a duke, I can write my own rules? Polite Society forgives a duke anything. The same goes for his duchess. You will break the mold of what a duchess is, Effie. I will give you the stability you need, but I will also provide you the freedom to be you. To do as you choose. You and I will never be puppets on a string, dancing to the tune that the *ton* plays for us."

He smiled. "No. We will write our own story. Make our own rules. If you do not wish to ever attend the Season, then we will not go. I know you were bored. I also know you missed your family."

Tears misted her eyes. He did know her well.

"Just think of it this way. Next Season, you will have your husband. You will not need to meet people you have no interest in and dance with gentlemen who annoy or irritate you. No more morning calls, with endless suitors fawning over you, wasting your time. For you, the Season will be the celebration it is meant to be. You can visit with various family members each afternoon. Attend only the events you wish to. Sit with those whom you love at suppers."

She bit her lip. "You make it sound . . . possible."

He laughed, kissing her hard. "Of course, it is possible. We will be the Duke and Duchess of Waterbury. We will do as we please. We will show a kindness and civility to others which has not been practiced in Polite Society in decades. We will find others who are likeminded and become their friends. We will celebrate family."

Malcolm kissed her tenderly. "And hopefully, we will build a family of our own." He gazed at her intently. "Effie Strong, you are the woman I want by my side. Without you, I am nothing. With you, I am everything. Say you will be mine for always."

She believed in what he said. She believed in him.

Effie believed in them. Together.

Smiling, she said, "You are a most persuasive man, Your Grace."

Suddenly, he was swinging her through the air, holding her waist, spinning her about until they were both dizzy. When he stopped, she collapsed against him. His mouth sought hers, and they kissed and kissed and kissed.

She knew the picture he painted of their life together was not false. They would make their contribution to Polite Society in their own ways. They would lead by example. She would get to spend time with her sisters and cousins and their husbands and children.

And she would have children of her own, with this man, this wonderful, incredible duke.

Breaking the kiss, he asked, "How soon can we wed?"

"It takes three weeks for the banns to be read," she reminded him. "Unless you purchase a special license."

Malcolm kissed her over and over, murmuring between kisses that a special license was an incredible idea.

"I want to wed here at Shadowcrest," she told him, barely able to catch her breath. "We have a chapel on the estate. It is where all Strongs wed."

"We will need to summon all your family. Mama and Ada, too. Will they be willing to leave the Season?"

Effie laughed, feeling free and alive—and very much in love. "They will for my wedding." She framed his face in her hands. "You need to hear this from my lips because I have yet to say it. I love you, Malcolm. I will always love you."

His smile warmed her as if she sat by the fire on a cold winter's night. It filled her with warmth. Hope. And love.

"I plan to love you a very long time, Duchess," he said huskily, kissing her lightly. "Now, shall we go and share our good news with your aunt Matty?"

Effie beamed at her betrothed. "I will race you," she declared, breaking away from him and flinging herself into the saddle, Juno taking off like lightning.

"Cheater!" Malcolm called, though she soon heard hoofbeats behind her.

Her spirits soaring, love filling her heart, Effie knew life with Malcolm would never be boring.

>>><<<

A WEEK LATER, Effie stood in the bedchamber she had shared her entire life with Mirella. Of course, it had been hers alone ever since her sister had wed Byron.

She looked out at the room, seeing nothing but jabbering Strongs. Her three sisters and two cousins were present, along with Sophie, Aunt Matty, and Mama. They had all come to ready Effie for her wedding. Frankly, she did not care what she wore and knew Malcolm wouldn't, either, but her relatives all wanted her to look her best.

Everyone had come from town for today's ceremony, including the Dowager Duchess of Waterbury and Lady Ada. Those two were already at the Shadowcrest chapel, along with Lord Ashmore.

Malcolm had asked Effie if she minded the viscount coming to the ceremony, and she had eagerly agreed to invite him. She could imagine a betrothal announcement coming soon for Lord Ashmore and her friend.

Suddenly, Effie saw Mirella climb upon the bed and stand there. She signaled Pippa, who let out one of her earth-shattering whistles. The room came to a halt.

"Thank you," Mirella said, addressing the group. "It is time for us to all head toward the chapel and leave Effie in peace. Mama, you stay with Effie, while the rest of us go and join our husbands."

For the next few minutes, she was the center of attention, being kissed and embraced, until only Pippa remained to say her piece.

Her sister hugged Effie tightly. "Malcolm is a good man. He is the one meant for you. You will have a beautiful life together. Oh, I am so happy for you, Effie."

The sisters embraced again, and then Pippa vacated the room, leaving her with Mama.

Her mother took Effie's hands in hers and smiled gently. "My baby girl. Getting married." Mama's eyes misted with tears.

"We still have to marry off Caleb," she said, trying to keep the mood light.

"Yes, your cousin needs to find his own soulmate, just as you have done with Malcolm. I am so glad you reconsidered things, Effie. While I know you would have had a full life if you had chosen not to wed, your life will be richer for doing so, especially because you have made a love match."

"Thank you for being patient with me, Mama."

Her mother cradled Effie's cheek with her palm. "Of course, my darling girl. And you will know what it is like one day when you have children of your own. I see you, more than any of the others, being fiercely protective of those children."

"You were a shining example to me. I hope I can be half the mother you were to all of us."

Her mother dabbed her eyes with a handkerchief. "Well, I had help, you know. Aunt Matty was always there for me, to lend a helping hand, and you had excellent care in the nursery, all the way up to Miss Feathers."

Effie had wished Miss Feathers could be here on this special day, but she was far away in York with her two new charges. Hopefully, she would be able to one day introduce Malcolm to the woman who had helped broaden Effie's education, while becoming a trusted friend to her.

A light tap sounded at the door, and Mama said, "That will be Drake, coming to fetch us."

Mama opened the door, and Effie saw the captain standing there, beaming with pride.

He opened his arms. "Effie, my girl," and she moved to him, allowing him to envelope her. He held her close, kissing the top of her head.

"Shall we see to this business?" he asked.

"Oh, Drake, it is not business at all when it comes to marriages in this family. It is all about love," Mama protested.

"You do not have to remind me of that, sweetest Dinah. My love for you knows no bounds, and it grows stronger every day."

The captain offered one arm to her and the other to Mama, and they went to where the carriage waited for them in front of the house.

Effie was glad that Mama and the captain would have some time to themselves. After the wedding, James and Sophie said they would return to town and stay for a few more weeks to handle shipping business. Because of that, Sophie had insisted that the captain vacate the Neptune Shipping offices for a while and take his wife and Jamie to the country for a much-needed respite. They would remain at Crestridge until it was time for James and Sophie to return with George and Ida to Shadowcrest at the end of summer.

As for Georgie and August, they were heading to Dalmara, their property in Scotland. Since Pippa and Seth had never seen Dalmara, they were accompanying Georgie and August north, along with their children.

Byron and Mirella would leave Kent, taking Aunt Matty with them as they traveled to the Lake District to visit with Byron's Aunt Flora and Uncle Hugh, Aunt Matty's lifelong friends.

Only her cousins would be returning to town for another month or so. Neither Allegra nor Lyric had made a traditional come-out, instead making their debut into Polite Society with the house party Mama had held for them at Shadowcrest. Sterling and Silas were happy to accompany their wives and children to town again, but even that foursome would be leaving by the end of June for their own country estates.

The carriage ride to the Shadowcrest chapel only took a few minutes, and the captain handed down Mama and then Effie. Her mother went directly inside the chapel, while she and the captain lingered outside for a moment before she made her grand entrance as Georgie played her down the aisle.

"You made a wise choice, Effie," the captain said. "If I had to choose for you this Season, Malcolm would be the only man I would have even considered for you. He is a good man, Effie. And you make him a better one every day. Love each other well, and always talk. Share even the smallest of things with one another. Most people think it is those large moments in life you remember. I disagree. I believe it's the small moments between a couple which are the cherished times of your heart."

She threw her arms around him, kissing his cheek. "Thank you for being the father I never had. And thank you for being so good to Mama and Jamie and loving them both so well."

He wiped away a tear and cleared his throat. "Are you ready to begin the next chapter in your life?"

"I am, Captain," Effie said with conviction, and they stepped through the doors.

Georgie began playing as they moved down the aisle, Effie's gaze upon her groom. Malcolm looked so incredibly handsome. It was hard to believe he would be hers. She could not wait for the life they would share together.

The captain handed her off to her husband-to-be, and Malcolm linked their fingers. He gave her a smile and mouthed, "I love you. Now and always."

They turned their attention to the clergyman before them. Long after this day had passed, she would not remember the exact words spoken between them, but she would always remember their joined fingers and the love in her heart for Malcolm Ware. Her husband—and Duke of Waterbury.

She would also recall the kiss which started their life as man and wife and vowed to kiss this man and tell him each day just how much she loved him and their life together.

Epilogue

Waterside, Kent—Ten years later...

MALCOLM MADE HIS way to the steward's office, hustle and bustle around him as their servants prepared for the family to leave for their annual summer visit to Shadowcrest. Ever since a family house party had been held when Pippa and Seth returned from their honeymoon with little Adam, it had been a tradition for the Strongs and their spouses and children to gather at Shadowcrest at the end of each August and the beginning of September, lasting two weeks. As the children grew older and needed to leave to go away to school, the party had been moved back to the final two weeks in August.

This year, they would be celebrating the return of Pippa and Seth again, whose latest adventure had taken them on a cruise throughout the Mediterranean during the summer months. They were to stop at small seaport villages in France, Italy, Corsica, and finally Spain before returning to England.

As usual, Byron and Mirella would be returning from their time in the Lake District, while August and Georgie would be joining them from their summer pilgrimage to Dalmara. James and Sophie would abandon town for a while, as would Dinah and the captain. Even after all these years, Malcolm still referred to his father-in-law not as Mr. Andrews or Drake, but as the captain, as the entire family did. The captain had become a grandfather to their three children, ages nine, six, and two.

It would only be Allegra, Lyric, and their families who had spent the entire Season in town. While the rest of the family came annually for the start of the Season and stayed until the beginning of June or so, the twins enjoyed the social scene in London, and their husbands were happy to indulge their wives in these activities.

Malcolm reached the steward's office and entered without knocking, seeing his beautiful wife scribbling away. Effie had become Waterside's steward a year into their marriage and ran the estate seamlessly, with the help of Mr. Marcus, who assisted her throughout the year in managing the estate and took the reins during the Season and while the Strong house party was being held.

"Last minute instructions for Marcus?" he asked.

Effie finished writing and set down her pencil. Looking up, she gave him one of her radiant smiles, a smile that still stole his breath each time she bestowed it upon him.

Rising, she came toward him. "Is it already time to leave for Shadowcrest?"

He rested his hands on her waist, and her palms flattened against his chest.

"Yes. We should head out in a quarter-hour or so."

"Then I need to go and change," she said, starting to pull away.

Malcolm held fast to her. "Why change? Your family has seen you in breeches before."

Her hands slid up his chest, and her fingers linked behind his nape. "It is Effie, the steward, who wears breeches, Your Grace," she flirted. "The steward is going on holiday so that Effie, the duchess, can make her appearance."

She pulled him toward her, their bodies pressing against one another as she gave him a long, delicious kiss.

Breaking the kiss, he said, "I wish we had time for more, love, but if you are changing clothes, you better do so in a hurry."

"Are you certain you do not wish to help me change?" she asked, battling her lashes at him in exaggeration.

"You know what happens anytime I play lady's maid for you."

Then he kissed her again, long and slow, his desire for his duchess ever strong.

She brushed her thumbs along his temples. "I see a bit more gray here today," she teased. "I find that very attractive, Your Grace."

It was true. He was starting to see gray hairs at his temples, and other men in the family also were spotting gray in their hair. In the past decade, the captain's hair had been so threaded with silver that, over time, the black waves had gone light, giving him an even more distinguished appearance.

Malcom kissed the tip of her nose, saying, "Ten years may have passed, Duchess, but you appeal to me more now than you did when we first met." His hand moved to her belly, his palm flat against the small bulge there. "Will we tell the others while we attend the house party?"

Her hand moved atop his. "Yes. We will announce the new babe and his or her arrival next March."

He released her after a final kiss, and Effie went upstairs to change. She did so rapidly, unlike other women who had to shed gowns several times before they were pleased with one. His steward-duchess was immensely practical. As long as she wore a gown and her hair was swept back into its usual chignon, she never worried about her appearance. The fact that Effie had only grown more beautiful through the years and was entirely unaware of it told the true nature of her character.

Malcolm marveled at the effect his wonderful wife had on him, in ways both small and large. Of the many gifts she had given him over the years, he was happiest with Effie teaching him not to fear anything. He had explored emotional depths with her, sharing about his own lack of maturity and sympathy in his first marriage. Effie had been the one to encourage him to visit where Imogen and Eunice lay, and she accompanied him to the crypt each year on the anniversary of their deaths. Effie had taught him to accept his past, which could not be changed, and embrace his present—and their future.

Shouting it was time to leave, Malcolm saw Miss Feathers appear, holding the hands of his son and older daughter. She was followed by the nursery governess, who held his younger daughter in her arms. When Effie gave birth to their first child, she had told him they simply must convince Miss Feathers to return to Kent once their son outgrew his nursery governess. She said she could not raise her children without the steadying hand of her former governess. Miss Feathers had joined their household when their son turned three and Effie was increasing with their second child. He liked Miss Feathers, who had become family to him, as the many Strongs and their spouses had over the years. Where once Malcolm was alone, save for Ada, now he was richly blessed with a large, loving, extended family.

His sister and Lord Ashmore had two children of their own, both boys, and Ada was still hoping for a girl at some point. She and her viscount had wed at Season's end, as Effie had predicted. Ada thrived in her role as Viscountess Ashmore and ran her household with ease.

His mother had moved to the dower house, saying that the new Duchess of Waterbury should be the one the servants looked to for direction. Though Effie split her time as steward and mother, somehow she also managed his household with aplomb.

Soon, they were in the carriages which would deliver them to Shadowcrest. It usually was between two and two-and-a-half hours to make the journey from Waterside to Shadowcrest, depending upon the state of the roads. No rain had fallen for the past two days, and the roads were in decent condition, allowing them to make good time to their destination.

They were shown to the usual room, the children taken to the nursery, united with all their cousins. That was what Malcolm found remarkable about attending the Season each spring. These Strongs, unlike the majority of the *ton*, insisted upon bringing their children to town with them so they might see them each day. Families called upon one another daily, allowing the cousins ample opportunities to know one another and make lifelong friends.

Malcolm escorted Effie to tea on the terrace, which proved to be a lively occasion, and then the ladies went out to stroll through the gardens, led by Sophie, while the men stayed where they were and caught up on their lives since they had parted from one another in early June.

He and Effie then spent time playing and reading with their three children, tucking them into bed before heading downstairs to dinner.

After dinner ended, they retired to the drawing room for one of their many traditions, singing bawdy sea shanties as they gathered around the pianoforte. Georgie and Mirella took turns playing for them, with James and the captain leading them in song.

A warm glow filled Malcolm, his arm around Effie as they sang. They had shared their news of the newest Ware's appearance and received heartfelt congratulations from the entire family. He looked out over this group, people who had become both friends and family to him, all the couples love matches, as were he and Effie.

James, the rough and tumble sea captain, who had defied the conventions of Polite Society, turning the *ton* on its ear when he had wed Sophie, a widow who ran her own business.

Seth, another sea captain with an adventurous spirit, who had found his soulmate in Pippa, who matched him for craving adventures across the globe.

August, the once-handsome army officer, who had returned to London bearing his wounds of war, capturing the heart of Georgie, the most beautiful girl of her come-out class.

Then there were Sterling and Silas, two notorious rakes who had bedded half the women in London. They were now satisfied husbands, tamed by Allegra and Lyric.

Byron, who had shared with Malcolm some of his story and how he had despaired of ever catching Mirella's notice, the most spirited of the Strong women.

And finally, the captain and Mrs. Andrews, a couple who had found love later in life, yet their passion sizzled as much as any other couple present.

Malcolm turned, taking his wife's hand and lacing their fingers together.

"Thank you for saying yes to me all those years ago," he said, his voice filled with emotion. "Your family welcomed me and claimed me as one of their own. These women are like sisters to me, and these men are the brothers I never had. I am grateful each day to be so blessed, having you, our children, and this group in my life."

His duchess smiled at him. "Thank you for not giving up on me. For chasing after me and letting me know how much love you held in your heart for me. For allowing me a glimpse of what our future could be together."

Effie paused, tears misting her eyes. "Our life together has been even better than I could have dreamed, Malcolm. Every morning, I am thankful to awaken in your arms, ready to see what the new day will bring."

"It brings love, Effie. Other things, too—but there will always be love."

With that, Malcolm kissed his wife, and then they joined back in the song.

About the Author

USA Today and Amazon Top 10 bestselling author Alexa Aston lives with her husband in a Dallas suburb, where she eats her fair share of dark chocolate and plots while she walks every morning. She enjoys travel and sports—and can't get enough of *Survivor* or *The Crown*.

Her Regency and Medieval historical romances bring to life loveable rogues and dashing knights. Her series include: *The Strongs of Shadowcrest, Suddenly a Duke, Second Sons of London, Dukes Done Wrong, Dukes of Distinction, Soldiers and Soulmates, The St. Clairs, The de Wolfes of Esterley Castle, The King's Cousins, Medieval Runaway Wives,* and *The Knights of Honor.*

Printed in Great Britain
by Amazon